MAY 1 4 ENTD

# PERSECUTED

Books by
# Robin Parrish

*Offworld*
*Nightmare*
*Vigilante*
*Persecuted**

DOMINION TRILOGY

*Relentless*
*Fearless*
*Merciless*

*based on the film written and directed by
Daniel Lusko

# PERSECUTED

## I WILL NOT BE SILENT

### ROBIN PARRISH

based on a Daniel Lusko film

BETHANYHOUSE
a division of Baker Publishing Group
Minneapolis, Minnesota

© 2014 by Daniel Lusko

Published by Bethany House Publishers
11400 Hampshire Avenue South
Bloomington, Minnesota 55438
www.bethanyhouse.com

Bethany House Publishers is a division of
Baker Publishing Group, Grand Rapids, Michigan

Printed in the United States of America

Library of Congress Cataloging-in-Publication Data
Parrish, Robin.
    Persecuted : I Will Not Be Silent / Robin Parrish.
      pages cm
    "Based on a Daniel Lusko film."
    ISBN 978-0-7642-1267-3 (cloth : alk. paper)
    ISBN 978-0-7642-1266-6 (pbk.)
    1. Evangelists—Fiction. 2. Malicious accusation—Fiction. I. Title.
PS3616.A7684P47 2014
813'.6—dc23                                                    2014003976

14   15   16   17   18   19   20          7   6   5   4   3   2   1

# Foreword

Persecution is a subject that calls to mind the most incredible sufferings from all over the world, dating back to the days of Christ. Writing a movie called *Persecuted* comes with it a heavy task. Everyone can relate to the feeling of being persecuted for one's beliefs. The truth is many people feel persecuted, even within the Church, but few for the right reasons.

I want readers to know why I undertook this cause and why this particular story sits in front of them today. The stakes are high. I believe this project means life or death to those who are suffering from grave persecution all over the globe.

In America, we have become insulated in our lives to the point that few people, if any, seem to understand what it means to take up their cross and follow Christ. We're raised to think the Christian life consists of following a celebrity pastor and being involved in exciting events. This is not the case in much of the world today, as elsewhere persecution is something that is understood as part of the package in accepting salvation. Jesus said: "Blessed are those who are persecuted because of righteousness, for theirs is the kingdom of heaven." There is a power in suffering for the purpose of God, a power few have experienced in the West.

When persecution comes, few will be prepared for what comes with it. The story of this film is just the beginning of an awakening to prepare believers for a choice that will have to be made. I fear many will be wiped away, for the cares of the world will swallow them up. There is a cost to following Christ. Those who believe will know that cost, and they will have their reward in heaven. If you're asleep, I hope this wakes you up, because truth is stranger than fiction. If you're suffering worse conditions than those depicted here, don't lose heart, for God is with you. Bottom line: There's much more beyond the pages of this story; this is a symbol of the bridge I believe we must cross if we're to be joined with the remaining body of Christ around the world.

This is a wake-up call. Many of our freedoms granted to us by God will surely be ripped away unless we make a stand. This story is just the beginning.

Daniel Lusko,
writer and director of *Persecuted*

*Congress shall make no law respecting an establish-
ment of religion, or prohibiting the free exercise
thereof.*

—First Amendment to the
Constitution of the United States

*The framers of our Constitution meant we were to
have freedom of religion, not freedom from religion.*

—Reverend Billy Graham

*A man who won't die for something is not fit to live.*

—Martin Luther King Jr.

# Prologue

*B*oom.

Shot to the chest, instantaneous heart explosion. Emmett Olson. Brooklyn, eight years ago.

The next target came up. Mr. Gray took aim . . .

*Boom.*

Precision shot to the head, dead on impact. Gino Mendoza. Columbia, seven years ago.

He pressed the reset button on the panel in front of him. It triggered a belt in the ceiling of the shooting range that carried new paper targets into place. It was a huge place, larger than most, and Mr. Gray was setting each fifty yards away. But even so . . .

*Boom.*

Shot to the stomach, right where he'd aimed. Terrell Cobb. Tallahassee, five years ago.

He almost allowed a smile. That had been a more difficult, and therefore entertaining, job. The target wasn't supposed to just die but actually suffer for a bit first. So Mr. Gray had aimed for lower body mass. It had taken eight minutes for Terrell Cobb to bleed out over his kitchen floor.

You got what you paid for when you hired Mr. Gray. He was a professional.

His name, of course, wasn't really Mr. Gray. That was how he was known to those who employed his unique talents. Only a handful of people had had the misfortune of discovering the name he was born with, and he'd silenced them. Permanently.

Other men of his vocation would frown on assigning emotional values to past jobs. Mr. Gray found that it enhanced his skills.

He was about to take his next shot when his phone vibrated. No. Whoever it was could wait. The best marksmen could make any shot, even amid distraction.

*Boom.*

Head shot, double tap. Colton Lind. Tulsa, three years ago. The last hit he'd completed before taking on his new broader security assignment.

After taking a moment to ensure that his shots matched up with how he remembered the Tulsa job, he placed his gun down on the counter and pulled the phone from his pocket. It was the phone whose number he'd only given to his employer. It had already stopped ringing, but it logged the caller's number with a 202 area code. Someone here in Washington, D.C., but not his employer. The phone buzzed once. A message had been left.

Interesting.

Mr. Gray slipped the phone back in his pocket and returned his attention to the range. He had fifteen more shots to complete before he was ready for any distractions. Discipline and focus had gotten him this far. It was a core value—of his and of his clients.

The remaining shots went cleanly, with only the fourteenth slipping outside his intended area by more than an inch or two. Mr. Gray cleaned and packed away his gun, stowed his earplugs, and left the range, nodding once to the guard who'd been waiting for him to finish so the place could be closed for the night.

Only when he'd made it to his car—an intentionally unremarkable sedan with an intentionally remarkable engine under its hood—did Mr. Gray finally retrieve his phone and listen to the message left for him. The caller had followed protocol, sharing nothing about the desired job and providing only a phone number to an untraceable cell phone.

"Your employer," the message concluded, "suggested you as the best he'd ever met. He's been quite pleased with your assistance these last two years. I think you're exactly the right man for this opportunity."

Even without the caller's name, Mr. Gray could tell he was a politician. Elected officials were all the same, always trying to get people to like them.

Their pockets were deep, however.

Mr. Gray pulled an unused burner cell phone from his bag and placed the call to the number that had been left. When the call was answered, the unmistakable sound of a party—glasses clinking, forced laughter, even a band—could be heard immediately. "Go where no one can hear you or I will hang up."

"Got to take this," he heard the voice on the other line say and then the rustling of him walking away. Thirty seconds later, the caller said, "I'm alone."

"What's your need?"

"Oh. So, uh, what I need to know is how quickly you can go to work, once you've been given approval to proceed."

"Define *work*," said Mr. Gray, his patience being tested.

"Well, it's like this. For some time now I've been trying to convince my friend to join me in a vitally important initiative. I believe I still have a chance of winning him over, but if I can't, if he won't play ball . . . I may have need of your services."

Mr. Gray considered the man's words. Politicians usually dealt in vague terms, because clarity was too incriminating.

"Services?"

11

"Not that. Hopefully not that. But if he's not for us, then he can't be an obstacle. Your boss said you could handle this kind of complicated situation. You've helped him in the past."

"My fee is nonnegotiable," Mr. Gray said.

"Money is not a concern. Only success—and discretion, of course."

"I can guarantee both."

"That's why I called you."

"Send me the details electronically, along with payment in full. One hundred percent, in advance. Once that's done, I will present you with options for removing your obstacle. And anything else you may need."

"Excellent," said the politician. "You'll have both within the hour. I'll be in touch."

Mr. Gray clicked off, opened the phone, removed the SIM card, and snapped it in half. He'd finish destroying it at home, along with the phone. He glanced at his watch—1:30 a.m. Another productive day.

Starting the car, he began the drive back to the flat he'd secured as his base of operations here in Washington, D.C. It amazed him, after spending time on the ground in Iran, Afghanistan, Chechnya, and Somalia, how this city, in some ways, could be just as vicious. Just as dangerous. It suited him well.

Car pointed home, knifing through the quiet streets like a shark through water, Mr. Gray thought of the job that might wait ahead, that just might prove interesting. It was another chance to test his skills, another opportunity to put his training to work.

# 1

They were chanting. No, they were shouting. Screaming. This mob stationed outside the front gate, in the pouring rain, was screaming in shared outrage. But what were they saying? There was no audio on the news feed.

There were two sides to the mob, each as angry as the other. On one side were signs adorned with slogans like *Heaven is not a gated community!* and *I like your Christ, I do not like your Christians.* The other half of the mob held signs that said *Jesus is the way and the light!* and *Grace and truth come from Christ!*

Good grief, now they were singing.

John Luther turned his attention away from the TV monitor on the floor to his left, which had briefly cut away to the protestors outside Truth Ministries' headquarters. Now his own visage was back on the screen, where he was being broadcast live.

"Freedom has been under attack in every generation, and ours is no exception." John's sincere, steady gaze locked tight on the anchorwoman sitting across from him. He fought the urge to stare into the camera just over her right shoulder, as well as a vague desire to loosen his silk tie.

His surroundings were unusually sparse for a TV newsroom. CNW was as high-tech a network as any, and during his prior appearances he had always been seated in front of a green screen so that audiences would see an old Gothic church behind him. It was a different church every time, and John didn't recognize most of them. Just a visual cue to his vocation and traditionalist leanings, but it wasn't the image he would have chosen for himself. If he had to have a representative image projected behind him, he'd rather it be the stark beauty of an old wooden cross. Or maybe a picture of two hands with holes in the palms.

A tired-looking producer had explained to him an hour ago that they'd decided to go with a simple setup for this interview so that the focus would be on him, on this all-important occasion. It sounded nice, but John guessed they were in such a hurry to get him on the air that they didn't have time to assemble the usual background.

Seated across from him was Diana Lucas, CNW's most well-known and respected journalist. Blond and attractive, Diana had the kind of steely gaze that let her interviewees know this was *her* interview and she was in total control. She listened carefully to John's every word, though she didn't miss an opportunity to jump in when he paused.

"Who better to speak on the subject of freedom than you, John," she said. "You've been hailed as 'God's Ambassador' by some of the world's foremost dictatorships: Sudan, North Korea, and Iran. But there are those who claim that your ministry is intolerant, that it's condescending to people of other faiths. Some in Washington have said that your crusades may even threaten the freedoms of others."

John had sat across from her enough times to know that Diana Lucas approached every on-screen interview as a game of tactical chess, measuring the tiniest of facial tics and the most subtle vocal modulations with the skill of a criminal profiler. She knew exactly when to listen, and when to pounce.

Her pointed statement might have gotten under his skin a decade ago, yet this sort of exchange was old hat now. He shook his head and affected a sad expression.

"Diana, if I thought for one second that I could look down on anyone else for their beliefs, I wouldn't be sitting here. I'm not a Republican. I'm not a Democrat. I don't belong to any particular religious denomination. My personal history is no better than any of your viewers. Do you know what kind of person I used to be? Who I *really* was?"

Diana said nothing. Maybe she was waiting for him to bury himself with his own words. Or maybe she was genuinely speechless for once. John couldn't tell.

"An abusive, alcoholic, gambling drug addict," he explained. "And I deserved nothing less than death when God came into my life."

Diana's eyebrow twitched; it was barely visible, but John caught it. She'd allowed him considerable leeway, though her patience was running out now. He knew she was about to change the subject.

"So, John," she said smoothly, "what is your opinion of the primary tenets of the Faith and Fairness Act? And I quote, 'To *publicly* declare your religious beliefs in a way that permits equal time and respect to other systems of faith.'"

For the first time since the interview began, John bristled internally. But he swallowed it quickly, refusing to let her ruffle him on camera. "Freedom is fragile and costly," he said with conviction. "It must be constantly protected and defended by work and by faith."

Diana waited with her eyebrows pinched upward. John knew she was hoping for more, a stronger, more controversial sound bite.

It was awfully tempting to give it to her. But then why not? Why not say exactly what he was thinking? It was true, wasn't it? Come to think of it, people needed to hear it. If this bill passed Congress, there'd be many who wished that someone had come out and said it beforehand. John would never get a better opportunity.

He squared his shoulders. Yes, freedom had to be defended by work and faith. But also . . .

"Even by blood."

His voice resounded like a judge's gavel closing a heated court case. It was his final word on the subject, and he could see that even Diana sensed it. She jumped at the chance to end the interview there, transitioning effortlessly to a wrap-up of John's statements before handing things back over to the anchor desk.

John sat still in his seat, listening to her talk. Even after she was done, after she'd risen from her seat to shake his hand and thank him for his time, he remained frozen in place. Had he really just said that out loud? What was he thinking?

Well, now he'd really done it.

The board wouldn't approve of such strong words, as if suggesting their freedom to worship as they saw fit had to be defended with blood. But he would remind them that this bill was really happening, making this no time to soft-pedal or hold back. The easy thing would be to stay silent, but too much was at stake. They would be judged for how they acted right now—or refused to act.

No matter how many people would condemn him for it, or how many times it would be taken out of context in repeated news broadcasts, John knew it was the truth and had to be said. If not by him, then who? There probably wasn't anyone else influential enough to say it so that it mattered.

Maybe it had come across as too trite or too practiced. He hoped not. John found it hard to gauge his own on-screen performances. But he didn't just believe the words he'd said. He *knew* them to be true.

Not that long ago he'd been a wretched example of humanity who deserved the worst punishment eternity could offer. Not every man could understand the all-encompassing depths of God's amazing grace the way John Luther did. Not everyone knew what could be defended by blood.

# 2

The gunshot was so loud, it hurt John's ears.

As the cop knelt to the ground to check on the victim—his partner—the drug runner doubled back the way he came and made a run for it. Blood slowly pooled the ground underneath the fallen police detective, an elder member of the squad, while his partner frantically pulled a black radio from his belt.

"Officer down! Corner of West 5th and Buena Vista! Get the paramedics here *now*!" screamed the cop into the receiver.

John's heart raced with excitement as he watched the scene play out in front of him. He'd never seen anything so visceral, so realistic. He still couldn't quite believe he was here. It was like a dream.

Just ten years old, he'd lived a fairly sheltered life. The old man had seen to that. His father was a priest, a very respected and respectable one who clung to old-fashioned traditional values until they choked like that collar he wore around his neck. As such, he'd forbidden his son from engaging in most popular forms of entertainment and media—including movies. John had been invited to the cinema many times by friends from school, but his dad always said no.

A week ago John had presented his father with a crisp new report card bearing straight A's. It was the first time he'd ever scored top marks across the board, and it had required some seriously hard work in several disciplines that John found more challenging than most of the kids in his class. As a reward, the old man had offered him a free wish. Anything he wanted—within reason, not to mention budget—he could have.

John's wish was to see the big-budget buddy-cop movie that all the guys in school were raving about. Reluctantly his father had relented on his standard policy and agreed to take him.

The movie was only fifteen minutes in, and it was already the most exciting thing John had ever seen in his life. He already knew some of what was going to happen—that this older policeman who'd been shot was going to die, allowing the other cop to take on a rookie partner, kicking the story off for real—thanks to the kids at school. But he'd just learned that there was a big difference between hearing about something, and seeing and hearing it with his own senses.

Despite this, it wasn't a perfect experience. He could feel the disapproval emanating off his father in the seat to his right. Every time somebody on-screen uttered a word John only heard shouted by rough boys on the playground—words he never dared use himself—his father would let out a loud sigh or angrily mumble something indiscernible.

A minute later the older cop on the screen died from his gunshot wound, just as John knew he would. His younger partner stood to his feet, turned his anguished, outraged face to the sky, and screamed a single curse as loud as he could.

John knew his father would bristle at this, yet he wasn't at all prepared for what happened next.

Charles Luther, local priest and single father, cleared his throat loud enough for the entire theater to hear and stood. Everyone within a twenty-foot radius craned their heads in his direction. Charles squeezed past his son to exit the aisle.

"Come on, John," he said, seeming not to care about how loud he was talking.

What did he mean, "*come on*"? They weren't leaving, they couldn't. This was his wish, the reward he'd worked months for.

"I don't want to leave!" John whispered in reply, panic flooding his heart. He knew it wasn't wise to argue with his father, and under any other circumstances he'd already be on his feet, right in step behind the old man. But this was different. He'd waited so long for this!

Charles Luther froze and pointed his hard, expressionless gaze at his son. John swallowed but stood his ground. Or rather, sat.

"Get. Up." His father's words came out with his usual calm demeanor, but the undertone was painfully clear. John was now in serious danger of stepping over the line.

"But *why*?" John whispered. "You promised!"

"I won't have this kind of filth and violence filling your mind. We're going."

John had been angry before, many times. But never had he felt a rage so searing or urgent as what he felt at this moment. He turned his eyes back to the movie screen and replied, out loud, with a single word. "No."

The word had barely escaped his lips when he felt a painfully tight grip on his left forearm, jerking him out of his seat. No longer speaking, Charles pulled his son physically into the aisle.

"NO!" John screamed, pulling against his dad as hard as he could to try to get back to his seat.

Undeterred, Charles kept pulling. A big bear of a man, in another life he'd worked construction before entering Episcopalian priesthood, and still retained his strength of both muscles and will. His ten-year-old son was no match for him.

Still John refused to cooperate, pulling and screaming, "No! No! No!" as loud as he could. He was, as his father called it when they witnessed other children exhibiting this sort of behavior, causing *a scene*. And he didn't care.

His father was strict and relentless in his insistence on sheltering John from all things "worldly," and he also ruled the house with stern control that so stifled John he had trouble breathing. This was the first time John had ever dared to fight back against the old man, and he surged with the adrenaline rush, the feeling of exerting power. He wouldn't win, of course, and he knew he shouldn't be behaving this way. But he was proving right now that he *could* resist his father and make things difficult for him. It was strangely satisfying.

Charles dragged him, literally kicking and screaming, out of the theater and into the lobby, where a few dozen patrons turned in their direction. John was red in the face, screaming at the top of his lungs. He began to cry.

"But you promised!" he yelled. "You *promised*!"

"Yes, I did, John," Charles replied calmly. "And now I have to break that promise. Because I love you."

"Well, I *don't* love you!" John screamed. "I hate you!"

He didn't mean it, of course. But it felt good to hurt his father.

It was the first time he could ever remember seeing his father's stoic face show pain.

# 3

PRESENT DAY

They were still there. The protestors brandishing their big wooden signs like pitchforks and torches, right outside the studios of Truth Ministries. The rain was coming down harder now. Someone—probably Ryan—had left the small TV in his dressing room tuned to CNW, which was again showing a live view of the protests going on outside the building.

A CNW cameraman forced his way through the crowd like a shark drawn to blood, slicing to a point close to the studio entrance, where two voices were growing louder by the second. A man and a woman stood opposite each other. The microphone didn't pick up what the woman said, but when she shoved her large *Faith for Everyone!* sign into the man's face, it was pretty clear where she stood. The man swatted away the sign and replaced it with a well-worn Bible held high like a medieval sword.

The man's furious words were audible over the TV. "This is all I need!" he shouted. "God's Word! This is all anyone needs!"

The female protestor smacked the Bible away and onto the ground. The fundamentalist stood there for a moment, his mind unable to catch up to the sight of his treasured possession being cast to the wet ground like so much trash.

Then he snapped.

He threw himself at the woman full of red-faced rage and pain. The protestor gave back as good as she got, and as the TV camera captured the initial blows of their violence, the rest of the crowd made up of protestors and supporters—separated like football players on either side of the line of scrimmage—surged toward one another, launching punches and kicks in a thunder of fury.

The left edge of the camera's view caught a young woman leaning over to pick the Bible up off the ground. She clutched it to her chest protectively while closing her eyes. Around her the hatred swarmed, yet she seemed to be shutting out everything else, retreating deep inside herself for protection from the madness on all sides.

The CNW camera panned out slowly, poetically capturing the rain-soaked pandemonium erupting on Truth Ministries' doorstep. John was about to turn away from the TV when Diana Lucas's voice added a soundtrack to the on-screen action.

"'Faith must be defended *by blood*,'" she said in her most sincere intonation. "Those were the bold words of evangelist John Luther earlier this evening. And as you can see, they appear to have been taken literally by the crowd gathered outside the studios of Truth Ministries. Were his words incendiary? Our panel of experts is itching to answer that question. . . ."

Beneath the live footage of the fight, words scrolled across the bottom of the screen that included *Evangelist Calls on Christians to Fight Senate Bill* and *John Luther's War Cry*.

John sighed, slowly and deliberately sliding his watch over his wrist. How many children were starving to death right now? How many Africans were dying of AIDS at this very moment? How many believers in hostile nations were suffering for holding firmly to their faith? And yet a petty fistfight outside a television studio was what the national news was covering, using John's own words to fan the flames of hatred and prejudice.

He idly wondered if walking outside into the crowd might do anything to calm the swelling riot. But the thought passed quickly, as he knew that his presence would only have the opposite effect, and he didn't need to make things worse right now. Like it or not, he was a lightning rod in the public eye when it came to matters of faith. Everyone had strong feelings about the Faith and Fairness Act, and equally strong feelings about John Luther.

All John really wanted was to preach the Gospel. It was his reason for breathing. He wanted to share with any who would listen about the love and grace and forgiveness that had been given to him.

He turned off the television and sat down at his modest dressing table. Thankfully it had only been a short drive from CNW's studios across D.C. to his own ministry's headquarters on the outskirts of the capital. It gave him the time he needed to prepare. Hands clasped together and eyes closed tight, he prayed softly, "Lord, make me a channel of thy life, thy truth, thy way, thy words. Pure, honest, clean. Pure, honest, clean . . ."

John smoothed his hair back over his left ear, thinking of how he was the last person to judge those people outside in the rain. God knew he'd done worse things than starting fights in his day. Besides, human beings had been fighting over the Gospel of Jesus Christ for thousands of years and weren't scheduled to stop until time itself came to an end. And he had a feeling this particular confrontation might have been . . . helped along. He'd been behind the curtain of the media long enough to know how far they'd go to drive up ratings.

He just hoped the authorities could end the fight before serious injuries began racking up.

The clock on the wall told him it was almost time. John stood and buttoned the top button of his shirt. Tightened his red necktie. Then he began bouncing and shadowboxing around the room, punching at the air.

Left jab. *Breathe.* Right jab.

It seemed like the whole world wanted a fight. Maybe he'd give them one. His sermon tonight would be one for the books. All eyes were on him, and his only move was to come out swinging.

John stopped to button up his sleeve cuffs. On the inside of his left wrist he saw the small cross he'd had tattooed there years before he knew what it meant. It had been a joke—a jab at his father. Now . . . he leaned over the still-open Bible on the dressing table and read a few more words. Closing his eyes again, he prayed, "All I want is the truth. All I want is the truth."

A tiny knock came from the dressing room door. "Mr. Luther," a small voice said. It belonged to a young staff member. What was her name? She opened the door and stuck her head in. "Senator Harrison is here to see you."

Donald? What was he . . . ?

Oh. Of course. John should have seen this coming. Still, his old friend's timing was terrible. He had less than five minutes to show time.

"I can't talk to him right now," he told the staffer. Didn't he know that time was short, and John was supposed to be on in a matter of minutes?

"He *really* wants to see you," the girl replied, her voice rising. "I don't know what to say to him."

John held up his hands to calm her. "It's okay, it's fine. Just send him in."

He sighed.

Donald was here for one thing and one thing only. But maybe it wouldn't be so bad. He could dream, right?

Meh. If Jesus Christ could hold himself to a wooden cross in unimaginable pain for three hours, John could survive five minutes with Senator Donald Harrison.

# 4

The young woman at the door ducked out, barely getting out of the way of Senator Harrison, who slid into the room on shiny, spotless shoes like hot knives cutting butter. His eyes were heat-seeking missiles that locked immediately onto John.

Donald was in his late fifties, his perfectly coiffed hair prematurely white. A two-hundred-dollar haircut, John knew. The majority leader of the Senate was famous for his elocution skills and his ability to dominate any conversation. John had always appreciated his support and his friendship, but things had changed since they were young men. They had changed. At least in some ways. Donald was still a man who had little concept of another's personal boundaries, and an absolute ability to never take no for an answer.

"Hey, John!" Donald called out with a smile. "How we doing tonight?"

John took his old friend's hand and pulled him into a quick bear hug. He didn't want to be rude, but he needed to get to his pulpit.

"Oh yeah," Donald went on, "I just wanted to say I saw your

piece on *Primetime*. I thought it was very, *very* nice. Your transparency was very moving."

John smoothed back the hair over his ear again and glanced in the mirror. He knew the senator hadn't come all this way just to congratulate him on his latest press appearance. He'd come here for one thing, and they both knew what it was.

Donald sighed. "I know this isn't your cup of tea, John—"

"Then why do you keep pushing when you already know my answer?" John asked, trying not to sound impatient or exasperated, yet knowing he was failing at both.

"I really need your full support on the Faith and Fairness deal," Donald continued, as if John hadn't interrupted. "Your ministry reaches more people than the evening news! I know it's all just bureaucratic hoopla to you, but you're a fulcrum, John. A nexus. You stand in the middle of a crowd and turn one way, and the whole crowd turns with you. It's time to put them on the right path. Now, I need you to get up there on national television and announce that you fully support the bill. It could be the turning point for the whole thing!"

John closed his eyes and let out a breath.

Donald offered a tentative smile. "I'm counting on my friend to come through for me here."

The female staffer opened his door again. "Your wife and daughter are here."

John nodded in her direction, and she was gone. When he looked back at Donald, the senator was scowling. The stately gentleman was gone, and an imposing Beltway power broker stood in his place.

John doubted that Donald would ever get it. How could he? The man was a politician—and a very good one. What did he know about matters of the soul?

"What did God say about appeasing the masses, Donald?" John replied, standing toe-to-toe with the senator. "He said, 'I am the way. I am the truth. I am the life.' Not *one of* the ways, *the* way."

The senator was unmoved. "This isn't about that. This is about fairness and equality for all faiths, not just yours."

"Look." John felt his practiced cool beginning to crack, his pulse picking up. He grabbed his Bible and held it in front of his friend. "I'm not asking an imam to preach the Bible in a mosque, am I? All I'm focused on is preaching this book. It's not illegal to teach the Gospel in this country yet, is it?"

The temperature in the room shot up. Donald's cheeks flushed, and he rolled his eyes melodramatically. "I keep forgetting you're the sole proprietor of the Word of God."

John had to turn away and choke down the desire to shout the truth in Donald's face. Fighting wasn't the way. It wasn't what God wanted.

Donald let out a big breath. "This is a fine way to show gratitude to the people who have really helped you."

John turned back around. "I appreciate everything you've done. But you don't own me. And you've been thanked, plenty."

There was no mistaking the disappointment on the senator's face. "This bill is going to happen, and I'm offering you the opportunity to be on the right side of history."

Enough. John had no more time for this. He threw his suit coat on. "I *cannot* water down the Gospel to advance anybody's political agenda."

"Not everyone believes that heaven is a gated community, John," said Donald. Why did he sound so sad? He had to have known what John's answer would be before he came here. Did he come to the studio tonight to give John a warning? Or one last chance to jump on board?

The young girl opened his door again. "Sir, it's time."

Donald stood his ground and took on a much more formal tone. "I think I can speak for all of my colleagues in Congress when I say that we have reached the terminal end of our patience with you."

John wondered what that meant but chose to let the comment fall away. Neither Senator Donald Harrison nor all of Congress nor even the president himself held any power over John or the Christian citizens of this nation that did not first pass through the hands of God. His will would be done, no matter what.

John couldn't delay any longer. Yet he didn't want to end things this way with one of his oldest friends and supporters. Moving for the door, he stopped for a moment and gave Donald a friendly peck on the cheek.

"God bless you," he said, and hoped it meant something to the man.

Discussion over. It was time.

## 5

Ryan Morris bounced. Bobbing up and down in his jeans, expensive T-shirt, and sport coat, he stood in his customary spot just offstage, waiting for John to go on. Ryan was a handsome thirty-something with dirty-blond hair and chiseled features. He was as loyal and hardworking as they came, having dedicated his entire existence to furthering Truth Ministries. He had no family remaining, and no friends outside of the organization. It was his whole life.

John's calm always balanced out the buzz Ryan got at show time. They'd become a complementary pair over the years, and each knew the other's strengths and weaknesses as well as their own. Ryan was the unrelenting optimist, driven and enthusiastic at every turn. Quick with a joke or a hug, the man was like John's younger brother or son even. Someone who occasionally got a little too wild, and tonight he looked even more wide-eyed than usual. Like he'd had one too many cans of Red Bull before the show.

John marched through the dark backstage area toward the bright beacon that summoned him. The spotlight could be an intimidating place, but John had grown to love it. As always, he focused on that light, marching straight for it, because standing in that light was where he was able to speak the Gospel into the lives of those with ears to hear.

As he neared the stage, Ryan stepped forward to stop him for a moment. This was their ritual.

"You are gonna kill this thing like you always do," said Ryan, revving up his pep talk and gesturing in spastic arm movements. "You're *on fire!*"

He hadn't spoken to Ryan since returning from the CNW interview, but unsurprisingly his subordinate seemed to believe he'd nailed it. Ryan was always so quick to heap praise on him. John had asked him many times not to stroke his ego, as it made him horribly uncomfortable. But he'd come to realize that Ryan simply couldn't help himself. He believed so fervently in this ministry that any and every feat they accomplished—no matter how big or small—got him excited. They all knew what the stakes of John's interview would be.

"Right," John said with a deep breath. His apprehension at how he'd left things with Donald should have been buried, yet something small still nagged at him. And Ryan knew him too well. The man could tell something was bothering him.

"How are you feeling?" asked Ryan. "You good? You need anything?"

John shook his head while Ryan continued to gaze on him with concern. John felt a single bead of perspiration at his hairline. Ryan saw it too.

"You know what I'm thinking?" Ryan said, worried but growing excited again. "I'm gonna get you a driver to take you home after the show. You've got to take it easy, John."

No. Ridiculous. John didn't need a driver. He was fine.

"That's all right. I'll drive myself home."

John tried to slide past him, but Ryan wasn't done yet. He mirrored John's sidestep.

"Listen, listen," he said, gaining speed as he returned to pep-talk mode. "This media scrutiny comes and goes. You know that. All this talk of persecution is gonna die, and who's gonna be left standing? You are! Why? Because you're John Luther. So forget the politics. You get back in that ring and you bring those people out there what they came to hear. You bring the truth, brother! Go get 'em!"

John wasn't sure if he appreciated Ryan's over-the-top encouragement on this night or if he was growing tired of it. He was disheartened that he couldn't escape all the politics stuff even from his inner circle. He wearily nodded and walked past Ryan.

Ryan smiled and patted him on the back. He gave John a soft nudge in the direction of the stage. John turned his attention back to the spotlight. *For you,* he prayed silently. He took two deep breaths and then squared his shoulders. Finally he felt ready. It was time to put everything else aside, to leave the politics and the maneuvering in the rearview. It was time to step up to the podium and do the thing he was born to do, the thing that filled his heart with more purpose and fulfillment than anything else in this world.

It was time to share the Good News.

# 6

From Asia to South America, from Australia to Africa, John Luther has broken stadium records preaching the simple Gospel truth for many, many years!" boomed the gravelly voice of seventy-seven-year-old Dave Wilson. A senior member of John's board of directors, Dave was a zealot, a fiery devotee of both Christ and Truth Ministries. He also possessed a brilliant mind. Analytical and quiet, he was as passionate as Ryan and yet he approached life in a completely different way. They made a great team, offering their own unique perspectives on the world.

Dave's face was wrinkled and red at the moment, but he made no move to wipe away the sweat from his brow. He'd introduced John hundreds of times and yet still gave it every ounce of energy and fire he had, even after all the years. "Please do me a great favor and let's give a really warm welcome to John Luther!"

John's adrenaline surged as he parted the velvet curtain with a burst and strode confidently onto the stage. The bright TV lights enveloped him; somewhere across the years he'd come to enjoy their warm glow. There was something comforting about it. The two hundred-strong crowd—a filled-to-capacity number in the main studio—jumped to their feet and exploded in a roar of applause and whistles and cheers.

Bible in one hand, John patted Dave on the back with the other, then slid coolly into place behind the clear acrylic pulpit. Suspended behind him hung the circular logo for the show—*Truth Live* in white letters on a blue background. Stylized stalks of wheat representing the harvest ringed the outside edge of the circle, and the second *t* in *Truth* was a red cross. John held his Bible in the air, which he intended as a symbolic reminder that the audience's praise should be given to God, not to himself.

John projected his powerful voice into the microphone while gazing across the crowd.

"Tonight, I believe we are headed, as a nation, toward a great spiritual awakening. And yet many are telling you that if the government can unite all faiths under this new religious reform bill, that somehow world peace will come. But the Bible says that no government can ever bring peace to mankind!"

Senator Donald Harrison stood quiet, listening intently as he remained rooted to his spot in John's dressing room. He'd really thought John might come around, that he could be reasoned with.

His eyes swiveled toward the small television set, which blinked dark and then came to life again, now showing John Luther preaching on *Truth Live*. He loved the man, but what a stubborn fool John had become, how blind to the momentum of history's changing tide. Their conversations these days too often had turned into arguments, and Harrison couldn't understand why his friend couldn't see that he was standing in front of a tidal wave about to overwhelm him. The time for worry or pity was over. Donald had made his overture, many of them, but John had chosen his path. Now all Donald felt were frustration and disappointment. John's way of thinking was a relic of the past. How could he not see that? What would happen next, John was bringing on himself.

On the TV screen John was building momentum, his voice rising in volume and his gestures getting more animated. "Why? Because mankind has a disease. It's either the world and its religions and its politicians and its pleasures, or it's the Lord. Every human being who ever lived has had to make the same choice."

Donald pulled out his phone and redialed the last number he'd called.

"He's not on board," he said softly. Donald sighed. "Go ahead."

He put the phone away and cursed John's stubbornness under his breath.

John was breathing hard and sweating, working up to his crescendo.

"Many believe that religious reform will save us from war, from fear, and from terrorism. When has it?!"

"Never!" shouted the crowd.

John scanned the audience, looking as many of his parishioners in the eye as possible.

"Of course not," he said. "We know that only the Word of God can bring peace to the heart of man. You cannot legislate the power of God! You can't change your past, but Christ can with his blood! You don't have the power to do it yourself. But if you surrender to God, he'll give you the power to change your life and shape your future. Jesus said, 'I am the way.' Come to him now!"

# 7

A few miles away from Truth Ministries' studios, Mr. Gray, in his usual gray suit and dark tie, put his phone back into his jacket pocket. He drove a plain-looking black sedan the way one might pilot a tank, with a dour expression and unflinching solemnity. Driving slowly through downtown, he turned up the radio's volume. The preacher man Luther shouted through the vehicle's stereo speakers. He was well into his sermon now; he'd be done soon.

Not much time.

Finding the address at last, he brought the car to a stop in front of an old brick tenement and honked once, just as he'd said he would. A young girl soon emerged from an upstairs fire-escape door and wound her way down the wire-frame balcony and steps. Once her feet hit the pavement, he could see that she was quite pretty, and young, likely no more than sixteen or seventeen. She snapped and popped bubble gum, adding to her youthful appearance, but her eyes looked old. She'd seen life. As instructed, her clothes were nondescript—not overly conservative nor flamboyant but somewhere in between. She was old enough to suit his needs, yet young enough to retain her youthful vitality. He knew what went on in the apartment upstairs. Another year and the girl would probably look ten years older. But right now . . . she'd do.

Mr. Gray looked away as she approached, pretending not to have noticed her yet. She slipped lightly off the sidewalk and strolled over to the car. She was in no hurry. He turned off the radio as she knocked on the window. Rolling it down, he made eye contact.

"Want a ride, honey?" he asked.

She eyed him playfully, seductively. "Do you?"

He unlocked the passenger door. "Get in."

She rounded the vehicle and slid into the seat opposite Mr. Gray.

"What's your name?" he asked.

"Aaliyah," she answered, studying him with a smile.

"Get rid of the gum," said Mr. Gray.

She rolled her eyes but complied, sticking it onto a single finger.

Mr. Gray poured a pill into her hand from a prescription pill bottle, keeping his thumb over the word *Rohypnol* printed on it. He saw the greedy gleam in her eye. That was why she'd agreed to tonight, but the pill wasn't what she'd been promised. Rohypnol was a powerful sedative that relaxed the nervous system and made the user highly susceptible to suggestion. Fraternity brothers had abused its powers for years. Mr. Gray had no intention of taking advantage of this girl; that would be far beneath someone of his station. Yet he needed her drugged for what was to come.

"You've never had a ride like this before, Aaliyah," he said with a smirk. "I guarantee it."

She grinned back at him and tossed the pill into her mouth without even bothering to look at it. Mr. Gray handed her a can of soda, and she swallowed.

"Good girl," he said, starting the car.

Aaliyah eyed him sideways. She bit the gum off her finger and resumed chewing it as he drove into the night.

Roughly ten minutes later, Mr. Gray and Aaliyah slipped into the *Truth Live* studio to find it was mostly empty. Luther's sermon was long over, and most of the crowd had gone home— fewer potential witnesses. A few families remained, chatting among themselves. Just as Gray anticipated, Luther was still there, standing in the center aisle, not far from the stage. He looked tired even as he patiently greeted the attendees who'd lingered, shaking their hands and smiling for photos and saying prayers.

Mr. Gray grabbed Aaliyah by the hand and walked as quickly as he dared down the center aisle, approaching Luther from behind. The man was speaking to a family of four, thanking them for coming, when Mr. Gray tapped him on the shoulder. He decided he'd probably get further with the man if he acted apologetic and grateful. It had been a long night and he couldn't risk Luther deciding to pack it in.

"Mr. Luther, do you mind if we take a pic with my daughter real quick? She just loves this show," he said, smiling warmly.

Luther responded just as Gray had expected. He amicably put an arm around Aaliyah and smiled, waiting for Mr. Gray's camera phone to flash. Mr. Gray couldn't leave it at just one photo, though he knew he was pushing his luck.

"Oh, thank you, that's so great. Just one more, please?"

Luther had already relaxed, but he smiled again and resumed the pose. Gray noticed it was harder this time for the man to hide his weariness.

"Big smile!" coached Mr. Gray. "Excellent."

Okay, enough. No need to antagonize him.

"Thank you," said Luther, smiling again. He turned to Aaliyah and shook her hand. "Thank you for coming. Bye-bye." The preacher turned away, to another family waiting to meet him.

"Come on," said Mr. Gray to the girl, his voice barely audible.

He led her back out the same door they came in. One job done. But the night was just beginning.

# 8

It was late. All John Luther wanted was to be in bed, asleep. He'd stayed far too long at the studio tonight, but so many had come to see him, to get a smidgen of one-on-one time with the famous evangelist. Some had driven hours to get to the D.C. studio, crossing entire states. One family had come all the way from Canada. How could he possibly disappoint them?

Except now he was paying for it. He wasn't as young as he used to be, after all. Still, what a great night it had been. God was so good. The sermon couldn't have gone better. He prayed that many, many souls would hear the message and give their lives to Christ. And if his viewers were inspired by his words to make their voices heard in opposition to the Faith and Fairness Act, all the better.

He loved getting one-on-one with people. It was way too easy to get bogged down in business matters and board meetings and talk shows, and forget the reason Truth Ministries existed in the first place. It was about winning souls to Christ. That was all that ever really mattered. Not the fancy studio, not his face on television, not his opinion being counted among the major issues of the day.

Sure, John was tired, but it was a *good* tired. He'd sowed the fields tonight, and it felt good. As much as he wanted his nightly swim, followed by deep, blissful sleep, he wouldn't have traded the chance to meet his parishioners for anything.

His eyes were glazing over as he drove out of town in his olive-green Toyota FJ Cruiser, off the highways and out of the bustle of the city, toward his home farther south in Virginia. A place with trees rather than monuments. He blinked suddenly, willing himself not to sleep yet. Home was just another twenty minutes or so.

Home.

He dreamed of climbing into bed beside Monica. What a woman she was; he loved her so much. Beautiful, kind, thoughtful, supportive, she was a great wife, and a truly amazing mother. He wondered if she would still be awake, waiting for him. She always said she never slept well when he wasn't home, but it was after one o'clock in the morning already. Besides, she wasn't terribly happy with him at the moment.

The same day that Donald Harrison had entered his dressing room and demanded his support for that idiotic bill, she'd shown up at the studios. He loved it when she made the trip in, though lately it seemed to mean that something was up. And usually something not good.

The dressing room door had flown open and in ran his daughter, Jodi, throwing her arms around his neck in that special way that little girls do only for their daddies. At seven years old, Jodi was as precocious as they came, and the everlasting sunshine in John's life. He'd almost given up on ever having kids—he was several years older than Monica, after all—but she wanted a child so badly. John was eternally grateful that she'd won that debate, because his little girl was more wonderful and beautiful and more filled with love and life than he could have ever imagined. He'd never loved anyone so selflessly in his life as he did Jodi, and it surprised him how easily she was able to pull that love out of him.

Monica walked in quietly behind her with an apologetic look on her face. The girl must have escaped her grasp and slipped down the hall. He smiled and shook his head gently, indicating that it was fine. He didn't mind.

He turned to Jodi. "What are you doing up?" he asked in mock disapproval.

"My recital is tomorrow and I needed to practice," she explained, wide-eyed. "Are you coming?" Her blond hair was in a ponytail, and she had on a polka-dot dress she adored.

John sighed, searching for words. How could he disappoint that beautiful face with its spray of freckles across her nose?

Monica walked up from behind and brushed a stray strand of hair out of the girl's face. "Sweetie, Daddy has a super important board meeting that's scheduled at the exact same time," she said. "He can't make it."

The tone in Monica's voice was unmistakable. John could hear the frustration and disappointment just below the surface. A quick sideways glance of her tired eyes confirmed it. When they fought, it was always about this. Balance. Time with the family. And guilt was always Monica's most effective weapon. But what could he do? Things were what they were and he couldn't change them. Truth Ministries was closing on some new properties tomorrow, the culmination of years of hard work. There was no way he could just skip it.

He and Monica had engaged in this argument year after year. Nowadays it was mostly fought with looks and inflections.

The ministry was important, there was no denying that. It was his mission, the purpose given to him by God. He was as sure of that as he was of drawing breath. But over the years, Monica had come to feel marginalized by it. It was a family affair at first, and then as the ministry grew ever bigger and the two of them finally had a child, things began to change. These days, Monica believed that as important as Truth Ministries was, it was always taking him away from his family—especially when they needed him most. Their little girl wouldn't be with them forever, she'd said once. And that he was just watching his board members get older. That had hurt. So did the pain in Monica's eyes when he missed another event. But what was there to say? John wished he could find a way to better balance the two sides of his life, but after twenty-plus years of ministry, he'd still not mastered that skill. There was always so much to do at Truth Ministries, and absolutely everything required his attention.

"Is there any way you can reschedule?" Jodi had asked in the dressing room, her eyes bright and hopeful.

Oh, how he hated disappointing his little girl. Nothing ripped his heart out more.

"I tell you what, baby," he said. "You go home with Mommy, straight to bed. And when you wake up, I'll be there. I promise."

"Breakfast in bed?" Jodi grinned.

John grinned back. "Breakfast in bed."

"Only I'm cooking!" proclaimed Jodi, full of glee.

John laughed. "Deal."

Even now, all alone in the Toyota in the dead of night, he couldn't help laughing again. There was truly no situation that could not be made better by Jodi simply being Jodi. He thought of waking her up in the morning and swinging her around her room in his arms. He thought of her adorable giggle, those mischievous eyes, and that smile that could light up the whole world.

John was still thinking of his daughter when he spotted the girl on the side of the road, trying desperately to get his attention by waving both arms over her head.

# 9

"What is she doing?" John mumbled. He leaned in toward the windshield to get a better look as he slowed the vehicle and pulled over.

Something in the back of his mind said *This isn't right.* Here he was, on a lonely old road in the middle of nowhere, and a young girl was flagging him down. There was nothing on this entire road except a Mini Mart gas station, lighting up a section of the road about a block ahead.

Before the SUV was fully stopped, she'd run frantically up to him and slammed her hands down on the hood. "Help me!" she screamed, staring wildly in all directions.

She looked drunk or high or something. But she was too young for that—probably fifteen or sixteen. And what was she wearing? Some kind of midriff-baring top and short shorts? It was cool out, and this girl was practically in her underwear.

This was very, very wrong.

But he couldn't just ignore her cries for help. She looked genuinely frightened out of her mind. What if something was really wrong?

He got out of his vehicle and rushed up to her. "Are you all right?"

"They're coming!" she screamed. She was completely crazed, just—

Wait.

He'd seen this girl before. Wasn't she at the broadcast tonight? Yeah, she and her dad had stayed late to meet him. . . .

"Who's coming?" he asked.

She spun around then and started to walk away.

John wasn't sure whether to chase her down or not. This was nuts. "Young lady, what are you doing out here by yourself?"

The girl paraded around the space in front of the Toyota, clearly not in her right mind. John was growing impatient; he wanted to be home and in bed. If this was just some stupid prank . . .

"Sweetheart, what are you doing?"

She faced him with a gleeful smile. A freezing chill ran down John's back.

"They're he-ere," she sang, grinning. "*They're he-ere.*"

A beefy arm suddenly had John in a headlock. His heart hammered hard against his ribs as he pulled frantically at the arm wrapped around his neck. It was hard like iron and immovable.

Something sharp stuck him in the neck, and darkness swallowed him.

🏛

John swam in and out of consciousness. He caught glimpses of moments that would be forever frozen in time as hazy memories. He was slumped in the passenger seat of his vehicle, with dark silhouettes of trees passing by the side window.

A hand ran across his body in places no one but Monica should be allowed. He wanted to squirm but couldn't get his body to move.

Who was driving his Toyota?

A flash of light made him stir again. He blinked just enough to see a camera phone being held out in front of him, taking photos of him with . . . with that girl. She was sitting on his lap, making vulgar poses and groping him. He wanted to tell her to stop, to force her off his lap, to take the phone out of her hand. But his mouth and body refused to work. He was so sleepy, he just couldn't stay awake.

The sound of a male voice roused him a third time. "Scratch his face."

John forced open his heavy eyelids for a moment to glance sideways. It was the girl's dad, the man from the studio who insisted on taking several pictures of John with his daughter. No, not his daughter. A father would never do this to his girl. Especially since he was watching her with calculating eyes, like a hawk watching its prey before striking.

The left side of John's forehead and face was suddenly on fire. He blinked and saw three of the girl's fingers withdrawing after scratching him. There were more flashes, forcing John to close his eyes again.

"You gonna teach me a lesson?" teased the girl between snapping pictures. "You're a bad boy, preacher man."

And then the darkness drowned John again.

# 10

33 YEARS AGO

I won't allow you to do this," said Charles Luther. He stood at their house's front door, his arms crossed over his chest. A tall, broad-shouldered slab of granite. Immovable.

"Doesn't matter. One way or another, I'm going," John said, glaring from behind the aviator-style sunglasses his father had given him for his last birthday. It helped—the old man not being able to look into his eyes. Made him feel bolder. A packed duffel bag lay at his feet.

He stared down his father from across the room, seething with anger. He was emboldened by three years of self-searching and teenage rebellion. And also three beers. He wondered if the old man could tell he'd been drinking. Probably could smell it on him, the bloodhound. It wasn't like it was the first time. But he'd always attempted to hide it before. Not this time. Not today. At sixteen it was entirely illegal for him to touch a can of beer, which was the main reason he'd done it.

But he liked the feeling of defiance. Doing something forbidden

51

was thrilling, and his every rebellious action added to his father's grief. Something he rather enjoyed.

The old man had always been strict. But it went beyond that. Charles Luther was so convinced the world they lived in was full of corruption and suffering and evil, that he was determined to shield his son from it completely. John's friendships were judged, his every word and second scrutinized. There was little laughter in his home, and every time John tried to engage in something from the culture at large, his father would recite Philippians 4:8. "Finally, brothers and sisters, whatever is true, whatever is noble, whatever is right, whatever is pure, whatever is lovely, whatever is admirable—if anything is excellent or praiseworthy—think about such things." And he would recite it until it became nothing but a clanging gong that John had grown to despise. Now his days were mostly filled with silence. No conversation. No words. Just sixteen years at home that felt like solitary confinement.

"I'm done, Dad. I can't live in this house another minute. I'm so stifled here, I'm choking. *All the time.* I feel like I'm dying."

Charles sighed. "John, if I've been overprotective, I'm sorry. But I love you, and I don't want you to walk the same path I did. I want more for you. The road you're on leads only to destruction."

John went on glaring at his father. He'd heard all this before, so many times, and had no desire to hear it again. As a young adult his father had become an alcoholic, and his life fell apart because of it. He couldn't keep a job, he slept around, he was even homeless for about a year. As he'd told John countless times, God met him at his lowest point, and everything changed. He gave up all his destructive habits, got a solid job working in construction, and eventually entered seminary. The only evidence of that old life was the occasional cigar the old man indulged in.

John knew all of this to be true, but he didn't care. His father was so intent on keeping his son from becoming just like him that John felt nothing but rejected at every turn. Everything was so unfair here. He'd had enough.

But before he left, there was one question he had to ask. One unspeakable topic that had to be spoken. In sixteen years he'd never asked. He couldn't. It was unquestionably, unequivocally *off-limits*. But what if he never got another chance to ask?

"Where's Mom?"

Charles looked as if someone had punched him in the stomach. He took a tiny step backward.

"Where is she, Dad?" John repeated. "Is she dead? You've never told me a single thing about her, not one word. I don't even know her name!"

The old man studied his own feet.

"Debbie," said Charles. "Your mother's name is Deborah Letts. It was never my intention to keep her from you, son. I kept waiting for the right time to tell you, and well . . . I guess it never came."

Charles shifted his weight, unable to look John in the eyes. John had never seen his father look this uncomfortable. It was so painfully awkward, he almost felt bad for the old man.

"Were you married?" John asked.

His father shook his head. "I had just started my big construction job. I was changing, God was turning my life around. But I was—*we* were—young. And deeply in love. I think she's the only woman I ever loved. We were together for about five months when she became pregnant."

John's pulse began to rise. He couldn't figure out why this was making him angry, but his bitterness rose with his father's every word.

"So why isn't she here?" John spat. "How'd you drive her away?"

Charles looked down again. "The day after you were born,

I found a note on her hospital bed saying she was sorry but she couldn't stay. She'd discharged herself, and that was that. Your mother was . . . unique. Special. I suppose you could call her a 'free spirit.' She always dismissed anything I said about marriage or family."

"And now . . . ?"

"I never saw her or heard from her again," Charles said, his voice growing quieter. "I don't know if she's even alive. She made her choice and she never looked back. But I still think of her. Every single day. She destroyed me when she left, but a part of me still loves her."

When his father fell silent, John's anger evaporated. Of all the ways he'd imagined this conversation going, all the stories he'd concocted in his head over the years to explain his mother's absence, the reality was nothing like he'd expected.

"It wasn't because of you she left," John said, his voice barely audible and his eyes wandering far into the distance. "She ran from *me*, Dad. I'm the problem. I always have been. It's me. She knew it the first time she looked at me. There's nothing good in me."

Emotionless, he picked up his duffel bag and walked toward the door. He pushed past his father, but instead of a rigid wall of stone, the old man was more like a deflated balloon. He made no effort to stop John from walking out the door.

"John?" his father said when John was just outside.

John hesitated but didn't turn around.

"No matter where you go or what you do, I will always love you," said the old man softly. "There's nothing you could ever do to change that."

John's eyes stung, and a lump rose in his throat. But he swallowed it and kept walking.

## 11

*Tick, tick, tick.* Mr. Gray studied his watch. Five more minutes ought to do it. He mashed down the gas pedal harder.

He glanced over to the passenger seat, where Aaliyah was having her fun. Doing her job.

The preacher was slumped in the passenger seat while Aaliyah sat in his lap, snapping suggestive selfies. She tossed her hair around, licked her lips, and stared melodramatically into the camera phone he'd given her.

She was better at this than he could have ever hoped. And only sixteen. What would come next would almost be a blessing for her.

One flash, then a second and third.

"That'll do," he said, then held out a hand in her direction.

She gave him the phone and popped her chewing gum back into her mouth.

Mr. Gray eased Luther's Toyota onto the side of the road, miles from where they'd tricked Luther into stopping. A red-and-white

Jeep was parked there, waiting for them. He stepped out of the vehicle, and Aaliyah followed suit, stretching her legs.

The phone still in his hand, Mr. Gray thumbed 911 and waited for the response. "Yeah, I'd like to report a car accident. One vehicle. Marker 134."

The operator repeated his words, "One vehicle. Marker 134."

"Looks like two people inside," Mr. Gray told her.

"Copy. Two persons with injuries?" she clarified.

"Yes. You're going to want to send an ambulance."

The call over, Mr. Gray threw his sports jacket over his shoulders and shoved his arms in. Aaliyah walked toward the trees that lined either side of the road. She lit a cigarette and took a long drag.

"Where do you think you're going?" he asked.

Aaliyah turned around and smiled. It was obvious she was enjoying herself, though how much of that was sincere and how much was thanks to the Rohypnol was anybody's guess.

"You just took his car," she said.

He smiled. "You like that, huh?"

She rolled her eyes but couldn't hide her sly grin. A light caught her eyes, and she turned serious. Mr. Gray knew she was staring at the red-and-blue lights of a police car. But no siren could be heard.

"The cops showed up?" asked Aaliyah, worried.

Mr. Gray shrugged. "Yeah. Are there any marks on you?"

She shook her head, then turned away from him again, so he could see there were no marks on her back.

"Come on," he prodded, smiling again. "Turn around for me."

Aaliyah spun to look into his approving face. She looked relieved that he was pleased with her work, and for just a moment he wondered what her story was. Was she an orphan? Had she never had a father and longed for that connection—even with a total stranger who'd hired her for a frame job? How did she end up here?

No one would ever get a chance to find out.

He backhanded her hard, and she was instantly unconscious. He lowered her to the ground and pulled out another syringe from his jacket and stabbed it into her neck.

The policeman, a big muscular man Gray called Mr. Broad, caught up to him just as Mr. Gray was pulling the syringe out of her neck. He stood to his feet.

"Get her in the car," said Mr. Gray and then headed back to Luther's vehicle, hearing Mr. Broad's grunt as he hefted the girl up. Gray approached the passenger side door and looked inside.

It was empty.

"He's gone," he said, no trace of worry in his voice. "Luther ran."

Mr. Broad, carrying Aaliyah, looked up in alarm. "But—"

Gray held up a hand, unconcerned. "Luther ran because that's what a guilty man does."

# 12

With great gasping lungfuls of air, John ran into the night. This was insane. He felt in his pockets, on his wrist. His watch was gone, as well as his car keys and wallet. They'd taken everything.

What was he doing, running through the woods in the middle of the night? He hadn't run this hard in years. How had it gotten to this? More pressingly, how long would it be before those two men noticed he was gone? There could even be gunshots fired in his direction any second now . . .

Wait. No, that didn't make sense. They wouldn't shoot at him. The man in the gray suit could have shot him in the car if he'd wanted John dead. So if they didn't want him dead, what *did* they want?

*Just go*, he told himself. He had to get as far away from them as he could. *Keep running*.

As he cleared a rise, he ran past something to his left between the trees, something just visible out of the corner of his eye.

His body was still sluggish from whatever they'd drugged him with, and it took longer than normal for his brain to catch up to his surroundings. Dazed, he stumbled to a stop and turned around. There stood two young people, probably twenty-somethings, both of them girls. One of them wore a hooded sweat shirt with the hood up around her head. She stood very still, holding a phone up at him. A camera, or video more likely. That was all he needed.

They shared a long, silent moment. The girls made no attempt to inquire about his safety or offer to help. But then neither did they rat him out to the two men down on the road below. John decided he should be grateful for small favors and let God worry about the rest.

*Be ye thankful in all things . . .*

The girl holding the camera phone looked pale, with heavily made-up eyes. Like a Goth, he thought. Is that what they were called? Goths? She had multiple piercings all over her exceptionally pallid face, and her clothes looked used and filthy, like they'd come out of a dumpster. Likely an addict, possibly even homeless. But why would she have a phone? Whatever she was, she certainly didn't seem to be interested in being his friend.

The camera girl's expression was blank, stern even. There was nothing on her face that he could discern—not even a fleeting curiosity. She was merely a bystander recording an interesting event.

Looking into her eyes and finding nothing there, no help, he turned and resumed his run.

A few minutes later, a small tree limb scraped across his forehead as he ran in the dark. He was so deep into the woods now, almost nothing was visible. He rubbed a sleeve against his head, found it stained with blood. He kept running.

Soon he had to stop to catch his breath. Without warning he doubled over and threw up on the ground, coughing and gagging. Was that the drug he'd been injected with? Working its way out of his system? Or just blind panic? John couldn't tell.

He placed a hand on his neck to feel his pulse. Predictably it was thumping harder than it had in years. He was so out of breath, he feared he'd never catch it. His lungs fought for air and his heart raced.

The darkness closed in once more, and John felt himself topple to the ground.

# 13

Monica Luther was afraid to turn over. She hadn't heard John come to bed last night, and she didn't want to find him *not there* now. But in her gut she had that horrible intuition. . . .

She rolled. His half of the bed was undisturbed.

Barring the occasional business trip, John always came home at the end of the day. Always. No matter what. Unless there was some big emergency to deal with, there was no way he would willingly not come home.

Okay, calm down, calm down. Maybe he was on the couch. Maybe he got in so late, he didn't want to wake her up. Or maybe he'd gotten up early this morning and was already downstairs, having breakfast with Jodi. Had she overslept? It wouldn't be like Jodi to stay quiet enough in the morning to let Mommy sleep in.

Monica rolled back over to glance at her nightstand. The alarm clock said it was 6:47 a.m. Well, that explained Jodi. She was a night owl like her dad; she rarely got up before seven. So what was going on with John? Monica told her heart to slow down, to stop trying to leave her chest. But it wouldn't listen.

Something was wrong. Terribly wrong. She could feel it.

Maybe she should call Ryan or Dave, find out if they'd seen John this morning. But she'd better do it quick; she'd have to get Jodi up for school in a few minutes.

Monica flinched and let out a clipped scream when the doorbell rang. Her heart jolted. Someone was at her door before seven in the morning. She wasn't even dressed yet. Who could possibly—?

Oh no.

She yelped again when a harsh banging reverberated throughout the house. Three knocks came from the front door, loud enough to be heard upstairs.

"Mommy?" called Jodi from down the hall.

Monica ran to her bedroom door, throwing her bathrobe on over her nightgown. "It's okay, sweetie. Just go back to sleep for a few more minutes."

Her heart thudded harder and harder as she descended the stairs as fast as she dared. She almost stumbled on one step, but caught herself just as the pounding on the door began again.

"Who is it?" she called out, rounding the bottom of the staircase.

"The police, ma'am" came the answer from a deep, gruff voice.

Monica hurried to the door, her fingers trembling as she unlocked the dead bolt and chain and flung the door open. Two uniformed police officers stood there, their expressions impossible to gauge.

"Is your husband home, Mrs. Luther?" asked the one on the left. The badge he held out to her said *Richards* on it.

Monica could barely process what was happening. The police were at her door, asking if John was here, and . . . *Was* he here? She'd never found out for sure. "Um . . . I don't think he is. I'm sorry, I'm a little disoriented. I just woke up."

The officer on the right, whose nametag said *Garcia*, spoke up. "May we come in?"

"Um . . . sure. I guess," Monica answered, still struggling to catch up. "What is this about?"

Officers Richards and Garcia ignored her question and stepped inside. They were followed by four more officers she hadn't noticed until now, each of whom slid into the house and moved off in a different direction. Just like that, the police were spreading out through her home.

"Wait," she said, her presence of mind finally returning. "Are you searching my house for something? Don't you have to have a warrant or something?"

Officer Garcia handed her a folded-up piece of paper. She didn't need to unfold it to know what it was.

She frowned at the two officers. "If you had this, why did you bother asking if you could come in?"

"Despite what you've seen on TV or read in crime novels, police officers do exercise common courtesy, Mrs. Luther," said Officer Richards.

There was a crash somewhere behind her, maybe the dining room? Monica frowned. Hopefully nothing was broken. More important, the noise had to have woken Jodi up. She'd be making her way to the stairs at any moment.

"In that case, I would appreciate knowing why you're here and what this has to do with my husband," said Monica.

Richards and Garcia exchanged a fleeting look. Were they under orders not to reveal too much to her?

"Do you know a teenage girl named Aaliyah Evans?" Garcia asked.

"No."

"You're certain?" asked Richards. "You've never heard that name before?"

"Never."

"Mommy?" said a small voice.

Monica spun in place. Jodi had moved very quietly down

the stairs and appeared right behind her mother. She sounded nervous.

"Why are the police here?" she asked.

Monica smiled at her daughter to lighten the mood. "They're explaining that to Mommy right now, sweetheart. Can you do me a favor and go get your school clothes on while I talk to these nice officers?"

Jodi obviously wasn't fooled. Monica knew her daughter could see her fear, and the girl glanced back and forth between the two officers and her mother, trying to find some answers. Greeted only with silence, she finally complied, shuffling across the hardwood floor and back upstairs.

The second she was gone, Monica faced the policemen again. "What is going on?"

"Aaliyah Evans is dead, Mrs. Luther," said Officer Garcia. "And I'm afraid your husband is our primary suspect. He hasn't been formally charged yet, but we have evidence that he was present at the scene of the crime when the girl died. And that he fled the scene immediately after her death."

Later, Monica would recall the sound of breaking glass at that exact moment. But she wouldn't be able to remember if something in the house had actually broken or if the sound had come from her world shattering into a million pieces.

## 14

Many hours later, John Luther slowly roused. He sensed a warm, dappled light on his face, and for a moment he forgot where he was. Why was the bed so hard? Why was that bird chirping so loudly outside his window? He was about to ask Monica to shut the window and put on a pot of coffee when he remembered.

His eyes opened tenderly, and he stared up into a maze of tree branches and bright sunlight beyond them. His lips felt swollen and cracked. Despite the sleep, he felt no more rested than he had before passing out. He was curled up in a burrow of leaves and fallen branches. With no small effort he pushed up onto his hands and knees, and then all the way to his feet. He steadied after a slight wobble and absent-mindedly put a hand over his abdomen. He was starving.

Worse, he was lost. He assumed he was still in Virginia, but he wasn't sure how long he'd been unconscious in the vehicle and how far they'd driven him. Turning in a circle he saw mostly trees, endless trunks of elms and oaks and firs. But there, finally, he saw the wreckage of his own flight. Bent branches and broken underbrush. Left without choices, he chose to backtrack down the path he'd carved last night.

$$\widehat{\mathrm{III}}$$

The scent and sounds of the woods were instantly recognizable to John, though he couldn't quite place why they felt so familiar. It was only on stopping to rest and hearing a particular bird sing a quick six-note chirrup deep in the woods that he was transported back nearly forty years to his childhood—to the first time he'd run away.

He'd been eight or nine at the time, up in the woods with his father as the old man visited and thought about cabins. It was a pastime of sorts for Charles Luther, planning his future hideaway in the wilderness.

John couldn't remember why they'd begun to fight—maybe something about an X-Men comic book John had hidden away in his luggage—but he did remember the outcome. Charles ordered John out of the cabin they'd rented for the weekend and into the woods. He was to spend a half hour sitting in and thinking over God's creation before he could come back in for the night.

John had grabbed his backpack, pulled his hood up over his head to hide the anger burning on his face, and stormed out. He walked down the crushed-stone driveway, crossed the road, and plunged into the woods, not stopping to look back because he knew for certain Charles Luther was not following him.

The power in walking, in defying, fueled his legs. For the first half hour.

But then he stopped and sat down and suddenly the immensity of the woods weighed in on him, and he felt how alone he was. *"Pray,"* the old man used to tell him whenever he was scared, but John refused. He was scared, but he would not pray.

And he didn't—even when the sun fell low, and evening's cool hand started to grip him.

His backpack had a bit of food in it but nothing for warmth, and John realized—while he wasn't in great danger, as it wasn't that cold—it wouldn't do him any good to just stand out in the open. Scouting around the area, while the sun dipped lower and lower, he finally found a massive boulder with a snug depression at its base filled with fallen pine needles. The perfect size to tuck himself into.

Quickly, before darkness fell, he gathered a few pine boughs to pull up around himself and then lay down in his little den, eating what little food he had. He guessed he wouldn't sleep, but the next thing he knew, dawn had lifted night's grip and he crawled out.

He could see his breath, yet he felt *alive*. He'd made it through the night. On his own. Without his father. Without even a single prayer.

Hunger followed quickly, though, and he had no interest in spending yet another night tucked next to the boulder. Instead he climbed the rock and looked around deep into the woods, hoping to gather some sense of which direction to head. He soon began to panic—every direction looked exactly the same at first glimpse—but then he caught a sharp reflection of light and heard what had to have been a truck rumbling to life.

It took forty-five minutes to reach what he'd seen.

It was a camp. A scout camp perhaps, probably used mostly in summer, and so all the buildings stood abandoned. John didn't care; he was just thrilled to find some evidence of other humans. He spent the morning exploring—few of the buildings had been locked—and even found a box of saltine crackers that had been left behind and were miraculously untouched by rodents. John opened a sleeve and wandered his way past a strange dome-shaped greenhouse and down a path to the pool. He sat on the edge of the pool deck, took off his shoes and socks, and dipped his feet in the water.

"Those were going to be my lunch," a voice said from behind him, and John nearly choked on a cracker. He bolted to his feet.

A man stepped out from the pool house. He had on a green flannel shirt and denims supported by a carpenter's belt.

"I'm sorry," John said. "Didn't think there was anyone here." He couldn't tell if he was disappointed to have been found or thrilled to no longer be alone. "My name is John. I . . . I . . . got lost in the woods."

Half an hour later, the camp's caretaker had escorted John back to the rented cabin. The family car was still parked outside, but John's dad was not around.

"Probably looking for me," John said.

"I can wait around, if you like," the carpenter offered. But John said he was fine, and so the man drove off.

Hours later, Charles Luther returned. He had a stringer of rainbow trout in one hand and his rod in the other.

"Clean these for dinner," he had said to John, handing him the fish, and never said a single word asking about how the boy had spent his night.

John remembered how powerful he'd felt at the time—standing there, gutting and filleting the fish. Because, at least for one night, he'd won. He'd survived and found his way back home, and with no help.

The woods brought all that back to John as he, again, found himself lost and desperate. This time, though, he'd been humbled enough to pray. For direction and guidance. For a safe path home yet again. Then he set off once more into the woods.

Two hours later, he found the edge of the woods at last and stepped out onto a main road. He couldn't keep walking or he soon would collapse. Weary, dehydrated, and famished, he emerged from the woods to find himself behind a familiar-looking gas station. It was the Mini Mart, the one not far from where the girl had first flagged him down. Where this whole mess began.

At the rear of the store, attached to a streetlight pole, was something red, and it caught his eye. Walking closer, he saw it was an old pay phone. Hope flooded his heart; at last he could call Monica and get some help. But his hope evaporated when he stepped up and found nothing but a cord that was broken off where the receiver had once been.

John closed his eyes for a moment and let his head sag backward until it rested against one side of glass. He was so tired, so disappointed.

But he had to keep going. Just keep going.

John walked to the Mini Mart. At least there would be a sink where he could wash the blood off his face and get a drink of water. How long would it be before the effects of that drug wore off? He still felt horribly disoriented.

Inside the tiny store, a female clerk stood behind a counter reading a tabloid magazine. She eyed him so warily that he wondered what he must look like. She had long red hair and was maybe a little overweight. Did she have her finger on a panic button right now, waiting to see if he'd try to steal something or brandish a gun?

He was too tired to care.

"Key to the men's room?" he asked.

The clerk didn't respond. She merely stared at him.

So he turned right and walked through the store, looking, looking . . . *there.* The soda machine was perched on a long table affixed to one wall, alongside condiments, napkins, a coffee machine, and more. He pushed the soda machine's button for plain water and caught some in his hand. After pouring the handful into his mouth, he splashed a little on his face.

"That's for paying customers only."

He looked up. The clerk was still watching his every move.

His face wet, John quickly grabbed a few napkins from a dispenser and dried off.

"I'm sorry," she said. "Company policy."

Despite appearances, did she actually feel some sympathy for him? Particularly given how he must look? He glanced down to see ripped clothes, bloodstains, and dirt everywhere. But still, was he really *that* unrecognizable?

"Don't you know who I am?" he asked. He hoped it didn't sound pompous; he hadn't meant it that way. He was just so worn out that any hint of familiarity would be nice.

The clerk shook her head. "No idea."

John's head sagged again. "I'm . . ."

Ah, why bother? He wiped water drops from his tie and shirt with the napkins, then threw them in the trash. He walked toward the door.

"I apologize," he said, exiting the building. He knew he should be thinking about what would come next, how he was going to contact someone, but at that moment he felt only exhaustion, thirst, and a simple wish that he could fall once more into darkness.

Only this time it didn't come.

# 15

The halls of power at the J. Edgar Hoover Building were filled with clusters of agents engaged in hushed conversations. Whatever the big news was that everyone was whispering about, Agent Ashley Rivera had the feeling she'd missed it. She'd only arrived at work ten minutes ago, and had barely walked in the door when her partner summoned her to his office as quickly as possible.

Of course, referring to Agent Preston Clark as her "partner" was a slight misnomer. It was true that the two were a pair when working on cases, but his twenty-some years of experience at the FBI far outranked her two and a half. No one ever said it, but Clark was her mentor.

Agent Clark was tall and solid, a college linebacker in his day and something of a maverick at the agency. He was known for following protocol to the letter, but also for employing methods of investigation that were entirely his own. He relied on his instincts more than most federal agents were comfortable with, though he was also highly skilled in many disciplines.

"Seen this yet?" he asked as she walked through his office

door. He nodded at the flat-screen TV hanging from the wall to the right of his desk.

Rivera took her customary seat at the front of his desk and focused on the television. It was tuned to CNW, where one of their anchors was breathlessly relaying breaking news about an evangelist named John Luther. Rivera knew who Luther was; most everyone in America did. He was the most popular preacher in the country—possibly even the world. Luther was an outspoken, unapologetic evangelical, a virtue that made him plenty of enemies in Washington. And plenty of allies as well. Some loved him, some hated him. But everyone in D.C. respected him.

In the game of politics, John Luther was one of the few major players who held no public office.

A scroll at the bottom of the TV screen revealed the gist of the breaking news. A teenage girl had been found dead in Luther's car, Luther was the primary suspect and had fled the scene of the crime, and he was currently at large. A fugitive.

"So *this* is what all the chatter's about," Rivera said, running a hand through her long jet-black hair.

CNW splashed a photo of Luther that filled the entire screen. Luther was standing in it, his hands clasped in front, with a serene but serious look on his face. Behind him was an American flag, hung so that the stripes ran vertically. It almost looked like a presidential portrait.

Clark stabbed at the TV's remote and paused the live feed. "What do you see?"

It was a favorite exercise of Clark's. He had an uncanny knack for accurately determining guilt or innocence by "reading" the suspect's eyes. "The eyes are the window to the soul," he'd once told her. "Everything you need to know is there. You just have to look hard enough to see it." Shortly after being made partners, Clark had begun frequently engaging Rivera in this game. Most people believed that instincts couldn't be taught, but Clark was determined to instill them in his partner.

Rivera cleared her mind and stared into Luther's gray-blue eyes. She saw sincerity, though she knew that could be faked. Luther's eyes practically glowed with conviction and certainty of purpose. There was honesty, and lots of it. Some measure of ambition as well—probably more than he'd admit to. Was that a hint of patience? If so, was it the practiced kind that didn't come naturally? His eyes weren't unkind, but there was a distinct lack of humor. He was not a lighthearted man, and there was a great deal of pain in his past.

"Gut instinct . . ." she said, "he's a complicated man. But I don't see a killer."

Clark, who'd watched her closely as she made her determination, gave a slight nod. "Neither do I. But if drug use was involved, that changes all the rules."

"What makes you think drugs could be involved?" asked Rivera.

"Just a guess. But you're right. We need more to go on. The call came in twenty minutes ago. This is ours. You and I are going to bring this guy in before somebody else winds up dead—including him."

Rivera hesitated. That didn't quite add up. "Aren't fugitives under Marshal jurisdiction?" The purpose of the U.S. Marshals office was to hunt down fugitives and bring them to justice. This kind of thing wasn't unheard of for Feds, yet it was a bit unusual.

"Luther's unique status makes lots of folks up on the Hill very nervous. They want the FBI to take point."

Of course. When it came to politics, perceptions were all that mattered. And Congress would have an easier time molding the public's perceptions of John Luther if the FBI was running the investigation.

Clark unpaused the TV and caught it back up to the live

broadcast. CNW was showing an interview with John Luther, which was labeled PREVIOUSLY RECORDED in tiny letters in the top left corner.

"Do you know what kind of person I was?" asked Luther to whoever was interviewing him. "An abusive, alcoholic, gambling drug addict."

The face of popular journalist Diana Lucas replaced Luther's. She was speaking live. "That was John Luther, just days ago, admitting to a history of alcoholism, drug abuse, gambling addiction, and spousal abuse. It is not widely known among Luther's followers that he is currently married to his *second* wife, after his first marriage ended in a bitter divorce following allegations of abuse on Luther's part. He and his former wife eventually settled out of court, and today Luther is married to Monica Luther, with whom he has a daughter. He claims to be a changed man, having been 'delivered by God' from the destructive behaviors of his past. But only time and more information about the shocking events that took place last night will prove if that deliverance has stuck. . . ."

Rivera glanced at Clark. "I'll pull his criminal file."

Clark nodded. "Good. I've asked the police to let the agency conduct the girl's autopsy, so we should have those results in a few hours."

"What about the car?"

"It's being held for us," replied Clark. "The scene too. Let's get to work."

## 16

As the police searched the house, Monica sat at the dining room table for half an hour. Silent and alone.

She had no idea who this Aaliyah Evans was. But the whole thing had to be a mistake. It just had to be.

John had made his share of mistakes in the past, but he was different now. A good man. He was *more* than a good man—he was a man that countless others looked to, following his example and teachings. Monica hadn't known John before God came into his life. She'd heard stories of the wretched example of humanity he was back then. But the man in those stories was not the John she knew. He wasn't *her* John. She never wanted to meet that man.

Was it possible he could have slipped? Well, anything was possible. John was a flawed human being just like everyone else. No one was perfect. No one was immune to sin.

But he wouldn't do this. Monica's husband, the man she fell in love with and with whom she shared her life, would never, ever hurt anyone.

He wouldn't, right?

No. Of course not.

Unless . . .

Had something changed?

Had she missed the warning signs?

She stood and walked slowly to the kitchen. After digging in her purse, she retrieved her phone. What was his number? He was the last person she wanted to talk to right now, but few people spent more time with John and would have noticed any changes in John's behavior.

After two rings, Ryan Morris answered. "Yyyyellow?"

"Ryan, it's Monica."

"Well hey there, beautiful," he said. "Have you seen John this morning? He's not in his office, and we—"

"Ryan, something's wrong," said Monica.

As he so often did, he breezed right past her words. "Hey, is John feeling okay? I told him last night he was looking kinda pale. I hope he's not coming down—"

"*Ryan*," said Monica again. "John is missing. The police are here at the house, right now."

A brief silence was followed by, "What? What do you mean, 'missing'? Where is he?"

"I don't know, Ryan," she replied, rolling her eyes. "Something happened last night . . . something about a girl. I don't know any details yet."

Monica heard some kind of commotion in the background, people calling for Ryan.

"Hang on," he said. She heard shuffling and decided it was the sound of Ryan walking or jogging. Then there was louder hubbub, followed by the emotionless intonations of what sounded like a talking head on the TV news. She couldn't make out what the newscaster was saying.

Ryan was quiet for so long, she wondered if he was still holding the phone.

"Ryan?"

"You, uh . . . You'd better turn on the TV," he said.

For the second time today, Monica felt like she was going to throw up. If the media had already picked up on whatever happened last night, then it was over. Even if he was innocent, the media would make him *look* guilty. There was nothing television news networks loved more than a scandal. John was going to lose everything.

The world felt like it was moving in slow motion as she made her way to the living room and looked for the remote. The sense of dread was physical and overpowering.

Was any of this really happening? How could it be?

She found the remote on the couch, dropped it—when had her hands started shaking?—picked it back up, and pressed the power button. It was still tuned to CNW from the last time it was on.

*Breaking News* was plastered prominently at the bottom of the screen, with a smaller headline underneath that read, *Girl found dead in evangelist's vehicle.*

". . . highly respected evangelist John Luther, who has ministered to millions around the world, including sitting presidents and other global leaders, is the chief suspect in the alleged murder of Aaliyah Evans," said the news anchor. "We currently have no details on Ms. Evans, but police have confirmed to us that she was found dead shortly before dawn this morning, inside John Luther's vehicle, which Mr. Luther had apparently abandoned in an undisclosed location . . ."

Monica couldn't remember sitting down, but she was on the couch now. What had John been doing with a young woman in the middle of the night?

". . . manslaughter, possibly statutory rape, child endangerment, drug possession, and leaving the scene of an accident. Talk about a relapse—I don't know how a judge could overlook . . ."

*God, please, no.*

This couldn't be real.

# 17

The worst part was still being alive.

Standing outside the Mini Mart, John came to that slow realization. His head was finally clearing from whatever drug they'd used on him. Looking up and down the empty rural highway, John knew they had deliberately let him live, had likely wanted him to escape. It hadn't been mercy or kindness. Instead, there had to be some darker reason that he hadn't yet discovered. And now he was lost. Left here without a phone or money, hours from his home. He knew he had to find people to help him, but there were few options for next steps. Looking to his left, he began trudging in that direction.

What was that passage in the book of Matthew? The one about Jesus and the time he roamed the wilderness after Satan had tempted him? It said that angels had come to him and cared for him there.

"Lord," he whispered, "I sure could use an angel or two about now."

He was staggering, exhausted and thirsty. He hadn't felt like this in a very long time, not since the dark days before God came into his life. He'd forgotten how horrible it was, how he never wanted to feel like this again.

Minutes later, a white van appeared next to him, slowing to a stop. A woman popped her head out the side window. She had bright, fierce eyes, sharp cheekbones and chin, and long, curly brown hair. She wore a black T-shirt, not one but two cross necklaces, and one of her wrists was loaded with multiple bracelets that were a rainbow of colors. Thirty years ago she would've been a hippie. Today he'd see women like her in the audience, and the same kinds of faces in the crowds protesting him.

"Sir!" she called out.

John stopped short and walked over to her.

"You okay?" she asked.

"No," he replied wearily, out of breath. "I'm not okay."

John leaned forward to rest his head against the side-view mirror. The woman looked deeply concerned, studying him closely.

"Thanks for asking, though," he added.

"I'm Kathy from Helping Hands," she said. "I've got water and donuts if you want some breakfast." She produced an ice-cold bottle of water and handed it to him.

John accepted it gratefully, looking at the bottle as if it were the most precious gift he'd ever received.

Kathy smiled at him. "Not so long ago I looked just like you."

Oh. She thought he was homeless. Maybe even drunk.

John poured water into his mouth, swallowing the gloriously cold liquid greedily.

"The arms of God aren't as far away as you might think," Kathy continued, and John had to hold back a bitter smile.

He didn't have time to explain his situation to her. "Kathy, I need to borrow a phone."

She looked mildly surprised. "Okay," she said, reaching for the van's console, where she grabbed a cell phone. She offered it to him freely. Whoever this woman was, she was a godsend.

"Thanks," he said.

John turned and walked away, back around toward the rear of the van. He just wanted to get far enough out of earshot for a little privacy. Kathy opened the van's side door and peeked out, keeping an eye on him. She didn't seem to have much regard for her phone, so he had to assume she was worried about him.

Leaning against the back of the van for support, John made the call. The one person he needed to talk to first.

"Hello?"

"Monica!"

"John!" Monica whispered. Only she didn't sound relieved. "The police are here, and they're going through everything. They're talking about you like you're some kind of murderer! Where have you been?"

John stammered, "I . . . I don't know. I'm trying to figure it out. Something happened last night—"

"A girl is *dead*, John! They're saying you're involved. They're saying you killed her!"

Dead?

She wasn't dead when he ran from the car. She was fine. Drugged probably, but up walking around under her own power and seemingly feeling fine. How could she be dead?

It hit him.

It was *them*. Those two men—the one in the gray suit and the supposed cop.

That poor girl . . .

Dear God in heaven, they killed her.

# 18

I didn't kill anybody!" insisted John. "I woke up in the middle of nowhere. They took all my stuff—my car, my wallet, my ID."

Monica's silence was crushing. She believed him, didn't she?

"I'm coming home," said John. He knew it was madness, but he was just so tired.

"No! Don't!" Monica whispered. "*They're watching me.*"

John's muscles went weak, and he took a few steps backward until he fell against the van. Did Monica mean the police? Or . . . someone else?

He quickly ended the call, tried to compose himself, and edged around the van to hand the phone back to Kathy. He looked at the area around the van with new eyes. An oppressive, bright sun burned his skin as he spun around on the old hillside road. Dirt bordered both sides of the road, with higher hills on the right and dense woods on the left. The hills were clear and easily visible for as far as his eyes could see. But within the trees there could be anything.

Was he being watched right now? Or was he being paranoid?

Surely he wasn't important enough to warrant constant surveillance from . . . well, from whoever was doing this to him.

Who *was* doing this, anyway? Why was this happening to him?

"Can I give you a ride somewhere?"

John looked up. Kathy was still leaning out of the side of the van. Had she overheard his conversation with Monica? He'd spoken of killing, of someone being dead. Why wasn't she calling the police on the phone he'd just handed back to her?

She studied him intently as he did the same to her. He could discern nothing on her face except a sincere desire to help. No hint of deception.

John blinked, realizing he hadn't answered her question. His head was swimming with too many thoughts, and he felt dizzy. "What?" was all he could get out.

"Can I help you get somewhere? Someplace safe?"

Someplace safe. Where would that be?

He couldn't go home. The police were there and would have the entire neighborhood staked out by nightfall. The same went for the office; he couldn't possibly show his face there.

*Was* there anyplace safe for him anymore?

Well, I *could* . . .

There was one place John was always welcome, no matter what. And his connection to the place wasn't widely known, though it was a matter of public record and would surely come to light sooner than later. He didn't want to risk endangering anyone.

But maybe if he got there first, before the authorities . . .

Short of leaving the country, it was his only option.

"Downtown," he told Kathy. "I need to get to St. Peter's Church."

## 19

S enator Donald Harrison shook his head as he stared at the television screen in his office. The coverage had been playing for over an hour now. Nonstop reporting and analysis on four different networks about John Luther's shocking alleged drug relapse, possible murder of a teenage girl, and subsequent fleeing from authorities.

Donald located the TV remote on the corner of his desk and switched it off. Enough of this distraction. The Luther train had begun rolling away from the station, and there was no stopping it now.

"Well, here we go," he said to himself, rounding his desk and grabbing his coat before exiting the room.

He rode the elevator alone to the bottom floor, then strode out of it with confidence of purpose. Where were they . . . ?

There.

Coming in sight of the building's glass front door, he saw them, just as he'd expected. A moderately sized gathering of reporters, photographers, and camera crews stood a respectable distance away from the building's exterior, waiting for him to emerge.

Donald ran over in his mind a few ideas he'd had about what he would say when this moment came. Then he blew through the main doors and braced himself.

"Senator Harrison!"

"Senator!"

"Sir!"

The cacophony of voices came at him all at once as the crowd of journalists quickly converged around him.

"Senator!" cried a female reporter he recognized from one of the major networks. "You're a close friend of John Luther's. Do you care to comment on the charges he's currently facing?"

Donald cleared his throat, and everyone fell silent. More than a dozen microphones and recording devices were shoved up close to his face.

Affecting just the right note of concern and disappointment, he replied, "John Luther is a fine man. This is an absolute tragedy that's happened."

Another reporter spoke up. "If this ever goes to trial, will you be pushing for a lenient sentence?"

They might as well have been working off a prearranged script, ticking off Donald's anticipated questions one by one.

"Well, my heart goes out to his family," he said, managing to sound both stern and compassionate. "But regardless of who he may or may not have had relationships with, I want to see justice served."

Time to get moving again. He couldn't take the risk of appearing to *want* to speak to reporters about this. He pushed through the crowd and attempted to keep walking, knowing the reporters wouldn't let him go that easy.

The questions kept coming, fast and loud as he walked away, and he kept waiting to hear one he wanted to answer. Careful not to let his frustration show, he was nonetheless annoyed that their questions were turning inane. For several seconds there was nothing worth answering.

Finally he spun, walking backward, and offered a polished, flat politician's smile. Spreading his hands wide, he said, "I can't clean the world with soiled hands."

How was that for a sound bite, America?

Donald estimated that the line would be the lead-in for the John Luther news coverage for the rest of the day and much of tomorrow.

# 20

There it was. It took the better part of two hours to track down Luther's records, since most of them were police reports that came from disparate sources. Seemed Luther had spent a lot of his youth and early adulthood wandering from place to place. He'd been all over the country, from the looks of it.

Of greater interest to Agent Rivera was how difficult it had been culling his complete criminal history from the FBI database. The system was so sophisticated these days that a simple criminal report could usually be found in less than a minute. But Luther's records had proven difficult to track down. And even now, she'd only been able to compile a *criminal* history. She wasn't entirely sure that it was complete, even now, and his noncriminal records—marital status, deceased relatives, school records, and so on—were missing from his file.

It wasn't the first time she'd seen a file with conspicuously missing data. When the interests of one's benefactors in Washington were involved, those kinds of "public" records had a way of getting masked behind red tape.

Rivera knew that most agents hated chasing down records, but she'd always enjoyed it. There was something fascinating in learning about the things people did, the lengths they went to in order to get what they wanted, the capacity for evil that rested in the human heart, and the depths to which they descended and how they justified it. It was like reading forgotten pages from a volume of modern history, with a healthy dose of psychology thrown in.

She'd just begun skimming the report when Agent Clark walked into her office.

"Hear from the coroner yet?" she asked.

"Shouldn't be much longer. Autopsy's in progress now. O'Neill's doing it."

Rivera blinked. Franklin O'Neill was a senior agent, one of the "big office upstairs" guys who gave orders and supervised the work of underlings like Clark and Rivera. Many years ago he'd been a medical examiner, but he hadn't performed an autopsy in probably twenty years or more. Someone in Washington had to be applying some major pressure on the bureau if he had scrubbed up to perform Aaliyah Evans's autopsy himself.

"That his file?" asked Clark.

Rivera nodded. "He wasn't kidding on that TV interview. His criminal record is *not small.*"

Clark leaned in, reading the computer monitor from behind her shoulder. "Huh. Multiple arrests on drug possession, enforced rehab at twenty-six, license revoked for drunk driving at twenty-eight, three charges of domestic abuse . . ."

"All three of which were later dropped," Rivera added, pointing at a specific spot on the screen. "That was his first wife."

Clark nodded. "That date on the last reported incident—she filed for divorce just a few weeks later."

Rivera glanced at her mentor and partner. An unspoken question passed between them. How did he know the details of

Luther's divorce? And what else had he already found that she hadn't yet been able to?

He smirked at her sideways, then returned his eyes to the computer screen. That was probably all the answer she'd ever get. She knew Clark well enough to know that he had ways of finding things out that others couldn't or wouldn't. Sources, methods—sometimes it was just that uncanny intuition of his.

She returned her attention to the computer report. "What about the gambling? He mentioned gambling on TV, but I don't see anything here."

"He took over a dozen flights to Vegas over the years, but hasn't been since he turned his life around. It's a smart bet that he probably frequented Atlantic City at the time too, but by car."

Right. There would be no records of Luther flying to Atlantic City when he likely drove there.

Again, Rivera couldn't help wondering how Clark had gotten access to all of these personal details about John Luther. Was someone on the Hill feeding him intel? Someone who wanted to see Luther fall? Or maybe even someone who wanted to see Luther vindicated?

"So what we've got here is a dividing line," she said, summing up the report. "There's his old life, where he was toxic and self-destructive. And then there's his current life, where all of that stuff went away and he became a respected religious leader. The dividing line was probably a 'conversion experience' where he 'met God' or whatever. The question is, when did it happen?"

"Somewhere between fifteen and twenty years ago," Clark replied. Now he was studying her again. "And this is relevant how?"

He wasn't questioning her reasoning. He was testing it. Always he was testing her and how she functioned as an agent. "If we understand the circumstances of when and how he changed his life so drastically, it might help us better understand why he's flipped the switch back the other way, if he has indeed relapsed."

"Very good," said Clark.

If he was happy with her reasoning, then she was happy too.

# 21

Kathy's Helping Hands van came to a stop across the street from St. Peter's Church. John slid open the side door.

"God bless you," he said. "And thanks."

Kathy smiled warmly and placed a hand atop one of his. "No matter what, God is still with you. Never forget that."

"I'll try," John replied. He tried to smile back at her but couldn't quite manage it.

He stepped out of the van and glanced around. In so many ways it was just another small Virginia town. Far enough from D.C. and Richmond that commuters hadn't totally taken it over, it felt like a place out of time. Partly because every time John walked these streets he couldn't help but see how it looked twenty and thirty years ago when he'd prowled the area as a teen. The downtown block was remarkably empty for early evening. There were usually people out walking on errands, vehicles speeding about. Was it luck that no one was around to see him, or was it a little help from above? He was grateful either way.

Coming here may have been a terrible mistake. What if the old priest didn't believe him? What if the police showed up at

95

the church while he was inside? What if that gray-suited man was hiding somewhere nearby, watching him right now?

He shuffled his feet, quickly crossing the street to the sprawling limestone church and entering through a set of double doors, painted red as the blood of a lamb.

The old priest stood at the altar at the front of the church, silently lighting dozens of votive candles in red glass holders. The red symbolized the blood of Christ, shed to redeem mankind. John recognized the votives as part of a traditional prayer vigil. Was he praying for John? Undoubtedly. But would he *believe* in John's innocence?

At least they were alone in the dark, cavernous sanctuary.

John struggled to move his aching feet down the center aisle, passing dozens of pews until he came within earshot of the priest.

"I didn't know where else to go," he said, an apology in his voice.

Charles Luther slowly raised his head, though his eyes stayed glued to the candles.

The relationship between the two men had improved over the years. They would never be best friends, but John had eventually let go of his self-hatred and the resentment he'd long carried against his father. And Charles had forgiven himself for his shortcomings as a father and tried his best to repair the relationship with his son.

"I don't know what you've heard," said John between weary breaths, "but, Dad, I didn't hurt anybody."

"I know you didn't, John." At last Charles turned to face his son. His black cassock was wrinkle free, his white clerical collar pristine. His expression was severe but not unkind. "Come with me."

John heaved a great sigh of relief as he followed his father through a side door into his personal chambers. Dingy brown walls were lined with shelves filled with hundreds of books. An old radio sent out a tinny news broadcast that was punctuated with occasional pops of static.

". . . victim has been identified as sixteen-year-old Aaliyah Evans, a runaway tragically found dead early this morning," said the newsreader. "The suspect in the alleged rape and murder of the young girl is John Luther, the renowned evangelist . . ."

Rape? It wasn't enough that they thought he'd *killed* her. Now they thought he'd raped her too?

Aaliyah Evans. So that was her name. Whatever her culpability in this crime against John, she didn't deserve to be murdered.

Charles crossed the room and turned the radio off.

"Monica and Jodi?" he asked.

John spotted a familiar painting hanging on one wall and scuffled slowly toward it. "They're at home, and they're safe. The police are there."

Something about the painting captivated him. It was a Caravaggio, a very well-known one, and a lifelong favorite of his father's. Entitled *David and Goliath*, it depicted David kneeling over the corpse of Goliath after his victorious battle against the giant. Goliath's head had been severed and lay in the foreground. It was simultaneously gruesome and beautiful.

Now John was facing his own giant, and he doubted it would go down as miraculously as the one in the painting. Or was he Goliath, having been toppled by a David he hadn't yet identified? Whoever had done all this to him was strong enough to have toppled his entire world with a single blow.

"Did I do this to myself?" he mused.

"It was only a matter of time, John," replied his father. "You're just a pawn in a much bigger game. It's about a powerful political movement based on deceit."

Political movement?

*Political . . .*

Donald.

Of course. John should have seen this coming. Donald had always been a dangerous kind of benefactor, but John never truly believed he would take the Faith and Fairness thing this far. Then again, maybe this went beyond Donald. The president himself was pushing the bill for all he was worth. But surely the leader of the free world had more important things to do than hanging John Luther out to dry.

How had he somehow become the linchpin in this big political power play? He was just a preacher of the Good News.

Charles crossed the room and handed John a small and very worn Bible. John looked at the leather-bound book in confusion.

"Why do these politicians hate me so much? Am I *that* much of a threat?"

Charles's features softened. "John, by the grace of God you were able to bring yourself up from the depths of degradation and form a wonderful ministry that has spoken the truth to millions of people. Now those who believe in nothing must bring you down. They have to destroy you to achieve their own goals."

John still couldn't believe all this. Why was it happening to him? How could it be that Donald and the rest of Washington's most powerful feared him so much that they had to eliminate him as an obstacle before they could get their bill to pass through Congress? It was impossible to get his head around. Sure, he'd spoken publicly in opposition to the Faith and Fairness Act a handful of times, but he couldn't possibly be so important as to single-handedly keep the bill from passing? Could he?

"Look," said Charles, "you're going to be charged with first degree murder. You have two choices now. You can turn yourself in, throw yourself on the mercy of the authorities, and hope for the best. I think you know how that'll turn out."

John's face was probably being printed on a bunch of those

Most Wanted posters right now. The evidence against him may have been circumstantial, but there was no way the police would ever believe him.

"So there's a second option," said Charles. "One you may not like very much."

"It doesn't matter what I like." John was tired but found his resolve growing with every passing second. He'd known Donald for almost a decade. How dare his friend do this to him? How dare he have an innocent girl killed to advance his agenda? "I'm going to prove the truth."

His father was resolute. "You do that, John," he said. "For that girl. And for yourself. You may be the only person who can."

# 22

**32 YEARS AGO**

How's the food?" asked Charles.

John smiled between mouthfuls of bread and tomato soup. "Better than I remember," he said, causing a line of soup to stream down his chin.

It was over five months since he'd walked out the front door of his father's home and never looked back. For a while at least. About a month into his self-imposed exile—or running away, depending on how you looked at it—he began second-guessing his decision to leave. His pride had prevented him from returning for quite a while, but soon he got so hungry and desperate for a warm, comfortable bed, he couldn't stand it anymore.

Not that he'd been exactly destitute or penniless, as they say. He'd managed to pick up odd jobs here and there, found some decent places to stay, though nothing fancy. There was the occasional homeless shelter, but he'd managed to avoid that sort of thing for the most part, sticking to motels and newfound friends willing to give him a place to sleep for the night.

He'd had to choke down a lot of ego to come back home. But it hadn't been as hard as he'd thought.

John knew the old man must be dying to ask him where he'd been and what he'd done while he was away, but to his credit he kept his questions to himself. While he welcomed John home with his typical stoicism after John knocked on the front door, John saw more going on inside the man than anyone else might have noticed.

Charles seemed to be fighting the urge to linger over his son as he ate his soup. He would disappear from the dining room and reappear every few minutes. He rarely said a word; it was like he was checking to see if John was still there. Or if maybe he'd imagined his son's homecoming.

"Your room is exactly how you left it," Charles remarked as John was finishing his last bite of soup.

John tried to offer a smile yet felt too awkward to pull it off. "Thanks," he said. "I could use a shower. Then I'll probably turn in."

Charles hesitated, searching his son's eyes with a trace of hope in his own. "So you're staying, then?"

John stood to his feet. "For now."

The next thirteen months were the most pleasant John could remember at home. Where his father had once been overprotective and domineering, he now swung to the opposite extreme. He refused to keep tabs on John's comings and goings, never remarked on John's attire, and pretended to be disinterested anytime he accidentally came across John engaging in any sort of personal activity, like listening to music or watching TV. Charles seemed determined to let his son live his life however he chose, but John knew the old man was terrified of pushing his son away again.

It was good to be home. But even though things were better, he still didn't belong there. Not really.

Late one night in the spring, John quietly packed his things and slipped out of the house before his father awoke. He knew his father would be awake by 5:00 a.m., and he didn't want to have to try to explain why he was leaving when he didn't really know himself. He knew only that he had to.

Unlike last time, he didn't want to leave the old man on bad terms. So he wrote a note and left it on his bed. It reassured his father that it wasn't about him—it was only about John. It answered what had to be Charles's biggest unspoken question, saying: I never found her. My mother. But I'm not done searching yet.

Atop the folded note he left the old pair of aviator sunglasses he'd been wearing the last time he left. The note explained why. *Hold on to these*, it said. *You need them more than I do. You spend all your time staring into the light. But I've never figured out how to.*

## 23

Steaming water washed away the muck of the last twenty-four hours, pooling blood and dirt under John's feet. It had very little pressure, and there wasn't much room to move in the tiny stall, but the heat felt wonderful to his tired muscles.

John felt old. Tired. He *was* tiny David staring down his own Goliath, and it seemed an impossible task. How was he supposed to uncover the truth about Aaliyah's death? How could he hope to expose a criminal conspiracy involving one of his oldest friends—activity of which he had zero proof? He wasn't an investigator, for heaven's sake.

But there was another thought nagging at John's senses. It had been there since this mess started late last night: How would Jesus react in John's place? What would Jesus do if someone framed him for murder?

The Bible said to turn the other cheek. Those were Jesus' own words, right out of the book of Matthew. John had read that passage many times. Christians loved to quote it, loved to hear it said aloud. It was a profound statement of mercy and grace and obedience. But John had always found it troubling, if not impossible to live out.

He'd never preached a sermon on this part of Scripture, because—though he would never say it aloud for fear of being judged—it struck him as another way of saying "lay down and die" or "encourage your enemies to crush you." Every time he read the fifth chapter of Matthew, he hoped that maybe the true meaning of the words had been lost to centuries and translations. Surely the Great Shepherd wouldn't expect his sheep to give themselves willingly to those who would gladly destroy them.

And yet the very next verse plainly stated exactly that. In it, Jesus compared being wronged to having your shirt stolen from you. His answer to this kind of injustice was not only *not* to fight back but to give the thief your coat too!

As hot steam entered his nose, throat, and lungs, John wondered how and if he was supposed to put this principle into action in the here and now. A girl was dead. Didn't the Bible also decry murder as a deplorable sin? Was John supposed to go to his enemies and ask them to kill him as well?

No. It couldn't be that. An innocent soul had been murdered, and under the perfect law of God's holiness, justice had to prevail. Evil could never be allowed to win. Always a price had to be paid for evil, a balancing of the scales. Jesus was a man of peace, but as God incarnate he couldn't abide injustice. Right had to triumph over wrong. If Jesus hadn't believed this, he would never have sacrificed himself to satisfy the wages of sin on the world's behalf.

In the end, vengeance would be the Lord's. Unquestionably. Only he was fit to judge and punish the guilty. But this wasn't about punishment. It was about stopping those who craved power at any cost from taking innocent lives to achieve their goals.

And yeah, John wanted his life back. Was that so wrong?

John ran a thick bar of soap across his arms and chest. The

last time anything had touched his chest, it was the girl, Aaliyah. She'd been just sixteen years old. The events of last night were starting to come back to him. She'd slipped her hand between the buttons on his shirt and massaged the skin underneath while snapping pictures. The thought made him shiver in revulsion.

More memories surfaced. The man in the gray suit . . . He'd watched with a kind of professional detachment as Aaliyah followed his instructions, running her hands over John's body . . .

He shuddered again.

Did that man answer directly to Donald? What was he, some kind of hired thug? Or was he an agent of the law gone bad? John squeezed his eyes tight, concentrating, trying hard to remember something he'd seen, some relevant detail about the man in the gray suit that was teasing at his mind. . . .

There it was. John opened his eyes and looked into his memories, where he stared down the barrel of a matte-black pistol that looked like molded plastic. Before becoming a preacher, he'd gotten to know a little bit about firearms, and he knew that this weapon was a Glock 22. The weapon of choice for most U.S. law-enforcement agencies.

Whatever he was, that man was a pro, and no stranger to taking a life.

How had he killed the girl? Did he shoot her in the head? Snap her neck? Did he choke the life out of her or did he poison her?

Did she have any idea when the two of them walked into the *Truth Live* studio that she would be dead by the end of the night?

John's eyes came into focus at the odd sight of a narrow spiral of blood amid the water at his feet. A red tendril slowly snaking through the shower water and into the drain.

The blood of the girl who died?

His own?

How much more blood would be shed in the days to come? And would he ever feel clean again?

# 24

Charles Luther was nothing if not prepared. As soon as he'd heard the news that morning, he'd known with absolute certainty that John would come to him for help. And that not long after John arrived, the police would follow.

He'd had most of the morning to consider this and make the necessary preparations. Soon he would find out if his plans were sound.

As John showered in the adjacent washroom, Charles stood at his office window keeping watch. The tall, narrow window offered a view of the downtown street that ran in front of the church. Today was Friday, which meant there were no services scheduled, just a few parishioners who would slip into the sanctuary to say their daily prayers. Any other visitors received would almost certainly be officers of the law. Whether they would be police, federal agents, or members of some other agency, he had no idea. But they would know that he was John's father, and they would almost certainly come carrying a warrant to search the premises on the chance that Charles was hiding and helping his son.

Which Charles had every intention of doing.

John had been at the church for over half an hour now, and every second he lingered he was in greater danger of being caught. But he had to get cleaned up and put on a fresh set of clothes. He was far too conspicuous, looking as he did before.

One of the first preparations Charles had made that morning was to find some street clothes John could change into. He'd considered running down to the local Goodwill store but worried he might be gone when John arrived at the church. Instead he'd raided the personal closet of one of his subordinates, a young priest named William. The two men's sizes weren't quite a perfect match, but it would have to do. William was a good man, and Charles promised himself he'd explain everything to the younger priest later.

The sun was drifting into the horizon when the unmarked sedan came to a stop in front of the steps leading to St. Peter's Church. At last. Charles was surprised it had taken them this long to come. Maybe it was divine intervention that slowed them.

He stepped quickly into the washroom, where John was getting dressed. His jeans were on, and he was just pulling a T-shirt over his head.

"It's time," Charles said. "Here's what I need you to do."

Less than two minutes later, Charles answered the ringing brass bell at the front door.

"Mr. Luther?" said one of the cops standing just outside the door. A woman, and a detective if Charles wasn't mistaken.

"Yes?"

"I'm Detective Millis, and this is Detective Chen," the woman said, gesturing to her partner. "May we come in?"

Charles smiled inwardly, knowing this was just a formality. These two could march straight into the church and do anything they wanted, and they good and well knew it. Still, he appreciated their manners.

"Of course," Charles replied. "The House of God is always open to those who seek him."

Detective Millis offered a friendly half smile as she stepped inside, while her partner appeared dour, unimpressed. "Why was the front door locked?" he asked.

Charles remained perfectly serene. "Purity of mind and body is one of God's commandments," he said. "Even priests must bathe."

Detective Chen examined him. "You don't look damp."

"The vestments of priesthood can take some time to gild oneself in, my son," Charles said. "Especially for those of us burdened with advanced years."

He led the two detectives down the church's main aisle, toward the altar, where the red votive candles were still burning. When Charles arrived, he turned to face the officers. "Now, how may I help you today?"

"You probably know why we're here," said Millis, her manner gentle.

"I know you're not looking for God."

Chen glowered. "Have you seen or heard from your son since last night?"

Charles was determined not to break his vows by lying to the officers. But he couldn't give John up to them either. Maintaining a perfect poker face, he replied, "John's no fool. He wouldn't reach out to anyone likely to lead you to him."

Chen and Millis exchanged a glance.

"If he isn't here, then you'll have no objections to us taking a look around," said Chen.

"If you find it reassuring, then by all means," Charles said. "I ask only that you not disturb our sacred vessels or other accouterments."

Millis said, "Of course," but Charles saw Chen roll his eyes as he looked away.

The two detectives first walked to the right side of the sanctuary, where the confessional was located. Charles took in a sharp breath as Detective Chen flung open the ornate wooden door on the right to look inside the priest's alcove. He found it empty. Chen next threw aside the curtain covering the opposite side of the confessional. Inside was a small bench for parishioners to sit on while confessing their sins. Like the priest's alcove, it too was empty.

Charles said nothing. He merely waited patiently and tried not to think about what his son was doing right now.

Once the door to his father's office had closed, John risked a peek around the corner. He was crouched at the end of the narrow hallway that led from the office to a storage closet where Eucharist supplies were kept. A tiny mechanical room was next door.

His father had the two cops inside his office, which meant John had to move. He was still clammy from the shower, and he wiped water from his forehead. John could hear the cops talking in muffled tones. He knew the office was a small room and that they wouldn't be in there long. He had to go, *now*.

As quietly as he could, he crept down the hall toward the office. His heart thudded heavily, his pulse racing. While hiding in the storage room, he'd put on some socks to help silence his footsteps. He prayed that the floors in the old church building wouldn't creak as he walked. The slightest sound and the cops would be on him. It would be over, all of it.

The voices were still speaking inside the office as he neared the door, yet it sounded like they were getting louder. Either the conversation had heated up or they were moving toward the door.

John slid past the office, gently opened the sanctuary door, and went inside. He heard through the door that the cops and his father had just emerged back into the hall. John knew his father would do his best to lead the detectives away from the sanctuary now, but he wasted no time in case they weren't compliant.

Still moving quick and noiseless, John shuffled down the altar steps and to the far side of the sanctuary. He entered the priest's confessional alcove and sat down. This was his father's plan; the old man had known the cops would check the confessional first. It was the oldest cliché in the book—hide the fugitive in the confessional booth. After checking it once, those searching would move on, and the tiny alcove would become the safest place in the building.

All he could do now was wait, sit still, and not make a sound.

# 25

"Aaliyah Evans wasn't raped."

Agent Rivera looked up. Clark walked in, his eyes scanning the girl's autopsy report on the tablet computer in his hand.

Rivera was kneeling on the floor next to the passenger's side door, which stood open. She'd been inspecting the interior of John Luther's Toyota SUV in the FBI's forensics lab for the last hour. So far her findings confirmed everything the police had deduced.

Clark continued, "She was sexually active, but there's no evidence of rape."

"What's the cause of death?" she asked.

"Broken neck."

"That's consistent with what I'm seeing," she said. "I don't think she was wearing a seat belt. It looks like she was flung forward into the dashboard when the crash occurred." Rivera pointed to two spots on the vinyl dash that bore slight indentations.

Clark leaned over above her to get a closer look. "Hm," he said, and then went back to the tablet.

Rivera knew what he was doing. He was checking the autopsy report for bruises on the girl's body that lined up with the dents on the dashboard. He gave a brief nod, indicating he'd found what he was looking for.

"Okay," he said, regrouping. "I'm John Luther. I'm high or drunk, and I pick up a runaway junkie to join in on the fun. I have consensual sex with her—or maybe there's no sex at all. But then I wreck my car. Maybe I'm enjoying the afterglow. Maybe I'm just hammered. Either way, when I come to, the girl's crumpled on the floorboard, her neck snapped from an impact with the dash. So I . . . flee the scene on foot?"

Rivera hadn't been sure where her partner was going with this until he got to that last phrase. Now she got it. "Why didn't he leave the body and take the car?"

Clark looked her in the eye and nodded. "Not only did he leave *his car* at the scene of the crime, he left the girl's camera phone *on her person*, the very phone that held incriminating photos of the two of them."

Rivera pondered it. Was there a flaw in her partner's logic? Probably not, but he expected her to try to find one. It was part of their routine.

"It's conceivable that he could have been so high out of his mind that he wasn't thinking clearly," she suggested, even though she wasn't even buying it herself.

Clark frowned. Then something occurred to him, and he looked back down at the tablet. He swiped sideways several times, flipping through the report's pages. His brow furrowed, and his expression turned even more serious.

"What?" she asked.

Clark let out a slow breath, still reading. At last he looked up. "Evans's bloodstream showed toxic amounts of cocaine."

"Yeah," said Rivera. "We knew she was a drug addict already, didn't we?"

"But there was no powder residue found in her nostrils."

So she didn't snort the cocaine. Insufflation, as it was called, was the most common method of ingesting cocaine. Everyone knew this. But it was hardly the only available method of ingestion.

"I don't follow the significance," Rivera said, watching her partner.

"Alone, it's probably not significant," he replied. "But two other findings in the autopsy make it troubling."

Rivera extracted herself from the vehicle and stood, stretching her sore muscles. "I'm listening."

Agent Clark referred once more to the tablet. "Cocaine wasn't the only substance found in her bloodstream." He held out the device for her to see.

Rivera scanned the tablet's screen. "'. . . trace amounts of . . . Rohypnol.' That's the date-rape drug, isn't it?"

"It is," replied Clark, taking back the tablet.

Rivera took a breath, her mind spinning. "Okay. So he drugged her. Maybe she wouldn't get in the car with him otherwise."

"Maybe," Clark echoed.

Rivera pursed her lips. She knew Agent Clark was still holding back the most significant piece of evidence he'd read in the report. "What else?"

"Not every coroner would even think to check for this," he began. "But our guy did. God bless O'Neill . . . The cocaine in the girl's system saturated her bloodstream, but at the time of death, it hadn't been *digested*. At all."

Rivera blinked, then grabbed the tablet out of his hands. "You're kidding."

Clark said nothing, waiting for her to verify what the report stated.

And there it was. In the autopsy report, figures stating the amount of cocaine in the deceased girl's system, and a percentage showing how much was found in her digestive system. The first number was quite high. The second simply read *zero-point-zero milligrams*.

"The cocaine entered her system *after* she was already dead?"

Clark nodded. "Injected, most likely. Quite some time after she'd taken the Rohypnol."

Agent Rivera gave him back the tablet and crossed her arms. Her mind reeled, carefully piecing together everything she'd just learned. As usual, Agent Clark studied her.

"I don't like what this is adding up to," she said, looking Clark in the eye.

"Neither do I."

# 26

"Obviously we're all in shock," said Ryan Morris. The man floundered in his seat, unable to conjure up words adequate for the situation. "I mean, the accusations . . . they're unbelievable."

Ryan was seated opposite Senator Donald Harrison, across his huge, ornate wood desk. Night had fallen, but that was of no concern—Donald considered himself always on duty. He watched this man he'd called to his office on *very* short notice. John always talked about Ryan's nearly hyperactive energy, and Donald could almost feel the man vibrating in the seat, barely able to stay still. His eyes shifted wildly around Donald's immaculate, intricately furnished office, visibly impressed. Each piece Donald had collected in his travels around the world. As a collection he knew they added up to prestige and power. But to be sure his visitor felt the full effect, Donald had asked his associate Mr. Gray to sit in on the meeting. His presence alone was enough to intimidate almost anyone.

Senator Harrison said nothing, allowing Ryan to squirm a little longer.

"But, uh . . . you tell me," said Ryan. "Where do we go from here?"

Donald smiled inwardly. People were so easily played. Like notes on a harp, he excelled at plucking them until they sang his tune. Not that he relished manipulating people, mind you. Or that he took pleasure from any of the actions he'd taken over the last twenty-four hours. They'd been difficult but necessary. It was all for the greater good.

Donald let out a measured sigh. "Well, what it is, is a tragedy. And the moment John comes in, I want to get him help and see him restored. Just as I'm sure you do."

Ryan nodded enthusiastically, but Harrison saw him shoot an anxious glance at Mr. Gray, who watched him with his usual focused intensity. As soon as he'd made eye contact with Mr. Gray, Ryan turned back to Donald fast, as if he'd done something wrong.

Harrison switched to his best fatherly tone. "Sometimes out of the ashes of tragedy comes opportunity."

If Ryan understood what Donald was hinting at, he didn't show it. He seemed to still be trying not to look directly at Mr. Gray.

All right then, Donald would just have to spell it out for him.

"How long have you worked with John?" asked Donald.

"Fourteen years," Ryan answered with a half smile.

"Fourteen?" Donald said, making himself sound impressed by the huge number.

Ryan smiled again and nodded.

Harrison knew exactly how long Ryan had worked with John Luther and Truth Ministries; he'd known long before tonight. He also knew that Ryan had entered full-time ministry after a bout with severe depression. His wife had left him, and subsequently they were divorced, plunging Ryan into the abyss of despair. He'd remained in a deep depression for almost a year, until he'd been dragged by a family member to a special church service—a service where the guest speaker was John Luther.

Donald would have felt sorry for Ryan if he hadn't found the man to be so grating. Fortunately his psychological profile made him the perfect candidate for the senator's needs.

"Well," he continued, solemn now, "to save this organization, it's going to take some bold leadership. We have a multitude in panic—millions of people who are going to feel unmoored, who are going to be looking for answers and direction. We need to show them all is not lost, and we have to speak into their lives a message of hope in these dark times."

Ryan leaned forward in his seat. He was a man desperate for hope, hanging on Donald's every word.

"How many people can you reach on your email database?" asked Donald.

"Oh, uh . . ." Ryan looked up at the ceiling, thinking. "We have a boatload. I'd have to check."

"But you *will* check, won't you, Ryan?" said Donald.

Ryan nodded again, eager to please.

Senator Harrison smiled a reassuring smile. He was coming to Truth Ministries' aid, and to Ryan's specifically. That was what he needed Ryan to take away from this meeting.

"I've been watching you for years now," Donald said. "You do fine, selfless work. Don't you?"

Ryan grasped for words again, but this time he blushed. "Well, I'd like to think God had a hand in it . . . but I appreciate that."

Still smiling with as much warmth as he was capable of, Donald went on, "This might be your time to shine. Great leadership knows when to seize opportunity."

Ryan looked overwhelmed, a dawning realization coming over him.

Finally. The simpleton was starting to get it.

"We need to bring this church together," said Donald, preparing for checkmate. "Now more than ever. We need to rise up and resurrect this ministry and take it in a brave new direction."

Ryan watched him with eyes wide. He was waiting to hear the senator's next words.

"Are you with me, Ryan?" asked Donald.

Ryan was clearly surprised to be offered the keys to the kingdom. But he was smiling. He let out a long breath. "I'm your man."

Donald grinned as Ryan rose from his seat and reached across the massive desk to shake his hand. "Glad to hear it."

He offered Ryan a fleeting, barely visible wink to seal the deal.

# 27

Just minutes after the police were finally gone, John was back in his father's office. The old man was offering John his best advice on how to proceed.

From one of the many books that filled the room's bookshelves, Charles surprised his son by pulling out a thick wad of rolled-up cash held together by a rubber band. John examined the book and found that a rectangular hole had been cut from the pages on the inside. A secret safe, made of paper. It looked like the old man had cut it out himself.

John knew his father cherished books, so he couldn't imagine any volume the old man would willingly carve up. He flipped over the hardback and couldn't help but smile. The spine read *The God Delusion* by Richard Dawkins.

He turned his attention back to the money. Charles Luther had never been rich. And the life of a priest was not exactly a lucrative one. Where had he gotten this much cash? Had he been saving up? For how long? There had to be five, maybe even ten thousand dollars in the roll.

He was about to pull off the rubber band when his eyes caught hold of something behind his hand. On Charles's desk was propped a small, square photo in a simple silver frame. John knew this picture. He'd given it to his dad a few months ago. It was a bright, sunny photo of John with Monica and Jodi. He had an arm around Monica, with Jodi situated in front of them both. John had his other hand on Jodi's shoulder. All three of them were grinning.

It had been a beautiful summer day—that day at the beach when they'd rented a three-seater bicycle. The photo was taken shortly after they'd returned the bike to that kooky rental guy who made Jodi giggle. Hearing her laugh always made her parents laugh, so they were all smiling extra big in this photo because of it. The rental guy took the picture for them.

That was such a great day. So much joy and laughter they'd shared.

How he missed them! He missed Jodi's laugh. Monica's touch. Her beautiful smile. Jodi's little hand in his. Her hugs. Monica's tender voice.

John suddenly couldn't remember why he always spent so much time working at the ministry. His wife and daughter brought out the best in him, and without them he was incomplete.

He picked up the photo and rubbed a finger across its glass surface.

Monica.

Jodi.

He needed them. And they needed him. No job—not even a ministry—was more important than that. They were his whole world, and he had to find a way back to them.

John wished he could hold both of them tight, right now. He didn't realize his father was watching until he wiped the moisture from his eyes.

"Don't do it, John," said Charles. John looked up at his father. "I know how much you want to be with them, son. When your mother left, I missed her more than I thought I was capable of. I would've done *anything* to be with her again. But you can't go to them. Not now."

John sighed. "I know. The police have probably staked out the neighborhood."

"Your head knows that," replied Charles. "What about your heart?"

"I won't, Dad. I can't."

"That's right, you can't. No matter how badly you want to. You'd only be endangering them."

John nodded and set the frame back down on the desk.

"I have something else for you," said Charles. He turned to a small, wooden keepsake box resting on one of the bookshelves. He pulled something out and returned to John. He handed it to his son.

John smiled when he saw the sunglasses in his father's hand. The aviator sunglasses. Was it . . . ? It was.

The same pair.

"You need these more than I do," said Charles with a half smile.

John accepted the glasses and turned them over in his hands. He couldn't believe his dad had kept them this long.

"Thanks," he said.

"Things are going to get worse before they get better," said Charles. "Don't you stop staring into the light, no matter what. You keep on looking into the light."

John looked down at the glasses again, and nodded.

"Now come on. We've got to get you out of here."

# 28

John followed his father down two flights of stairs into the church's basement. He'd never been down here before. The big, windowless room was partitioned off with makeshift walls, and there were old pews, tables, and chairs scattered about, along with other items like tarnished brass crosses, white cloths that were worn and dirty, and candles that had burned down almost to nothing.

Everything seemed damp, ancient, and gloomy. He imagined this as the kind of place slaves on the Underground Railroad might have been sheltered and hidden back in the nineteenth century. The kind of place no one in their right mind would expect any living creature to be found.

"Through here," Charles said. He led John through a narrow door made of rotting wood, into another partitioned room. They turned left and entered yet another tiny space in the basement.

This last room was somewhere in the middle of the basement, if John was estimating correctly. His father pulled on a chain hanging from the ceiling, and a single light bulb came to life.

The room was more or less square, and filthy. John imagined that his father's priests and other staff must've rarely had reason to venture down here.

"Grab the crowbar," said Charles.

Crowbar?

John glanced around, not seeing a crowbar until he looked back toward the door they had entered through. There, resting right beside the doorway, was the iron device in question. He picked it up, wondering what they needed it for.

"Here," said his dad, pointing at a rug on the floor in the center of the room, right under the hanging light bulb.

John moved forward as his father pulled up the rug. Underneath was a grimy old manhole cover.

He looked down at the metal cover, then glanced back up at his father. "And this is . . . ?"

"Your way out, John," replied Charles. "It goes right down into the sewer."

John's shoulders drooped as he thought of what it probably smelled like down there.

"The police are outside," Charles explained, "watching the building. If you have a better idea, I'm listening."

John frowned at the manhole, unable to think of another way to escape the police.

"Here," said his father, holding out a key chain with a single key dangling from it. "There's a ladder leading back up to street level a block and a half south of here. Use it and you'll find a burgundy sedan parked nearby."

John took a deep breath. This was it then. This was where it began. From here he'd either prove his innocence and get his life back or he'd be caught and probably lost forever behind endless reams of political red tape.

It wasn't like this was the first time he'd had to survive on his own. He'd left home many times as a teenager and then roamed the country alone as a young adult. He might be older now, but he was as mentally equipped for this as anyone could be.

"Thanks, Dad," he said, "for helping me."

"It's what I do," said Charles with a knowing smile.

"It's what you've always done," said John.

Ten minutes later it was starting to rain as Charles watched from his office window. He prayed John had the strength and faith to do this. His son was up against a lot more than one or two rogue federal agents. This was a political juggernaut that wouldn't go down without a fight. Could one man alone take down this Goliath?

Charles glanced at his Caravaggio painting.

No, that wasn't right. David was never alone, and neither was John.

Charles lit a cigar as he continued to look through the window. There he was. He watched as John's silhouette peeked around the brick corner of a building. A few seconds later, John emerged and walked with casual aplomb to the sedan that waited nearby. Soon he was gone, the old Volvo speeding off into the night.

The old man took a slow drag on the cigar as the car left his sight. Shaking his head, he mumbled to himself, "Dear God . . . This is really happening."

# 29

On the far end of town, John stopped the Volvo at the first motel he saw. It was a little after seven o'clock. The building looked on the gaudy side, all neon and chrome, as if the designers had tried too hard to make it hip and trendy. But it would do. Past the glass-brick front wall, John found a silver check-in desk with a clerk at the desk, who appeared far too young for the job. As he stepped closer to the counter, he noticed that she was pregnant—at least six months along—though her attire was far from modest.

Trying his best not to look conspicuous despite his sunglasses and crisp new leather jacket, he approached the attendant. "Hi."

"Hey," she replied.

"I'd like a room. Just for the night."

The attendant smiled. "I think we can manage that. Let me see what we have." She began typing on the desk's computer.

John glanced around the spacious foyer. A handful of people were coming and going, all of them a lot younger than himself. There was a flash of light beyond the glass entrance, and John sucked in a breath, jerking his head in the direction of the door. It was only headlights from a car outside.

He mentally kicked himself; the attendant had noticed his squirrelly reaction.

"Something wrong with your eyes?" she asked. Her voice was casual, unbothered. Just making friendly conversation.

But John was long out of practice at this sort of thing. How could he answer without making himself seem even more peculiar?

After way too many seconds had passed without his saying anything, he simply smiled, trying not to look sheepish. "No," he said with a shrug.

The girl waited, as if expecting John to remove the sunglasses. But he didn't.

She gestured at her temple, and it took John a few seconds to realize she was referring to the fingernail scars visible on his forehead and the side of his face. When he made no reply, she smiled a nervous smile and mumbled something John couldn't understand.

"How's the room?" John asked, trying to speed things along. She was trying to act normally, but he could tell that this pregnant girl couldn't have been more wary of his appearance and behavior. If he lingered much longer, she'd figure him out.

"Good," she replied. "I just need a credit card and a valid ID."

Before he could answer, a flat-screen TV affixed to the wall behind her caught his eye. It was CNW with breaking news. A young, clean-cut male reporter was speaking to the camera from a sidewalk in front of the U.S. Capitol. Under the young man was splashed the words *FBI Manhunt for Evangelist John Luther Under Way.* And in the top right corner of the screen was a sight that made John nearly double over.

It was one of the lurid photos Aaliyah had taken of herself with John when he was borderline unconscious. At least his eyes were closed in the photo, although now that he thought about it, he wasn't sure if that was a good thing or not.

At home, Monica was seeing this. What must she be thinking?

The board of directors at Truth Ministries were seeing it too. They had to be.

Not to mention his millions of supporters, the faithful viewers of his nightly broadcasts.

One thing he knew for certain was that Donald Harrison had just upped his game. Was he sending John a message? The senator *had* to know that John was out there somewhere, a fugitive in hiding yet hoping to exonerate himself. So he'd leaked this photo—and probably several others—to the media anonymously. Tightening the noose.

Donald knew John's agenda, and vice versa. And Donald knew that John had figured out his involvement. That he was likely the mastermind behind this whole mess.

So their friendship was over, and the game was on.

John blinked when he realized the attendant was staring at him as he was lost in thought, waiting to see the credit card and ID that he didn't have.

In the background, he heard the man on the TV saying something about "Mr. Luther's actions sending shock waves throughout the entire religious community . . ." He chose to ignore it.

John pulled out his roll of greenbacks and slid a hundred-dollar bill across the desk. "Will this work?" he asked in a hushed voice.

"It should be fine," said the girl. She didn't seem at all surprised to see the money, and John wondered how often people did this sort of thing. Or was she just really good at acting nonchalant?

John ran his fingers behind his ear, tucking back his hair, as she picked up the bill.

"I'll be right back," she said, flashing a winning smile. "I just need to go check on something really quick. Can you just wait here a moment?"

John's pulse jumped. This felt wrong. Was she pushing past

the usual paper work to give him a room anonymously, as he hoped? Or was she . . . ?

". . . reported history of crime and addiction in Luther's apparently unstable early years," said the CNW reporter.

John frowned at the TV. Then he heard a voice whispering.

"I'd like to report a suspicious person, please," said the voice. It was the attendant, in an office adjacent to the front desk. She wasn't being nearly as stealthy as she seemed to think.

It had been a very long time since John had uttered a curse, but he was powerfully tempted to now.

He ran.

# 30

The police were gone, finally satisfied after hours of turning the house upside down. Or maybe it was Monica's life that was upside down, inside out, twisted and crumpled and gnarled beyond recognition. Again and again she kept coming back to the same question: How could this be happening?

John didn't do it. Of course he didn't. He wouldn't. He'd never in a million years.

But, quietly, in the back of her mind, she could hear the same awful whisper of doubt. He'd *been* this kind of man once in his life. Sure, it was long ago, but if he'd done it once, he could become that man again.

Monica's train of thought was interrupted by the sound of an acoustic guitar and a man's voice singing out the first line of "Amazing Grace."

Oh. Right. She'd almost forgotten Ryan was here. He'd arrived a little while ago, and he seemed . . . different. Monica had never been crazy about Ryan, but he was usually tolerable. Now something had changed. He held his chin a little higher, a smile played at the edges of his mouth, and he appeared rather pleased with himself. What was going on?

She didn't want to hear him sing. She was curled up on one end of the couch with one of her favorite handmade quilts—a gift from John for their tenth anniversary—deep inside her own world, watching nothing at all behind puffy eyes. She would have gone to sleep if her every muscle weren't so tensed up.

And Ryan wasn't helping.

"Ryan, please stop," she said.

He kept singing, ignoring her.

"*Please*," she repeated.

Ryan stopped. "I thought that was your favorite."

He was trying to comfort her, she realized. For some reason it made her uncomfortable. Unable to think of anything to say, she just looked away. The living room's big picture window was to her left; she kept staring out of it, wondering where John was, praying for his safe return, and hoping against hope to see him come walking down the sidewalk.

"All right," said Ryan.

She was vaguely aware of him standing and crossing the room to the kitchen. He soon returned and started talking again. Why couldn't he just leave her in peace? If she hadn't been so consumed with thoughts of John, she would have been able to think of a nice, not-terribly-rude way to get rid of him. As it was, she kept her mouth shut for fear of saying something she'd regret.

"Listen," he said, "I am *not* going to let you feel guilty for trying to take care of yourself."

Still she said nothing. She didn't care about herself at the moment. She cared about Jodi, and John, and about her family being whole again.

Something new occurred to her then. Had her father-in-law heard from John today? She'd be more surprised if he *hadn't*. If only there were a way to contact him, but the police had wired a tap to her phone before they left. Somewhere out there beyond the big window, police cars were on every corner throughout the neighborhood. She couldn't breathe without their knowing.

Ryan walked near and seated himself on the couch right next to her. This was quickly moving from uncomfortable to downright awkward. And now she saw what he had gone to the kitchen for. He'd poured himself a glass of white wine.

"I get it," he said. "Nobody saw this coming. Obviously. And now John is out there running around, doing . . . whatever he's doing. Personally I can't figure out what he must be thinking. If it were me, I'd put the needs of others before my own—you, Jodi, the ministry. I'd turn myself in."

Monica couldn't believe it. Ryan actually thought John was guilty. Which meant she had no use for this man. None whatsoever.

"I don't know if you remember," Ryan went on, trying his best to sound smooth, "but back before Jodi was born, I promised John that if anything ever happened to him, I'd watch over you like you were my own."

Monica had to fight hard to keep from rolling her eyes. Was he seriously hitting on her? *Now?* In the middle of all this?

"And as you know, I'm a man of my word." Ryan poked her playfully in the arm.

Monica wasn't feeling remotely playful just now. She glanced at Ryan with heavy eyes. Was he for real?

But then maybe she was being too sensitive. What if he was just trying to help her? Why should Ryan—John's right-hand man for over a dozen years—be the person whom she piled all her anger and frustration on? Did he deserve her ire?

Well, he certainly wasn't doing much to avoid it.

"In any case," he said, "have you heard from John?"

Monica looked away again. She didn't know what to say. Instead she simply closed her eyes while fiddling with her wedding ring.

"That's my point," said Ryan. "See? Me neither! I know how you feel. I feel the same way. And I can't stand what this is doing to you. I mean, he's left you alone here like you're a single mother or something."

She snapped, rounding on him. "No! He is *coming home* to this family."

Ryan looked at her with pity. "You have to accept this, Monica. Your husband is a fugitive."

Monica's eyes burned, but she refused to give him the satisfaction of seeing her cry. "No!" she said.

"He's a fugitive," he said again, this time with a harder edge that made him seem almost angry.

Monica *was* angry, and growing more so by the minute. "No!"

She stood and walked to the window. Arms crossed, she stared out into the night.

*Where is he?*

There was a beep, and Monica watched in the window's reflection as Ryan pulled his phone out of his pocket and read a message.

"Sorry," he said. "We're having an emergency board meeting in an hour."

Wonderful. Now Truth Ministries was regrouping to decide how to go on without its founder.

"Anyway, I pray you're right about John," said Ryan. "I really do. All he has to do is show up, tell everybody what really happened, and we'll get to the bottom of this. But you know . . . God works in all things."

Monica watched the street out front as tears spilled from her eyes. She wanted to break down, to let it all out and cry on somebody's shoulder.

Yet it wasn't going to be a shoulder belonging to Ryan Morris.

## 31

John flicked off the headlights as he pulled the Volvo to a stop. After fleeing the motel, he'd driven away as fast as the car would go. He had no idea where he was going; he just put as much distance as possible between himself and that place. For over half an hour he drove in a panic, not thinking about the direction he was going or where he might spend the night. He barely noticed stoplights, traffic signs, other cars on the road, or any other landmarks. He just drove.

So it was quite a shock for him to find himself coming up on his own neighborhood. Entirely without meaning to, he'd driven home. Ahead on the left was a little-used road that had recently been paved to make way for a whole new row of houses, most of which hadn't begun construction yet. From the outside looking in, most drivers had no idea that this dark, unlit, unmarked road connected with the neighborhood where John and his family lived. It was never used by locals, as parts of the street were still nothing but dirt.

He'd told his dad he wouldn't go see them. He knew he shouldn't. But he was so close to them now. They were less than half a mile away, and the itch to see them was so powerful . . .

Maybe if he just stayed in the car. It wasn't even eight o'clock yet. Monica would still be up, and the big living room window would probably be open.

John turned left onto the dark road. It was narrow, unmarked pavement for several hundred feet, and then a stretch of dirt at the end connected it to the street on which John lived. In no time at all he was less than a block from his house.

He saw no police cars or any marked vehicles anywhere near the house. In fact, the only car he didn't recognize as one of the neighbors was a red convertible, a 1957 Corvette. It was Ryan's car, and one of his prized possessions—a sporty little thing the man had bought after a nice bonus two years ago. A car as fast as the man himself. John hadn't expected Ryan's car here, but he guessed it made sense. Ryan was keeping the promise he'd made a long time ago.

Where were the police? Shouldn't they be watching the house?

With the headlights off, John pulled up the hood of the sweat shirt he wore under his leather jacket and circled the cul-de-sac a short way from his home. Driving past his house, he turned down a side street that gave him a perfect view through the picture window in front, if he craned his neck around to look out the back of the car. He turned the engine off and dropped lower in his seat, trying to hide as much as possible.

Monica rose from the couch and walked to the window. Behind her, Ryan sat on the couch and—was that a glass of wine?—talked. And talked. And talked some more. A pain struck John's heart when he realized Monica was crying. He could see a tiny reflection of light glistening on her cheek.

She wasn't crying because of anything Ryan said. John knew it was because of him. This big crazy mess was destroying her.

Did she believe in his innocence?

*God, please give her strength. Ease her pain. Help her. Help me now.*

The squawk of a walkie-talkie echoed down the street, and John's heart tried to escape from his chest. A patrol car was coming straight at him on the street ahead. The officer behind the wheel was sweeping a flashlight back and forth, examining every car, every trash can, every tree or bush he passed.

John quickly sank further into his seat, then pitched himself sideways so that he lay across the floor in front of both front seats. He heard the police car drawing closer and lay as still as he could, not moving an inch, not even breathing.

He heard the crackling sound of the patrol car's tires grinding slowly against the pavement, coming nearer, nearer, then stopping altogether. A light shone onto the seats just above him and lingered there for several seconds. John pressed himself into the floorboard as flat as he could.

His mind raced almost as fast as his heart. Why had he risked coming here? And why was the cop spending so much extra time on his car? Did they know what he was driving? They hadn't seen him exit the church. There were no cops at the motel, and he never saw the attendant come running out after him. There was no reason he could think of that anyone but his father would know what kind of car he was driving.

And yet here was this lone cop, scrutinizing his car more than any other on the block.

If the patrolman had been circling the neighborhood all night, then he would know that John's burgundy sedan was new. Maybe that was it. He was just making sure the car belonged here.

Except it didn't belong here.

At last the light receded and was gone, and he heard the car door open and slam closed before the cruiser rolled away again. John popped up and peeked over the edge of the passenger side window. He gasped.

All he got was a fleeting glimpse, but the driver of the police car looked terribly familiar. He'd seen this policeman before, and John didn't believe he was a cop at all. The last time John saw the broad-shouldered man, he was picking up the unconscious—or was she dead already?—body of Aaliyah Evans, next to the man in the gray suit who'd knocked her out.

He worked for Donald Harrison; he had to. And Donald had him here, watching to see if John attempted to go home. At least that meant they were leaving Monica and Jodi alone.

He needed to get out of here.

John glanced back at the house one last time, tears filling his eyes. Would he ever be with his wife and daughter again? He honestly didn't know. These people were dogging him at every turn. They seemed to have thought of everything.

Just as he was passing out of sight of the house, he saw Ryan emerge from the front door and walk toward his car.

# 32

Senator Donald Harrison glanced at his phone as it vibrated. He'd been expecting this call, having left the phone just to the side of his desk computer. He answered via speakerphone.

"They're starting, sir," said the voice of Mr. Gray.

Harrison said nothing, merely hung up. He turned to the computer and opened a program that played audio feeds and clicked the play button.

From the computer's speakers came the sound of several voices murmuring, as well as the screeches of sliding chairs. They were taking their seats. Good. The sound was coming through nice and clear. Donald would be able to hear the entire meeting.

Just a few hours ago, Donald called Ryan Morris to his office, pretending to back the man as the next and future leader of Truth Ministries. And that was important. Equally critical was when Mr. Gray opened the door for Ryan as he was leaving, and casually brushed against his sleeve, placing a tiny electric bug on his sleeve, just near the wrist. So long as Ryan didn't change clothes before tonight's board meeting at Truth Ministries—and why would he?—Donald would be able to listen in on the whole thing.

"I, uh, I think we all know why we're here tonight," Ryan

Morris began. Ryan had called the emergency meeting himself, at Donald's suggestion. "The accusations against John Luther have left us in a mighty awkward position, and now we have to decide where—"

"Let's not jump the gun here, Ryan," said another voice. Donald knew this one; it was Dave Wilson, the man best known for introducing John at the start of his telecasts. Donald had never had a formal conversation with the man, but he knew that Wilson was one of John's oldest friends. They'd known each other since before John became a minister. If anyone was going to be a problem on the board, it was likely to be Wilson.

"No," replied Ryan. "But we do need to look to the future. We're in a very precarious place here, and I think we need to establish governance for our unanimous cooperation with the Faith and Fairness Act, *prima facie*."

Wilson jumped in again. "According to our bylaws—"

"I think we're all very aware of the legal ramifications, but thank you, Dave."

A voice Donald didn't recognize spoke up. "Let him talk, Ryan." Some board member, Donald didn't know who, was reproaching Ryan. Wilson, several decades older than Ryan, was deserving of more respect than he was being given. Even Donald understood this.

It was one of the biggest risks in backing Ryan—the man was volatile, overly excitable, and a taste of power could make him seem too desperate. Donald needed the man to rein himself in.

There was a silent pause before Dave spoke again. "I just want to state for the record that I find the very origins of this meeting extremely distasteful. John Luther has more than earned our trust—many times over—and he deserves the benefit of the doubt. Before we do *anything*, we should hear the situation from John's perspective."

Dave Wilson was a hard-liner, always had been. A true believer, and absolutely loyal to John. But then, until a short while ago, Ryan Morris had been the same. Ryan was easily influenced, however. Donald doubted the rest of the board would be so easily swayed. Especially Dave.

"Look," said Ryan, "let's cut to the chase. We all hope John didn't do this. I for one believe the best of him. But we have to take into consideration not just our interests but the needs of the millions of people who've supported this ministry for years. We have a shared responsibility on their behalf."

Donald signed in relief. That was definitely a better path, and as speeches go, it wasn't bad. Certainly better than Donald had worried Ryan might be capable of.

"None of us would be on this board if not for John Luther," Ryan went on. "This ministry has changed all of our lives for the better. Unfortunately, John is *also* the reason we're having this meeting right now. We all believe he didn't kill that girl. But the fact that he hasn't taken into consideration our needs and the needs of the ministry . . . I don't know. Maybe that tells us something."

This was good, Donald thought. Ryan was hitting just the right note of fear. The room may have been filled with John's most faithful supporters, but they were also the people responsible for one of the biggest, most wide-reaching ministries in the world. Tapping into their fear of losing the organization, not to mention the human need for self-preservation, was a smart move.

"If our signing some piece of legislation sends a message to Washington that we're balanced, that we're in this for the long haul, then *I am for it*," said Ryan. "And written into this legislation for every single member of this board who complies—"

"Earmarks," interrupted Dave Wilson, his tone taking on a bitter quality. There was something else in his voice as well. A hint of resignation could be heard. Dave was losing this fight, and he knew it.

Donald smiled.

"There's a very generous tax package too," added Ryan, smoothing over Dave's animosity. "Dave, you're the one who's always told us to be prepared for the worst-case scenario. Well, brother, we're here! This is it."

A long silence followed, and Donald knew the dozen or so board members in that room were absorbing Ryan's words. The young man had been remarkably persuasive. Was it enough to get them all to agree? Or was the room filled with more nay-sayers like Wilson?

A new voice spoke up, another Donald didn't know. "I'm sorry, Dave, but I'm with Ryan on this. The individual tax benefit alone knocks this right out of the park."

Wilson said nothing in reply. Donald imagined him sitting stiffly in his seat, glaring at the rest of the board members, all of whom must've been in agreement with Ryan since no one was offering a counterargument. The old man was seriously outnumbered. At this point, he could either fall in line or abstain from the vote altogether. The latter option could even lead to his expulsion from the organization.

Donald very much doubted that Wilson's convictions would be strong enough to pit him against the majority. Or maybe he'd elect to side with everyone else in order to remain on the inside so that someone would still be there to represent John's interests.

Donald didn't care either way. It would be a unanimous vote, and that was all that mattered. Truth Ministries was officially on board with the Faith and Fairness Act.

At last.

# 33

John had to get out of there. He hated everything about this place: the stench, the scenery, and especially the company. The only good thing the abandoned duplex had going for it was that it had a roof to block out the rain.

He hadn't tripped in days and was longing for a good high. It wasn't that the goods were hard to come by here—dealers were in and out of this neighborhood all the time. He just didn't have any money to pay them.

John had spent the last decade moving, always moving. He'd chase work where he could, bum rides and food and shelter when he couldn't. He hadn't seen Virginia in years, and now he was as far west as he could get without drowning in the Pacific. Work wasn't that hard to get in Southern California, but there were precious few employers willing to hire a guy who spent his spare time chasing whatever high he could find. He spent one night a week at the local shelter to get a shower and a decent meal, but he didn't like how the people there were always down on him, trying to help him "turn his life around" or whatever.

At least he wasn't an addict. John refused to let himself be called that. Not like the two dozen or so other squatters who came and went from this old condemned house they shared. He didn't even know most of their names. Thankfully they left him alone most of the time.

John had claimed a small upstairs bedroom as his own a couple of weeks ago, but that didn't stop Crazy Karl from letting himself in and crashing in the corner every night. It wouldn't have been so bad if Karl hadn't snored so loudly. It hardly mattered. John rarely slept anyway.

It was somewhere in the middle of the night, and he was stretched out on the mattress on the floor he called his bed, listening to Karl snore, when he heard a familiar voice.

"Well, aren't you a sad sight."

John sat up and rubbed his eyes. Standing in the doorway was Charles Luther.

John blinked. He'd had a hallucination or two, but they'd always been wilder, fanciful. This one was as real as anything he'd experienced, and John just stared at his father in silence. Had the old man died and this was his ghost? He was dressed in his typical black attire and white collar. He hadn't seen the old man in more than six years, and yet he looked exactly the same.

"Can't say I'm surprised you ended up in a place like this," Charles went on. He stepped inside the room and closed the door.

John's brain was reacting slowly. This wasn't a poltergeist or a hallucination. This was real. His father was here. How in the world had he found him? "Dad?"

"Tell me, John," said Charles, walking closer. "In all this time, did you ever find whatever it is you're looking for?"

John opened his mouth to answer, then snapped it shut. It was the kind of question he expected from the old man, but why was he interrogating him now? Usually the first thing he did was try to help his son somehow. This was a new approach. Maybe it was his father's idea of tough love.

"No, Dad," John replied. "I haven't found it."

"That's because you're looking in all the wrong places," Charles said.

A moan coming from the corner gave way to Karl sitting halfway up and rubbing his eyes. "Who you talking to, man?"

"This is my father," said John.

Karl looked confused.

"Just go back to sleep," John added.

Karl did as he was told, collapsing back into his sleeping bag.

"You're such a disappointment, John," said Charles.

John shook his head, trying to clear away the fog inside it. "Why are you here?"

His father ignored him. He walked over to the nearest wall and leaned back against it, crossing his arms. "You've *always* been a disappointment."

Wait a minute. The old man had his flaws, but it wasn't in his nature to insult anyone—much less his own son. He'd never spoken to John like this before in his life.

And if John hadn't tripped in days, why was the room so bright? It had to be two or three o'clock in the morning, and there was no electricity in the building. Yet the entire room glimmered with a silver sheen.

Then he remembered. He'd scored some stuff a few hours ago, using the cash he'd lifted off a businessman down at the bus station. While the dealer promised that the stuff would bliss him out, what John was actually experiencing had a very different effect.

With a sudden panic he wondered what he'd taken. He glanced up at his dad, who merely stood there staring down at him with a frown, his arms still crossed. Only this wasn't his father at all. It was all in his head.

That train of thought was interrupted by a thunderous crash from downstairs, followed by a lot of yelling and screaming. This was no hallucination; John could tell that these sounds were the real deal. Even Karl heard them, because he'd bolted upright with a wild look in his eyes.

One voice overpowered all the rest. It took John a few moments to understand that it was being amplified somehow.

"Nobody move!" the voice called out. "This is a raid, and the entire place is surrounded!"

John swallowed and then jumped to his feet. He was extremely unsteady, and the room seemed to tilt back and forth like a boat on choppy waters.

The police were here. Someone must've tipped them off that this ancient place was being used as a safe house for people like him. What was he going to do?

He couldn't run; he was barely able to stand. John was used to the clarity and euphoria his drugs usually gave him. Tonight his brain was full of clouds, moving slow and filling his eyes with visions of things that weren't really there.

He was still pondering what to do when three policemen rushed into the small room and placed handcuffs on him and Crazy Karl.

"There were about five different ways you could have escaped from this," said his dad in a resigned voice. The old man shook his head sadly and looked at John with those heavy-lidded eyes of his. "If only you'd cared enough to get out."

Get out? Get out of what? This place? This lifestyle?

One of the cops grabbed John gently by the arm and escorted him from the room. He looked back one last time on his way out.

But his father was gone.

# 34

Ahead and to the right was a trailer with a big banner at-tached to its front that read *American Woman*. It looked like some kind of tattoo parlor. There were a few leather-clad characters milling about just outside, even though the place was closed.

After driving for almost forty-five minutes, John brought the car to a stop in the dirt patch of land that served as the tattoo parlor's parking lot and switched off the engine. He was wheezing with labored breaths, taking in oxygen that was reluctant to fill his lungs. John had never experienced asthma, but he wondered if this was what it felt like. But no, it was more than that. His stomach churned, his pulse had shot up, and his head felt as if it might explode.

Was it a panic attack? Maybe.

He couldn't find a hotel where he could risk staying. He couldn't go home. He couldn't stay with his father. Was there any such thing as a safe place anymore?

John turned on the car's overhead light and reached into his inside jacket pocket, where he'd left the tiny Bible his father gave him back at the church. Shaking and unable to read, he pressed the small book against his forehead with his eyes closed, trying to draw enough strength from its worn cover to calm himself.

After a few minutes he was able to hold the Bible without shaking, so he opened it to a passage his father had left bookmarked using the book's frayed ribbon. A yellow highlighter made a few verses of Psalms, chapter seven, leap off the page. His eyes flitted back and forth over the words.

"'In you I put my trust,'" he whispered, nodding in agreement with the text. "'Save me from all those who persecute me. . . . If I have done this, if there is iniquity in my hands . . . let the enemy pursue me and overtake me, let him trample my life to the earth.'"

The psalmist's writing was so powerful, John felt as if it had been written with him in mind. The Word of God was speaking beautiful truth into his circumstances, into his life, and the thought of such providential writing that applied so perfectly to him today was too much. Combined with his loss and his longing for home, John was overcome.

He burst into tears, his shoulders shaking and his chest letting out heaving sobs. John couldn't remember the last time he'd cried like this, and it felt good.

He cried himself to sleep.

Consciousness returned to John slowly, his eyes squeezed together tight as he trembled. Harder and harder he shook, almost unnaturally fast. Was he really waking up? What was going on?

At last his eyes snapped open. He was lying on his side in

familiar surroundings. He was at home in bed. Morning light made the room incredibly bright, though his eyes adjusted quickly.

Even before he'd opened his eyes, he was aware that someone else was in the room. There was only one person it could be, but he was facing away from her.

"Monica?" he asked, turning over and sitting partway up.

She sat in a wooden rocking chair on the far side of the bed, rocking and staring out of the upstairs window. She was perfectly serene, her slow rocking oscillating in a steady rhythm. After a few moments, Monica turned to face him. Her mouth moved as she looked at him. She was saying something, yet no sound came out of her.

What was she saying? She was just a few feet away. Why couldn't he hear her?

When she finished with whatever she was saying, she turned back to the window, continuing her rocking as if he wasn't even there.

Confused, John lay back and found himself breathing much too fast. But he couldn't stop. He stared at the ceiling, wondering if he was going to hyperventilate, why he couldn't hear Monica's voice, why the room was so very bright . . .

He sat up straight with a jolt.

John was awake. His head had just jerked upright away from the car's headrest.

He looked around; it was morning. He was covered in sweat and breathing hard, and for a moment couldn't remember where he was. Then he noticed the tattoo-parlor trailer off to his right. He wiped sweat from his face and felt sandpapery stubble on his cheeks.

John opened the door and stepped out. He was a bit wobbly but managed to stay on his feet. Instantly his ears were filled with noise. It sounded like cars racing by. He looked around and saw the interstate about a hundred feet away and down a short ravine.

The morning air cleared out the cobwebs, allowing him to walk with purpose toward the American Woman tattoo parlor. He'd seen this place the night he'd been drugged. It was one of the only memories he had. Dashing away from the car, up and up and up, until he'd stopped and shared that strange moment with those girls. And the camera.

He'd remembered the camera only after Charles had asked him what his next step would be. How could he clear his name without proof? Only then did John remember there *was* proof. Those girls had everything, and after leaving them, he'd run past this shell of a building. He wasn't sure the two were connected, but it was his only shot of tracking them down.

He climbed the wooden ramp out front and marched through the front door.

# 35

It was a "blue jacket" day. Agent Clark was already wearing his when Rivera showed up at work, and she knew what that meant. Anytime they wore their navy rain jackets—the familiar ones with the big letters FBI emblazoned in yellow—it was a day for fieldwork. In this case, most likely interviews.

She hoped that didn't mean they were going to have to talk to the dead girl's family. Rivera hated interviewing victims' family members. It always left her feeling sick. Besides, the police should have already spoken to whatever parent or parents Aaliyah had.

"Manage any sleep?" she asked, trying to start the day in a bright place.

Clark looked up from his desk. "You know I don't sleep," he said. "Anymore."

Rivera closed her eyes and tilted her head toward the ceiling. Of course she knew that. "I'm sorry, Preston—Agent Clark. I wasn't thinking."

Clark waved it off with one hand and returned to whatever he'd been working on when she walked in.

A few years before Rivera joined the agency, Clark had lost his wife to a carjacking. Her body was found a few days after the crime, but the perpetrator was never caught. Agent Clark had almost cinched the noose around the guy ten months ago, but he managed to slip away yet again. Coming so near to finally closing the case had opened up all the old wounds once more, even though Clark worked his hardest to shove aside the anger and pain.

Still, he couldn't hide it from her. Rivera saw the subtleties in his facial tics that others didn't seem to notice. Clark himself had taught her how to read a person for the slightest of expressions. She guessed he never thought she'd be using the skill on him, the teacher.

Rivera never brought the subject up, having learned most of the details of the case from other agents. If Clark didn't want to talk about it, she would abide by his wishes. Rivera knew that the two of them had gained enough respect for each other that if he ever did decide to talk about it, she would most likely be the one he would go to.

"So what's on the agenda?" she asked him.

Agent Clark stood and rounded his desk. "Come on. I'll tell you on the way."

John Luther's home was surprisingly modest. Rivera had expected the world-renowned preacher to live in something more . . . palatial. But the house he shared with his wife and daughter was remarkably average. A simple two-story house in an ordinary residential development.

She actually respected Luther a little more for his living so modestly.

Clark reached over and rang the doorbell.

Soon a blond woman a good ten or fifteen years younger than John Luther answered the door. She was nicely dressed, but her mascara had turned to faint streaks running down the sides of her face, and her eyes were red and puffy.

"Monica Luther?" asked Rivera.

Her expression was vacant as she answered, "Yes?"

Clark spoke up. "We're with the FBI. I'm Agent Clark. This is my partner, Agent Rivera. May we come in?"

Monica looked them up and down. "Where's your warrant?" she asked. It wasn't said in a rude way. In fact, the woman sounded almost confused.

"We're not here to search your home, Mrs. Luther," said Rivera. "We're trying to find your husband before anyone else gets hurt, and we'd just like to talk to you for a few minutes."

"Oh," said Monica, still confused and distracted. "Um, okay. Sure."

Rivera and Clark exchanged a glance as they followed Monica into the house. She led them to the living room, where she sat in an armchair, the two agents on the couch.

"Can I get you coffee or anything?" asked Monica. The question sounded habitual, as if she was used to entertaining, but it wasn't warm or welcoming. It was sort of robotic.

"No, thank you, ma'am," replied Agent Clark. "You haven't seen or heard from your husband since all this began, have you?"

Monica looked him in the eye for the first time. "I wouldn't tell you if I had. John is innocent. There's no way he would ever kill anybody. He didn't do it."

The room fell silent for an uncomfortable few moments.

"Does your husband have any enemies?" Rivera finally asked. "Can you think of anyone who might want to frame him for something like this?"

Clark shot her a stern look.

"No, of course not," Monica said. "He's a preacher."

Rivera nodded slowly.

"Wait . . ." said Monica, her eyes growing wider and her voice louder as she added, "Why are you asking me about John being framed? Have you found something? Something that can vindicate him?"

Monica leaned forward, her eyes bouncing back and forth between the two agents. Rivera, meanwhile, wanted to shrink into her seat. She knew she'd said the wrong thing.

Clark stepped in with his smooth calm. "We're not prepared to rule out any possibilities at this time," he said. "What can you tell us about how and when Mr. Luther underwent his . . . conversion experience? The event that turned his life around?"

Monica sat back and collected her thoughts. "It happened before we met. John calls it his 'Damascus Road' moment. He was thirty-two or thirty-three at the time?—I forget now—and he was at the lowest low of his life. Drinking hard, addicted to drugs, recently divorced from Jackie, his first wife. He was angry at the world, at his father, even at God. Someone dragged him to this old-fashioned revival camp meeting thing, the kind they used to hold outdoors under a giant tent. His father's an Episcopal priest, you know, so he'd grown up knowing all about the Christian faith. But this was different from anything he'd experienced before. He says that the 'simple Gospel truth' he heard at that revival opened his eyes and his heart. That was the day everything changed."

"And he's never relapsed into any of his old habits—no drinking or gambling or anything?" asked Agent Clark.

Monica shook her head with conviction, but a tear escaped her eye. "No. Absolutely not."

Rivera found herself feeling for this woman. She didn't know why; she was well practiced at staying detached from individuals involved in a case. But Monica Luther obviously believed in her husband, even if some small part of her was terrified that her faith in John had been in vain.

"Please find him," Monica said with more tears. "His little girl needs him. I need him. Get him home safely to us."

Rivera was about to open her mouth to tell Monica that they would do their best when Clark, perhaps sensing her empathy with Mrs. Luther, cut her off. "We need to speak to your husband's friends. Can you tell us who he's closest to, outside of yourself and your daughter?"

Monica looked away, thinking. "Just members of his staff, I guess. There's Dave Wilson. He's known Dave for something like twenty years, I think. Some others on the board of directors. Oh, and Ryan. Ryan Morris."

Something about the way she'd said that last name caught Rivera's attention. It was a kind of vocal grimace. Was there an odd vibe between her and Ryan? Or was it between Ryan and John? Rivera filed that little tidbit away for later.

"Thank you for your time, Mrs. Luther," said Clark, standing to his feet.

Rivera followed suit, and Monica rose to see them to the door. Clark shook her hand and thanked her again.

"You've been very helpful," said Rivera, shaking Monica's hand. Before she could stop herself, she'd put her other hand on top of Monica's and gave it a reassuring squeeze. She immediately regretted the action and hoped Clark hadn't seen it.

But he had. He never missed anything.

When they were back in the car, Clark asked, "What was that about? You know better than to make a personal connection like that."

"I don't know," Rivera replied, and it was the truth. She didn't.

"Well," said Clark, "I suppose you were following your instincts, which is good. But personal feelings will always influence your objectivity as an investigator. What was it about her?"

Rivera wasn't sure she could explain it, but she decided to go with her gut. "She has so much conviction about her husband. It was something about the way she *believes* in him. She's one of the 'good guys.' I want her to win."

# 36

A blue haze hung near the ceiling, and the pungent, unmistakable smell of marijuana enveloped John as he walked into the tattoo parlor. It was an odor he hadn't been around for years, but one that was hard to forget. In the dim light, John could see that the place was even filthier on the inside than it was outside. Grime covered every window, and the heavy haze made the small space feel claustrophobic.

A man who appeared to be in his early twenties lazily looked up from a little welcome desk next to the door. The man was clearly stoned. "How can we help you?" he asked.

John didn't bother replying. He couldn't imagine anything he said would be taken seriously by this guy. Instead he stepped around the desk and headed toward the back of the trailer, where he saw another man, this one busy tattooing a woman's back.

He'd only made it a few feet when the stoner at the desk spoke again.

"Hang on a sec," he said. "I know you. You're that guy . . . that guy from the TV. Hey, man, what happened to your face?"

John instinctively put a hand up to hide the scratches on

the side of his face. In the back of the trailer, a short African-American decked out in a Capitals hockey jersey turned from his work and looked at John. The client, the woman with her back exposed, faced away from the man. Already the outline of a dragon snaked its way up her spine.

"You can't just let people walk back here like this," the tattoo artist scolded, pointing a tattoo needle at the one manning the front desk.

"Don't talk to him like that," replied the stoner. "Learn some respect, man. Nolan, this is that famous preacher from the television. You know?"

Nolan glanced at John. "Nope," he said, and turned back to his work.

A narrow door behind Nolan inched open, and a thin wisp of a girl emerged. She wore dark, baggy clothes that accentuated her skeleton-like appearance. Her eyes were as hollow as her expression. She stood there quietly, studying John.

He thought she looked familiar but he couldn't be sure.

"Sorry it's such a mess around here," she said, her voice lethargic. "I try, but he never cleans up after himself. Neither of them do."

"Scorpion woman," remarked Nolan, eying her with disgust.

The girl gave a half smile while keeping her eyes glued to John. "And you are?" she asked.

"I'm John Luther. I was assaulted near this shop the other night, and I was hoping one of you might have seen what happened."

The girl nodded as though understanding now what he was after. "He's here for the show," she said to Nolan.

Nolan looked at John again. "So you're a preacher?"

John nodded. "Yes, I am."

"He's a fugitive, Alex," the stoner said to the girl before turning to John. He looked giddy at the notion. "Aren't you? Man, that's hardcore."

"I know where you're coming from," said Alex. "That was some madness that went down. I even taped it."

John's breath stopped cold in his throat, and his mouth fell partly open. He'd been right! She was the one who'd been there making the video that night. John's heart began to swell; he just might be able to get himself out of this whole mess. But then he looked at the girl again—her cloaked expression and her wary eyes. No way was it going to be easy. Who was to say she wasn't lying to him?

"You really taped it?" he asked her.

Alex grinned and stepped closer until she was right up in John's face. And then he knew—she wasn't lying. But, just like that night, she wasn't going to help him either. At least not for free. She had him right where she wanted him, and they both knew it. "We got needs too," she said matter-of-factly. "You understand?"

He nodded. He didn't even want to think about what the girl meant by "needs," though he certainly could guess. Yet what other option did he have? He'd pay any price for her recording. If she wanted the clothes off his back, the watch on his wrist, even the car outside in the parking lot—she could have it all.

"So, my brother," she went on, "you better believe it's gonna cost you."

# 37

Senator Donald Harrison normally prided himself on being able to sleep through any turmoil or stress. He'd been in this game too long to let the worries of the day follow him into his dreams and knew that exhaustion was one of the worst things to pile on to a problem. Working in the Senate, running a campaign, dealing with angry lobbyists—such things took a focused mind, and that wasn't easy to maintain through the fog that came from an interrupted night. Even so, sleep had proven difficult as of late, and so he was wide awake, staring into the dim light of his bedroom when the phone rang. The phone he'd been instructed to keep for only one caller.

"Tell me you've found him," he couldn't help but grumble into the phone once the call was answered.

"The plan was to let him escape and resurface in his own time. He won't stay underground much longer," said Mr. Gray. There was an edge to his voice, and the slightest hint of surprise. Donald didn't like that at all.

"I need to know *what* he's doing, *who* he's talking to, and *where* he is!" insisted the senator. "Do you understand me?"

This part of the plan had never seemed like it would be a problem. How could John Luther manage to evade a man with as much training, resourcefulness, and cunning as Mr. Gray, a professional? It would almost be impressive if it weren't so maddening.

"I paid you in advance," he said, his blood pressure rising. "I hired you because you're supposed to be the best. But you've been outsmarted by a *preacher*!"

There was silence on the other end of the line. Beads of sweat popped onto Donald's forehead. He wondered if he'd gone too far.

But that would be ridiculous. *He* was the one calling the shots here, not his hired hand. A hired hand who was failing to deliver.

"Don't worry. I'll find him," said Mr. Gray, his voice like sandpaper rubbing against stone.

The line went dead.

Donald threw the phone down, took a deep breath and counted to ten.

He had to forget about John Luther. He had to forget about Mr. Gray and let the man do his job. Unfortunately they weren't the only challenges he was dealing with at the moment. The real reason he couldn't sleep right now—the thing that had been occupying the majority of his thoughts—was something far more positive thankfully. A light at the end of the tunnel for what had been some of the most difficult work he'd attempted to do in his entire career. Today, the final piece would fall into place. And not even John Luther, wherever he was holed up, could stop the march of progress any longer.

The world was ready for change. The world *would* change, and Senator Donald Harrison would be at the front of the line, leading the procession.

Glancing at the clock once more, he knew his night was over. There would be no more sleep for a while.

Donald rose, slipped on his robe, and stepped into the bathroom, where he splashed water on his face. He looked at himself in the mirror. Those that changed history were remembered forever. *That* was eternal life. He might just get there after all.

Donald practiced his smile. It looked flat and . . . *practiced.* He made a slow count to ten, clearing his mind, and then let the first positive thought he could find fill his mind.

Tonight's meeting. Tonight's meeting was the start of everything. His smile found its true shape but then just as quickly vanished. Senator Donald Harrison found himself looking at a tired man.

It had been such a long road to this evening. He still remembered the first discussion, years ago, about the greatest challenges facing the country in the next century and how he'd spent a long evening talking about religious polarization, both in the U.S. and around the world, with another senator from Oregon.

"The world doesn't need to be torn apart further. It needs to come together," the senator had said, and Donald had heartily agreed. He'd had his own reasons back then, but over the years he'd not only come to see the value of those words but embrace them as well.

The senator was addressing the very heart of spirit and body.

Donald had been raised a good Christian boy. His parents took him to Sunday school. He memorized verses from the Bible. He even went on a missions trip once.

But he knew now that Christians were too insular—too frightened by the ground they were losing, too focused on a message that was narrow and exclusive. Few of them really understood what matters of faith looked like to the rest of the world. They were too wrapped up inside their own self-serving little bubble. The real world was quite a different place than what was seen inside the small, white street-corner churches or the megachurches of America.

God, Donald Harrison knew now, was a story so much larger than any single religion could claim. And all acts of faith would lead to him. Donald had sat in a temple in Japan and saw God in the face of a young boy meditating. Good Minnesota Lutherans had shown him hospitality when he'd been snowed in for three days in Duluth. He'd heard the energy of the prayers of Muslim men faced toward Mecca in Abu Dhabi. For two hours he'd once sat in silence in a Quaker prayerhouse and left without anyone claiming to speak for God. He'd even taken in a sunrise with a group of atheists at Virginia Beach and heard them talk about nature's beauty in words common to every church and temple and mosque and synagogue across the world. God was everywhere.

But the people of the world could not find him by clamoring in different directions. They all needed to be heading in the same direction.

If it took a flute and a song, so be it, but the world needed a melody to follow. And for years now the Faith and Fairness bill had been developed to play that very melody.

It was fools like John Luther who were holding back progress. He was a relic of another time. A bully, in some respects—and the world had had enough of bullies.

John's face came to mind again.

He'd been a friend once, but the man was standing in the way now. Donald wondered if John had pieced together yet how this whole thing had come to him. He wondered if he would see the man in the future and whether he would see the recognition in his eyes that Donald had brought him low.

The thought did not give him pleasure. This was not about revenge. He didn't *want* this to go down the way it had, but John Luther and the Christians of this country had had their chance. Almost two hundred and fifty years of claiming to have all the answers, and yet those answers had solved nothing. Why did they have the same problems as everybody else? Shouldn't they have solved the world's issues by now?

Should human beings not, in these modern times, be more enlightened so as to rise above their petty differences? The fact that war was still so prevalent in the twenty-first century was proof enough that *unity* was the key to peace, the key to ending conflict around the globe. And the United States was poised to lead the way, to usher in that unity.

At long last it was time for the world to coexist.

Today's meeting would bring the final key player into the fold.

With that thought, Donald Harrison's smile formed wide and true again in the bathroom mirror. He stared into the face of a man who was ready to change the world.

Charles Luther had heard of the Sumac Alliance organization; he just never expected to receive a call from them. Ever since his son had risen to prominence, Charles had made it his duty to watch out for him—no matter whether John wanted him to or not. That often meant finding people who didn't necessarily want to be found. Early on, Charles focused on religious radicals from other nations, revolutionaries who might target his son to make an example of him as a "false prophet." It didn't take too long to realize that such threats might not come from outside America's borders but within. And that those who stood opposed to what John Luther valued might not threaten him with violence, but more quietly, with trying to silence him through the force of laws and politics.

The Sumac Alliance had come up as he'd made these inquiries. Each meeting of the Sumac Alliance went unadvertised, and attending was strictly invitation only. Just a dozen or so hand-picked individuals, representatives from a spectrum of religious orders, a few of whom choosing not to publicize the fact that they were members. But each had been specifically chosen and was a believer in the cause.

Well, almost all of them.

Charles Luther was still trying to shake off his surprise at being asked to attend this meeting when his bishop called him to say an emergency would keep him from attending. Charles would normally have passed, but he couldn't deny the serendipity of this chance to see the people who, if not responsible themselves for framing his son, had certainly laid the groundwork.

"Besides," the bishop said, "I really believe you'll enjoy the sharing of ideas that takes place." He'd been pressuring Charles for years to "think in new ways" and to "ready the church for the new world." This was probably Charles's last chance before the man wrote him off forever.

Up a driveway ramp behind a wrought-iron fence, Charles walked until he reached the front door to the lavish manor. A security guard stood watch on the brick porch in front of double doors that led inside. The man eyed Charles as if he were a rodent.

"How can we help you?" the security guard asked in a decidedly *un*helpful tone.

When Charles reached the bottom of the porch steps, he looked up at the man. "I was asked to fill in for the bishop."

Without another word, the man escorted him to the door and opened it for him.

Charles had never been inside a place like this before. Ornate and extravagant, no detail had been overlooked. Every end table was handcrafted with an intricate design. Exquisite draperies framed the windows. Even the doorknobs appeared to be carved out of solid brass and polished to a high shine. He had no idea which room the meeting was in, but he didn't have to go searching. He just followed the sound.

That sound was the deep voice of Senator Donald Harrison, the man who was chairing the meeting.

"I think you all know that the Faith and Fairness Act is a dream I've had for quite some time. I want to thank Warner for hosting this—"

Harrison stopped abruptly when he saw Charles Luther enter the room.

"Father," he said, warm and inviting. "Thank you very much for joining us. Would you have a seat, please? I think it's time we got started." The senator gestured to an empty seat in the back row.

Charles dutifully complied, feeling dirty sharing a room with the man who'd turned John into a fugitive. Did Harrison even know that Charles was John's father? Surely someone as well informed as the senator would have access to those kinds of details. But then it wasn't exactly Harrison's idea that Charles be present at today's meeting; he'd been invited by the bishop, after all.

Had the bishop known of the pressure Senator Harrison had been putting on John? Did any of the members here know? Charles doubted it. But in their quietly uniting to back this bill, they'd made their stand. For most of them, someone like John Luther was simply behind the times, preaching a faith that didn't matter in today's world. Only someone like Senator Harrison understood how important John's voice behind the bill actually would be.

Harrison resumed his spiel. "As you all know, the Faith and Fairness Act is very close to my heart. It's been quite a struggle . . ."

Charles tried to focus on the senator's words, but from the moment he took his seat, his attention was drawn to a figure standing above Harrison on an overlooking balcony. The man leaned on the balcony railing, his hands clasped together, and watched the participants in the meeting. No, that wasn't right. He was watching only Charles.

So Charles stared right back. The man was half hidden in shadow, but he appeared to be dressed much like the security guard outside, wearing a crisp gray suit. There was something ominous about this person, whoever he was. His gaze, the blank stare of a predator sizing up his meal, triggered an instinct in Charles to shrivel, but he fought it. This man was bad news. Charles could *feel* it.

As Harrison droned on, expounding the infinite virtues of his multi-faith alliance, a battle was taking place in this very room. A war without weapons, without movement, without even words. Miles of animosity filled the short space between Charles and the man in the gray suit. Charles felt his mouth stretch into a scowl while his eyes grew harder and harder.

*I'm watching you*, the man on the balcony seemed to be conveying.

*I'm watching you too*, Charles sent back to him.

Donald Harrison was the kind of man who would stab you in the back while giving you a great big bear hug. He'd already proven that, and Charles disliked him for it. This man on the balcony was altogether different.

Hatred was beneath a person of his station, but Charles couldn't escape the feeling that as he looked at this shadow-cloaked man, he was staring into the face of the enemy.

# 38

A quick check at Truth Ministries revealed that Ryan Morris hadn't made it in to work yet today. So Agents Clark and Rivera positioned themselves right outside the adjacent parking garage in order to catch him on his way in. Clark parked the black SUV on the curb next to the garage's entrance.

"I'm sorry about before," said Rivera. "With Luther's wife."

"I know," replied Clark, his eyes on the parking structure. "It's not important."

If Clark decided it didn't matter, then Rivera knew to let the matter drop. Still, she wondered what it was about Monica Luther that had brought her own emotions to the surface like that. As an FBI agent, she'd been well trained to put personal feelings aside while doing her job. It was like an on/off switch. You went to work, and the emotions got switched off. You headed home and, *flip*, they're switched back on. History had proven time and again that sentiment was a liability—particularly in the field.

She thought again of Agent Clark and his personal tragedy. At least he'd had someone at one point in his life. Rivera occasionally wished she had a significant other at home waiting for her, but she was too busy with work to have time for pursuing a relationship. The simple fact was, her partner was the man in her life right now—even if there was no attraction or romantic interest between them. She didn't look at him that way, and she was certain he felt exactly the same.

"There he is," said Clark.

Rivera followed his gaze through the windshield to see a tall man with dirty-blond hair just emerging from the parking garage on the ground level.

She and Agent Clark exited the vehicle in unison and converged quickly on Ryan Morris. Rivera did a quick profile on the man as they approached. His clothes made a bold statement. He wore clean-cut jeans, a crisp black T-shirt, and a pastel-pink sports jacket without a wrinkle to be seen. His hair was styled with a healthy amount of gel, ensuring that even if it moved, it always fell right back into place.

But none of these things told her more about Morris than what she observed from his walk. There wasn't mere confidence in his gait. There was a *swagger* to it. Ryan Morris was a man awfully pleased with himself.

Morris was humming some indiscernible tune, and smiling at nothing in particular.

Already Rivera disliked this man. It wasn't hard to deduce that he had tasted power very recently—probably having taken over as interim president of Truth Ministries in Luther's absence—and found it quite to his liking.

Was it poisoning him? Too soon to tell.

"Excuse me, sir," said Agent Clark.

Morris faced them with surprise on his face, though Rivera thought it may have been an act. He should have easily seen them coming from his peripheral vision.

"Ryan Morris?" Clark asked.

Morris broke into a smug grin. "The one and only."

Rivera saw no reason to humor him. She cut to the chase. "We'd like to have a word. That okay with you?"

"For the FBI, I'd be honored," Morris said with a little too much sincerity. "Tell you what you do. If you'll go to my office, they'll set up an appointment, and *boom*, we're good to go."

So that's how he was going to play it. The *I'm so important that I'm much too busy to deal with you* routine.

Rivera was about to tell him what he could do with his precious schedule when Clark spoke up.

"This will just take a minute," he said.

Morris glanced back and forth between the two of them, still smiling but registering disbelief. Were they for real? Didn't they understand who he was?

Rivera understood him all too well.

"Well, I'm sorry but I've got a critical meeting I simply *cannot* be late for," replied Morris. He was trying hard to keep things light and jovial, but his true intentions were quite clear. "I will help you in any way you need, but as I'm sure you're aware, we're in crisis mode here."

"We really need to talk," said Clark in a tone that left no room for further argument, and for a brief moment, Rivera flipped her internal switch so she could enjoy watching Ryan Morris squirm.

# 39

John was ecstatic.

The girl at the tattoo place, Alex, had come through. It'd cost him a sizable chunk of the cash his father had given him, but it was worth every penny. He'd left that place with a digital thumb drive containing video of Aaliyah Evans's murder. John could plainly be seen as unconscious in the vehicle while the man in the gray suit struck her and then injected her with a syringe. The camera then followed John as he fled his attackers, and by the time it returned to John's Toyota, the two men there were positioning Aaliyah's body inside the vehicle. It looked as though they were *posing* her.

God was good. John would probably be cleared of all charges before lunchtime!

He pulled out the phone he'd found waiting for him in the burgundy car the other night and dialed his father's number.

"I have it, Dad," he said, his words pouring out in an excited rush. "I'm going to the police. Can you meet me there?"

"John," said Charles, his voice disappointingly less than enthusiastic. "I've been doing some digging and . . . there's something you need to know."

Whatever it was, it didn't matter. Hadn't the old man heard him? "Dad, *I have it!*"

"It's not that simple."

Not that simple? Of course it was. What was he saying?

Charles sighed. "You're in their way, son."

Forty-five minutes later, John was on a secluded bench at a park just outside of town. His father wore a grave expression as he walked the dirt path and seated himself to John's left. Whatever the old man had to tell him, it was bad enough that John's heart thudded louder at the sight of him.

For a moment they sat together in silence, listening to the birds chirping in the surrounding trees. Clouds had rolled in late in the morning, and the sense of dread building inside John seemed to feed them, turning them darker and darker. He almost hoped his dad wouldn't say anything at all.

John looked his father in the eye. An unspoken question passed between them. *Why are we here, Dad?*

Charles pulled out a photograph and passed it to his son. John's eyes fell on it and saw three people at what looked like some kind of inner-city charity event. On the far right was Aaliyah Evans, looking much as she did the night he first met her at the studios of Truth Ministries. On the far left was a black woman John didn't recognize. And standing between them with a broad smile on his face was Senator Donald Harrison.

John studied the picture for a minute, trying to get his mind around what he was seeing. It was hard to concentrate because he felt like he'd just been sucker-punched in the stomach.

He knew he'd been set up. But by *Donald*?

What was this?

"We were like brothers once," said John. "He supported Truth Ministries for years, when we were just starting out and he was a state senator. We had our differences these past years, but I just can't believe it's him."

Charles's expression turned bitter. "That girl was adopted by a woman named Shanice Evans just two days before she was found dead. This woman was able to bypass the waiting list and a lot of other formalities thanks to the assistance of your friend the senator—the majority leader of the United States Senate."

This was much, much worse than John initially thought. Did Donald really possess this kind of limitless power at his command?

"Now, aside from the president," Charles continued, "I don't know of many people who are better equipped to withstand a bullet like this. Nor better equipped to make sure your evidence never sees the light of day.

"Senator Harrison isn't in the video you have, and you won't be able to connect him to it. The media has already tried you and found you guilty. You need to be more careful than ever about who to trust and how to expose this darkness."

John had a feeling that was an understatement. Donald Harrison suddenly seemed positively untouchable.

"Look, son," said Charles. "For Senator Harrison, it's about power and money. But more important, it's about what he's a part of here. The people he's associated with. What the Sumac Alliance is trying to do. What this legislation is bound to do to Christians all over America.

"Look at China, Russia, Iran, North Korea—these nations where we don't bat an eye when the authorities drag people out of their beds in the middle of the night and imprison them under false charges. People are even relieved to see this happening, because they think their government is cracking down on crime."

Was the old man saying what John thought he was saying? Was he comparing the persecution and martyrdom of Christians around the world with what the Faith and Fairness Act would result in? Even with what John was experiencing right now?

"You ask most people in this country, right now," said Charles, "about the persecution of Christians, and most of the time they'll just smile at you and say, 'No such thing. Not here. Can't happen here.'"

John thought of a quote from the Bible, after Saul's Damascus Road conversion, when it was said that "something like scales fell from Saul's eyes." John's eyes had never been more open. When he'd argued with Donald these past years about the Faith and Fairness Act, they'd been religious arguments, about truth and grace and what set Christianity apart from Buddhism, Islam, and the other religions. Donald had made the argument again and again that no one religion could corner truth and that God was big enough to serve all religions, but he'd never talked about his pet bill as a threat. But the old man was right. There it was, plain as day. If it passed, the bill could be used to silence anyone they targeted.

It was overwhelming. Goliath had just grown about ten times bigger, and John felt smaller than he'd ever been.

"There's one thing you need to understand above all else," Charles went on. "The eyes of all Americans are on you now. People are looking for a symbol of truth and freedom. Someone who'll stand up against the cabal of thorny, powerful politicians. Who'll be unbending amidst all the lies and slanders that can be thrown at him. Who'll get back up when he's knocked down. And that's exactly what you're going to do, son. You're going to get back up."

John looked sidelong at his father, thinking only of his own insecurities and inadequacies, and of the many failures of his past. How was a man with so many flaws supposed to be a symbol before an entire nation? He was neither deserving nor capable of such a feat.

He sighed and closed his eyes, half in exhaustion and half in prayer. If this really was what God wanted of him, then God was going to have to take the wheel. John swallowed hard and then blinked back the tears suddenly filling his eyes.

"God will decide who's found wanting," said Charles. "They can't silence the truth."

John held out the USB drive he'd acquired at the tattoo place. "I want you to watch this, Dad."

Charles accepted it, turning the tiny piece of plastic over in his hand. He exchanged the flash drive for a keycard inside a paper sleeve. "Here," he said. "I got you a room. Go get yourself cleaned up. And get some rest. It'll do you good." He clapped John on the shoulder.

John stood, slow and unsteady. But before he left, he looked back. "I *am* going to expose the truth about Donald Harrison." John feared his words sounded as if he was trying to convince himself as much as his dad.

The old man smiled at him, and John knew that he was proud of his son, proud of the man he'd chosen to be.

John only hoped he would be found worthy of such approval.

# 40

Suck it up, Rivera told herself. She'd wanted this job so badly and had worked crazy hard to get here. She had the best partner of anyone in the agency. She couldn't just pick and choose the most palatable tasks. She took a deep breath and squared her shoulders. She needed to take the good with the bad.

Even so, there were two or three dozen things she would rather have been doing right now than climbing the steps to Shanice Evans's apartment. It had taken some time to find the right place. Evans lived on the third floor of a crowded inner-city apartment building. The place had to be at least forty years old.

Rivera watched as Clark knocked on the door.

"Who is it?" called out a female voice from inside.

"FBI, ma'am," answered Clark.

Rivera heard the hasty sliding of latches and turning of locks. When the door opened, a tall, slender black woman stood at the threshold. Modestly dressed in a simple T-shirt and jeans, she didn't look as tired or grief-stricken as Rivera had expected a mother who'd just lost her child to look. Instead she looked like someone frustrated that she'd been interrupted from watching her afternoon talk show.

Clark held up his badge and introduced himself and his partner.

"Come on in," said Shanice. She held the door open and stepped aside.

"Thank you," Rivera said as she walked by.

When they were seated on an old but clean-looking couch in the apartment's living room, Shanice patiently waited for the agents to speak. Rivera glanced around, noticed crosses hanging on the walls spread all around the room. They were made of various materials: wood, ceramic, glass, and chrome.

"Our condolences for your loss," said Clark.

Shanice nodded. "Thank you."

"May I ask, when was the last time you saw your daughter?"

Shanice sighed and said, "I'm sorry, I still haven't gotten used to Aaliyah being called my daughter. . . ."

"Why is that?" asked Clark.

Shanice looked back and forth between the two of them. She seemed unsure of how to respond. "Don't you know? I'd only adopted Aaliyah just two days before . . . well, before what happened to her."

Rivera and Clark exchanged a look, both thinking the same thing. Only *two days*? No way was that a coincidence.

Clark recovered quickly from the shock. "How long had you known Aaliyah before the adoption?"

Shanice looked at the ceiling, thinking. "About two months, I think."

Rivera raised her eyebrows. "That's a remarkably fast turnaround."

"And I never would have gotten custody of her so fast if not for the senator's help."

"What senator?" asked Clark.

"Senator Harrison," said Shanice.

Rivera knew that name. She shot another look at Clark.

"He accelerated the process?" said Clark.

"That's right."

"Why?" asked Rivera, unable to suppress her curiosity.

Shanice looked uncertain. "We were like a test case . . . or whatever you call it. There was this bill he was working on. I read some of it on the computer, but it was way beyond me. It was something to do with supporting different religions. I'm still not sure what it all had to do with me and Aaliyah."

Rivera looked to Clark, uncertain what question to ask next. This interview was not going anything like what she'd expected. She'd heard of the Faith and Fairness Act, as the bill had been in the news a lot lately. But what did that have to do with a teenage girl's adoption—and murder?

"Hang on a sec," said Shanice, jumping to her feet. She left the room and retreated to what was most likely a bedroom. About a minute later, she returned carrying a photograph. She handed it to Clark, who looked at it and then passed it to Rivera.

It was a photo of Shanice, Senator Harrison, and Aaliyah, all of them smiling into the camera. Harrison had his arms around both Aaliyah and her new mom.

"When was this taken?" asked Rivera.

"Um, about a week ago. There was this big dinner thing he invited us to."

Clark let out a breath. "Well, I think that's about all—"

"Just one more question, if that's all right," said Rivera, playing a hunch. "If it's not too personal . . . how would you describe Aaliyah?"

Shanice's lower lip quivered. "Beautiful. Troubled. She had a difficult childhood. But she was a good girl. Whatever she was doing that night . . . she didn't deserve this."

Five minutes later, as she and Clark were descending the stairs, Rivera began thinking out loud.

"The deeper we dig, the weirder this gets. Senator Harrison . . . isn't he the one who's a big supporter of Truth Ministries?"

Clark looked at her, nodded.

"So what's he doing clearing out the red tape for a teenage girl's adoption just two days before she's murdered?"

"That," replied Clark, "is all I can think about."

# 41

Hotel Blue turned out to be an almost entirely forgettable little spot just off the highway and about an hour outside of D.C. and a few towns over from Truth Ministries' headquarters. Each ground level room had a parking spot right outside, so John could slip in without his being seen. His father could not have chosen a more perfect hideout.

John showered, and as the scorching needles of water stung and burned, he closed his eyes and prepared for what was to come. He was done playing the victim. It was time to put a plan of his own into motion. But before he could play Donald Harrison's game, he needed to know that his family was okay. More important, Monica had to know he was innocent, and believe in him. Without her support and trust, all of this was meaningless. Of everything he'd lost in the last days, his wife and his little girl were the only things that kept coming back to mind. Everything else could vanish, but without them . . . he couldn't imagine how he'd go on.

Two hours later, John used side streets to make his way over toward Truth Ministries. He had no doubt, if they were looking for him, that his headquarters would be one of the places there'd be a set of eyes. But he knew the area better than most, and he had more experience than they realized with finding shadows and vanishing when needed. The years he spent wandering as a young man had taught him some hard lessons, yet they'd also made him adept at dodging others' notice. And cutting through alleys toward the parking garage of his headquarters, those lessons all came flooding back to him.

He found a dark corner to crouch in, right around lunchtime, and watched. Soon enough, Ryan's Corvette whipped into the garage and squealed into a space—John's designated spot at the parking garage. John winced. He'd assumed Ryan would have taken charge in his absence, but wasn't parking in John's spot taking it a little far?

He put it out of his mind. He had much bigger things to worry about.

John slipped out of his corner and stepped behind a pillar in the garage, watching Ryan with eyes shaded by the hood of his sweat shirt. When Ryan headed for the elevator, John grabbed a cart of janitorial supplies he'd grabbed earlier from a supply closet the staff always left open, and followed Ryan.

The sound of whistling reached John's ears. Ryan was in good spirits.

When Ryan reached the elevator, John was close enough to tap him on the shoulder. Ryan jumped and spun around.

"Hey," said John. "It's me."

Ryan's eyes nearly leaped out of his head, and his complexion blanched lily white. "John!"

John was so happy to see a friendly face, he threw his arms around Ryan and wrapped him in a tight bear hug.

Ryan pulled gently away and spoke in hushed tones. "What are you doing coming here? It's too dangerous!"

"I need your help," said John.

"You—you need money?"

"Whatever you've got on you."

Quickly, Ryan pulled some bills out of his wallet, folded and handed them to John. "John, the whole country is hunting you!"

John suddenly felt self-conscious and glanced around the garage's interior.

"It's unreal what they're saying," Ryan added.

John had no time to explain himself. He handed Ryan a piece of paper on which he'd scrawled *Hotel Blue, 717 Central Ave.*, and the name of the town.

"Can you get this to Monica?" he asked.

Ryan glanced down at the paper. "Sure," he said.

Behind his shoulder, John heard the familiar squawk of a walkie-talkie. He turned to see a patrol car idling in the garage entrance, the cop inside talking to the booth attendant. Instantly he began backing away from Ryan.

"I'll be in touch," said John before turning and striding away.

Across the street from the garage, Mr. Gray waited. He scanned the street back and forth, watching for Luther. The preacher had shown up half an hour ago in an ugly maroon sedan and disappeared into the garage, but he hadn't come out yet.

On the orders of the senator, Mr. Gray had been trying to track down the preacher. The man had turned out to be a much more entertaining and elusive prey than Mr. Gray expected. After following him to the church, Luther had somehow escaped unnoticed. There was a report of him showing up at a motel on the outskirts of town a little while later, but he was long gone by the time Mr. Gray got there. The clueless girl who'd called the police was no help at all. While Luther had kept a low profile since then, Mr. Gray knew that sooner or later he would show up at Truth Ministries. Men with power couldn't stay away from their thrones for very long.

His associate Mr. Broad was busy patrolling Luther's neighborhood in case he returned there. As far as Mr. Gray knew, there'd been no sign of him yet.

Wait. There he was. Mr. Gray saw Luther pushing a cart down the sidewalk just outside the garage. He looked spooked. He was wearing those ridiculous sunglasses again. Luther soon ditched the cart and sprinted across the street, back to his car.

Mr. Gray watched him back out, and when he was sure Luther wasn't looking, he did the same.

Harrison would be relieved. He'd grown worried that they had nothing tangible on the preacher, but now that he knew the preacher's vehicle, Mr. Gray had more than enough information. He memorized the license plate and if needed would be able to affix a GPS tracking unit on the car. The full resources of the CIA and NSA were at his disposal, thanks to the efforts of Senator Harrison.

There was nowhere the preacher could go now. Mr. Gray had him in his sights and imagined circling him—drawing ever closer until he finally got the call. And then the real fun would begin.

# 42

23 YEARS AGO

Anyone sitting here?"

John glanced up at the source of the question, a middle-aged man standing next to him. He shook his head and returned to his meal.

It was a busy Thursday night at the shelter. At least a dozen other guests were eating at long tables in the small dining hall. This guy taking the seat next to him didn't look much like he belonged here.

"Enjoying your meal?" the guy asked.

Oh, wonderful. John had no desire to talk to anyone, but this guy wasn't picking up on his expression or body language. Or maybe he was, and he was ignoring it. Either way, John was annoyed.

He'd never been to this shelter before. He'd been in Chicago looking for work for less than a week, but he was coming up dry. John was thinking of moving on to Cincinnati or maybe somewhere to the south in the morning. But his tired body needed fuel first.

"Yeah," he replied, not making eye contact with the nosy guy.

"I made it," the man said with a smile.

John couldn't hide his surprise. "*You* cooked this?"

"Every bite," said the man, quite pleased with himself. "Do I make a mean corn-bread casserole or what? Come back next week and I'll make you some more."

John shook his head and rolled his eyes. This guy was wearing a white dress shirt without a single wrinkle to be found, pleated black dress pants, and well worn but stylish loafers. "You look more like a stockbroker than a cook," said John.

The man chuckled. "Not far off. I'm an accountant."

John sighed and took another bite of his food. "This is the part where I'm supposed to ask why an accountant is at a homeless shelter."

"Is it?" the man replied. "I thought that seemed pretty obvious. I volunteer once a week."

"That's *what* you're doing," said John. "Not *why*."

The corners of the man's lips playfully curled up. "Tell you what. I'll give you my 'why' if you give me yours. Why are you here?"

"Been traveling around, looking for work. Can't seem to convince anyone to hire me. Guess they don't like my hair." John's long locks extended past his shoulders and hadn't been cut in over a year.

"Or," said the man, "maybe it's the smell."

John felt his cheeks burn red. "What's that supposed to mean?"

"Sorry, my wife tells me I'm too blunt sometimes," the man said, looking sheepish. "You volunteer here long enough and you learn about various scents on people who come in off the street and what they are. And I know the burning-plastic-crossed-with-a-dollar-bill scent that's pouring off you is the distinct smell of cocaine."

John clenched his fists. How dare this total stranger—

"I've offended you! I apologize. Truly," said the man, and John had to concede that he seemed sincere about it. "You hang around here long enough and certain topics just become old hat. I shouldn't have opened my big mouth."

John relaxed but held on to his frown. "Forget it. You're not wrong, anyway. I'm not proud of it. I'm trying to kick the habit."

The man smiled. "You will. I'm sure of it."

John took another bite of food. "You are, are you?"

He nodded. "Absolutely."

"You don't even know me."

"True. But I see something in you that I don't see very often in the people who come here."

John stopped chewing. "Like what?"

"You're hungry."

John looked at him blankly. Was the guy making some kind of joke?

The man smiled. "I know, I know. That sounded ridiculous. But I'm not talking about food. You're hungry for *more*. You *crave* something more from this life. I can see it in your eyes. On your wrist."

John looked down and saw the small Celtic-style cross he'd had tattooed on the inside of his wrist. It had been a gag, just one more thing to annoy his dad. But *sometimes* he looked at it and felt uncomfortable. Not that he was going to give this man the satisfaction of being right. "Maybe," he replied. "Or maybe I just really like corn-bread casserole."

The man chuckled again. "Fair enough."

John took a big bite of the casserole and studied the man beside him. "Your turn. What's a successful accountant doing at a run-down, nasty old homeless shelter in the bad part of town?" John didn't know that the man was successful, of course, but he figured it was a safe bet.

The smile receded from the man's face. "I suppose . . . I'm soothing a guilty conscience."

John continued eating quietly, waiting for the man to explain.

"I make a lot more money than my family needs. And when I think of how many people in the world go hungry one, two, even three meals a day . . . I feel frustrated. And guilty. And a whole bunch of other things. We donate a lot of money to worthy causes, but it doesn't quite feel *real* if I'm not getting my hands dirty. So I come down here once a week and I cook."

John was surprised to find himself empathizing with this man he didn't know. He sat in silence and allowed the man's words to roll around in his head. Finally he finished his meal. It felt good to be full again. And he had to admit, the food was tasty. He stood. "Well. Thanks for the meal. And the rest."

"You're very welcome. Before you go, may I ask your name? I like to have names to go with the people I pray for on a regular basis."

John was surprised and really had no desire for this man or anybody else to spend time on their knees, lifting up his name to a God who probably wasn't even there. Yet for some reason his mouth formed the words anyway.

"John," he said. "John Luther."

The man put his hand on John's shoulder. "Thanks for the conversation, John. Stop by the next time you're in town. I'd be happy to cook for you again."

John nodded, then broke away from him. He was almost out the door when he stopped and turned back. "You didn't tell me your name," he called, not caring that everyone else in the room stopped talking and looked up.

"Wilson," the man replied. "My name is Dave Wilson."

# 43

Senator Donald Harrison had turned in early and just drifted off to sleep when the phone rang. Tomorrow was a big day. The Sumac Alliance was holding its benefit luncheon tomorrow, and there was much to do beforehand.

Fighting the urge to grumble, Donald reminded himself that calls in the night came with the job. He was always on duty. Besides, it wasn't even that late yet.

Donald turned on the lamp on his nightstand, reached over, and grabbed the receiver. It was attached to an antique-style phone, a Christmas gift a few years ago from his wife.

"Hello."

"Senator," said an official-sounding voice, "I have the president on the line."

Donald quickly sat up, swinging his legs over the edge of the bed. "Put him through," he replied.

On the other side of the large four-poster bed, his wife rolled over toward him and groaned. He waved a hand, motioning for her to be quiet. "*The president*," he whispered.

"Donald," said the president in his trademark Southern drawl.

"Yes, Mr. President," said Donald. "How can I help you, sir?"

"I'd like to share a story with you, if that's all right." The president's drawl sounded even slower and more rounded than usual. In front of the press, the accent would almost disappear, but in more casual situations, and especially in the presence of bourbon, one could clearly hear the man's deep Georgia roots. Donald wondered if he'd had a drink or two tonight.

"Please," said Donald.

"You know that feeling you get in your gut when something just ain't right?" said the president.

Donald's breath slowed. He and the president had only been talking about one subject recently.

"Yes, I know the feeling, sir," he said.

The president was quick to continue his story. "When I was about eight or nine, I was walking barefoot on the back porch and I heard a rattling sound, like a kid's toy. There it was, all coiled up. An eight-foot-long eastern diamondback rattler. Its fangs were dripping, the whole bit. Do you know what I did?"

"Uh, no," Donald said, even though he had a good idea of where this was going. "No, sir."

"I wrapped my little nubs around it and I squeezed until that devil didn't have any fight left. Do you know why I did that?"

A cold shiver ran up and down Donald's spine. This story of the president's was detouring to a very dark place. "Why?" he said, his voice much quieter than he'd intended.

"Because if I hadn't done that," said the president, "the safety of my entire family would have been in jeopardy."

Something had spooked him, Donald realized. But what had changed? Had the president heard about Mr. Gray spotting John Luther at Truth Ministries this afternoon? Was he worried that Luther was going to go on the offensive, turning the tables on them? Did he know something Donald didn't? Or was he just losing his nerve, chickening out?

"Do I make myself clear?" asked the president.

He most definitely did. But Donald wanted to try to lighten the mood. The two politicians were still allies, after all, and friends. There was no need for this to turn ugly.

"By the way, sir," said Donald in a jovial tone, "did you happen to see the polls tonight? They looked superb."

"I don't think you're understanding what I'm saying," the president said. It wasn't a warning; it was a threat.

"I certainly do, sir," Donald assured him. "In a few months, this is all going to be forgotten and you'll be in your second term. Please, just let me handle this, Mr. President."

After a short pause, the president said in his most authoritative voice, "Donald, I wash my hands of this thing. John Luther is *entirely* your misfortune."

There was a sudden click, and the president's voice was replaced by a dial tone. Donald pulled the receiver away from his ear and looked at it. He had to fight the urge to pitch it and the entire phone across the room.

He silently cursed the president. And yet Donald knew he should have seen this coming. All politicians had in common one driving motivation, one overriding purpose above all else, and that was self-preservation. It was only a matter of time before the president withdrew his part in the plan connected with John, thus denying any culpability. It had always been their objective for John to remain on the run for a while as a fugitive; it was so much easier to discredit and marginalize him that way.

Now that the plan was under way, however, and John was out there, moving in the shadows—obviously trying to prove his innocence—the president had thrown it all back on Donald. It was his responsibility alone now. He'd get no credit if everything worked out and would take all the blame if it didn't. None of it could be traced back to the Oval Office.

Donald was angry at the president, but even angrier at John. Why did the man have to be so stubborn? Why couldn't he have just gone along with the Faith and Fairness bill to begin with? Then none of this mess would be happening now.

If this was how John wanted to play it, then Donald had no choice but to oblige him. Maybe it was time to take the game to the next level.

Thinking fast, Donald picked up the receiver again and dialed Mr. Gray's number.

He had to send John Luther a message.

# 44

Charles Luther fired up his old record player, moving the needle to a piano concerto by Mozart. One of his favorite pieces.

It was otherwise perfectly quiet in the old log cabin. Charles loved this place. He'd bought it ages ago and came here whenever he had some free time. It was situated deep in the woods surrounding Kings Mountain, just forty-five minutes from the North Carolina border, untouched by the lights and commotion and noise of even the smallest of towns, let alone the big cities. It was his sanctuary from the demands of a life of service.

Above his desk was a wall filled with newspaper clippings. It looked like the obsessive work of a criminal profiler or a private detective, but a great importance and purpose was behind Charles's collection. He'd been assembling evidence for months. Well over a year, in fact. Few others saw the mounting signs, but that hadn't stopped Charles.

He sat down at the desk and placed the tiny USB drive John had given him into a slot on the side of his laptop. Already open on the screen was a web browser window showing CNW's front page. The top headline read, *Truth Joins Sumac in Fight for*

*Religious Reform.* Sumac had made the announcement early this evening, yet astonishingly not a single journalist had made the connection between John's supposed sudden "relapse" and Truth Ministries' shocking policy change.

Charles frowned when a video window popped up as a red light on the little thumb drive flickered. Looking down through his reading glasses, he clicked the play button. The video showed John's Toyota, pulled over to the side of the road in an isolated area. John was slouched in the vehicle's front seat and looked to be unconscious. Just outside, the girl, Aaliyah, stood talking to a tall man in a gray suit. Was that the man from the balcony at the Sumac meeting? Aaliyah turned to face him, and he struck her, hard. He then stuck a syringe into her while holding her in a headlock.

Charles turned sharply in his seat. He'd heard something, a creaking maybe. His heart sped up, his nerves on edge. But the house was perfectly still.

He went back to the video and kept watching.

A moment later, he turned again. This time he looked in the other direction, but again there was nothing but silence—save for the record that was playing in the background. What was it he'd heard? Was he imagining it? Maybe it was some kind of feedback coming from the video.

He returned to his computer. John was right. If they could get the media behind it, this video could at least clear John. Nailing down the true guilty party would be another matter entirely. Tying the man in the gray suit to Senator Harrison, though, would be trickier, if not impossible. Still, there had to be a way.

Charles reached across the desk for his phone and dialed John. It rang for several seconds until an automated voice message finally answered. "Call me when you can," said Charles into the recording, rubbing his rosary beads. "I've found something."

The woods were deathly still, the only visible light coming from the moon. Well, that wasn't completely true. There was a soft orange glow in the distance ahead that must've been from the cabin.

Mr. Gray waved Mr. Broad on with one hand, a nickel-plated pistol in the other. By his own orders both men were wearing latex gloves and hairnets. They may have looked silly, but it was unavoidable. This operation required zero residual presence. Not a single strand of hair or the tiniest piece of flaked-off skin could be left behind.

It took some time to weave between the gnarled trees of this ancient forest, but they couldn't allow their approach to be heard by anyone.

At last they made it to the cabin and slowly climbed the outside stairs one at a time, making sure their footsteps made no noise whatsoever. The front door wasn't even locked.

Inside, Mr. Gray identified the music being played as Mozart's Piano Concerto in D minor. Second movement, if he was not mistaken. This man had exquisite taste.

He and Mr. Broad traced the music to its source, a side room off the main living area. A wooden door was shut tight between them and their target. Would it give them away when they opened it? Mr. Gray was considering searching for an alternative entrance to the room when he heard a voice speaking inside.

"Call me when you can . . ." Mr. Gray recognized it as Charles Luther.

As the man kept talking, Mr. Gray seized the opportunity to grab the doorknob and turn it, assuming the man's voice would mask any sound this made. He needn't have worried. The door slipped open soundlessly on well-oiled hinges.

Mr. Gray quickly took in the details of the room. Across the room, his back to them, Charles Luther sat at a small desk up against one wall. There was a laptop on the desk. The rest of the room had warm, inviting fixtures. A beautiful end table that held a record player. A lovely brass floor lamp with a stained-glass shade. Religious iconography and art adorned the walls.

Noiselessly, Mr. Gray padded across the floor toward the desk. When the old priest hung up the phone, he leveled a silver snub-nosed pistol just inches away from Charles Luther's right temple.

Without hesitation, he pulled the trigger.

The priest's head snapped sideways, then slumped forward.

Mr. Gray and Mr. Broad went immediately into cleanup mode. Mr. Broad lifted a black duffel bag and set it on the desk. He unplugged the laptop and placed it inside the bag, with the USB drive still attached to it. For good measure he took the telephone too.

Mr. Gray carefully placed the pistol in the dead man's hand. Might as well make it look like suicide. Even if John Luther would never buy it, the police might.

Five minutes tops. Whoever Charles Luther had called could return the call or be headed here any minute, and they needed to clear out fast.

Double-checking their work, Mr. Gray nodded to Mr. Broad, and the man slipped back out of the office. Mr. Gray followed, stopping only for one second to reach out a gloved hand and turn off the record player.

Music that beautiful needed an audience. For Charles Luther, there was now only silence.

# 45

It felt great to swim. John took lap after lap in the hotel's swimming pool, clearing his head and rejuvenating his sore muscles. He'd taken advantage of the fact that it was too late at night for anyone else to be in the pool, and now he had the whole thing to himself. In the water he was weightless, and in the water there was silence. Everything from the last days dissolved, at least for a few moments, and he actually allowed himself to feel normal for the first time in days.

He pushed himself, hard. Much harder than when he swam at the fitness center near his house. It felt as though he was trying to prove something, but he wasn't sure what. Several times he thought he'd be done, on his last lap, but then decided to do one more. Just stroke and kick and breathe, over and over and over.

When finally his legs and lungs burned equally and he could go no more, he retrieved his belongings from the side of the pool and stepped back into his room. He was inside drying off when he noticed a light flashing on the phone his father had given him, which had been poolside while he was swimming. He wasn't used to this thing yet, and so it took a moment or two to figure out what the light signified, finally realizing that someone had left him a voice mail.

John pressed for the message to play and heard his father's anxious baritone on the other end of the line. "Call me when you can," said his father on the message. "I've found something."

John's heart fluttered, but not because of his father's words. Something in his spirit was unsettled, though he couldn't say what. He recognized the feeling. He'd only had it a few times before in his life. Almost always he found out later that it was the Holy Spirit tugging at his senses, coaxing him to pray for Monica or Jodi, at a moment when they were in dire need.

He called his father back right away. It was on the sixth ring when John knew in his soul that something was terribly wrong.

John grabbed his leather jacket and raced out the door.

After a frantic drive up the road leading to Kings Mountain, John finally arrived at the cabin. The lights were on inside the place; he could just make them out from the road. His dad was home, yet he hadn't answered his phone. A short hike through the trees and soon John was standing on the front steps, breathing hard.

He burst through the door. "Dad?" he called.

No answer.

Any chance the old man could be asleep? It was pretty late, after all. Almost eleven o'clock now.

Maybe he was in his study . . .

He ran to his left and flung open the door. "Dad?" he cried.

Charles Luther was slumped over to one side in his desk chair, his eyes closed. John froze, terrified of moving closer, because that would make this real. One foot in front of the other, he slowly inched across the room, hoping his father would wake up and John would discover this had all been a bad dream.

When he reached his dad at last, John leaned around and confirmed his greatest, darkest fear. On the other side of the old man's head was a bullet wound, blood streaking out of it and trailing down his arm to his hand. Dangling from his hand was the string of rosary beads he was never without, blood dripping from the beads into a pool on the floor. A nickel-plated pistol was clutched in his father's hand, but John knew instantly it had been placed there by someone else. Staged. Just as Aaliyah's body had been arranged for the police to find in John's Toyota.

"*Noooo . . . !*"

All of John's strength rushed from his body, and he collapsed to his knees. He knelt next to his father's crumpled form and pressed his head against the old man's. He squeezed his eyes tightly shut and let all his pain and grief pour out in sobs.

When the initial gust of sorrow passed, it was replaced by a rage unlike anything John had ever felt. He clenched his fists and looked around for something to hit, but there was nothing in his father's home that he was willing to destroy.

With a dread-filled start, John glanced at the desk. It was empty. No computer . . . no USB flash drive. He yanked the drawers from the desk and rifled through them, but the drive was nowhere to be found. John ripped the gun out of his father's hand and then, just as quickly, collapsed into a ball on the floor, wracked once more with sobbing.

He'd fought this man. For years and years, they'd fought. And then for years he'd run. So much had passed between them, and only recently did John feel like all the wounds of the past might truly heal one day. But now there was no chance. Now . . .

This couldn't be happening.

Several minutes later, John managed to get to his feet. He staggered out onto the back porch. In one hand he held the pistol; in the other he carried his father's bloodstained rosary beads. His limbs were heavy and numb as he tottered over to the edge of the porch. He leaned out and looked back and forth, half wondering if he might spot his father's murderer. And he knew exactly who the killer would turn out to be—the man in the gray suit. But that man was acting on someone else's orders.

When John was satisfied that no one was around, he tilted his face skyward, trembling with anguish and fury. With all his might he screamed at the top of his lungs, "*Are you not true to your name?!*"

He heard no answer.

After John had exhausted himself screaming to the heavens, he shuffled back inside the cabin.

His father's body sat there in the desk chair where he'd left him. It was as if the old man had been frozen in time. What should John do with him?

Should he bury his father? No, he couldn't. A coroner would need to examine the body before it could be laid to rest. And even before that, there were procedures for this kind of thing. In any murder, police considered the body as evidence. In fact, he shouldn't disturb anything in this room; it was a crime scene. A crime scene he'd placed himself right in the middle of. He'd touched his father. He'd taken the gun from the man's one hand and the rosary from the other. It was too late to put them back. His fingerprints would be on them both.

But he couldn't just leave his father slumped over sideways like that. The very notion felt horribly disrespectful. In just a few short days the body would start to decay, to smell . . .

John felt a sudden nausea, thinking of his father in these kinds of terms. Could this really be happening? *No.* He swallowed hard. He wasn't going to desecrate the scene of the crime any further. There was enough of that already with the old man's blood.

Maybe he could call in an anonymous tip to the police. Yes, that would work!

John dialed 9 . . . then hesitated. He couldn't call it in. There was no way he could report what happened as a suicide. It was too late for that, with his fingerprints on the gun. More than that, it would be a lie—a lie so revolting he couldn't stomach the thought of it.

Besides, any murder connected to John himself would put an even bigger target on his back. John knew how the media worked. They knew he'd had a complicated and often strained relationship with his father. What reconciliation had come between them these last years had been out of the public eye. If there was any suspicion of foul play at all, he'd be guilty in the court of public opinion almost immediately. He was already a desperate fugitive wanted for killing a young woman. Would the murder of his father be that hard to add to the list?

John wanted justice to be served toward those who'd done this evil act, but he could hear his father's voice in his head, reminding him over and over that what was important now was for him to focus on the first task—proving his innocence. Doing that would certainly bring the men who'd executed his father right to him. They'd have no other choice.

John sighed. He had no choice either but to leave the old man exactly as he was. The first chance he could, once everything was settled, he'd make it right. But for now . . .

Looking once more into the study, his eyes caught sight of the wall behind his father's desk, where dozens of newspaper clippings had been cut out and taped to the wall. His father had attached a long string to the papers, making links and connections between various articles. For just a moment, John wondered if they were about him, cuttings and publicity from his past.

He took a step closer. No. The articles weren't about John at all. Not a single one showed any mention of him.

They were about Sumac. It was remarkable really, his father's charting a complete history of the Sumac Alliance. The time-line began with a piece on the formation of a Senate Judiciary Committee on International Religious Freedom, chaired by—surprise, surprise—Senator Donald Harrison. It was dated three years ago. From there, it was easy to see now, in hindsight, that Harrison had begun gathering like-minded supporters through contacts and associations he'd made on that committee. Donald had talked to him once, eighteen months or so ago, about Sumac and whether it was something John saw Truth Ministries being interested in, but John hadn't even given it a second thought. His organization's focus was on sharing the Gospel. That was all.

John wondered how long Donald had been planning the Faith and Fairness bill, putting the pieces into place to build support and momentum in order to get it passed someday.

Many other headlines charted the growth and shaping of the group, which called itself a "nonprofit organization devoted to protecting religious freedoms." John wanted to spit at the irony. There were ups and downs recorded here, triumphs and setbacks on Donald's mission to unite all the major religions and require them to play nice with one another. Plenty of pious quotes from the senator on the importance of religious entities respecting one another and being friends.

"Too long have the religions of this nation focused on what divides them, when there is so much we have to share in common," Donald had said in one article.

It all sounded so nice and friendly—on the surface. So much talk of "mutual respect" and "the inherent cultural and historic value of every system of belief." Nothing wrong with any of it, except that John knew all this rhetoric was merely the public face of Sumac. Donald's true motives went much deeper.

It had been bothering John since the very beginning. What was Donald really after with the Faith and Fairness Act? Was the goal of world religions standing side by side worth killing for? Something about it didn't ring true.

The last article was an analysis of the contents of the Faith and Fairness Act, which ended by pointing out that the bill was scheduled to go before the Senate in just a few weeks' time. The article was dated a little under a week ago.

John took a step back and examined the timeline as a whole. Why had his father been following Sumac's formation and progress all this time? This had to have taken him years to compile.

It came to John in a rush of understanding. The old man had known all along. He'd come to see Sumac as a powerful organization that would one day stand in direct opposition to his son's ministry. Truth Ministries had risen to become one of the most popular evangelistic ministries in the world. John himself had become something of a celebrity, his name well known around the globe.

Of course, Truth and Sumac would come into conflict. It was inevitable.

Charles couldn't have known that his son would one day be the target of a conspiracy to frame him for murder, thereby discrediting him. But he had been watching and waiting for a very long time.

John had always despised politics, but his father had demonstrated a keen eye for it and tried to convince his son of the importance of staying on top of international legislation. Although he'd been trying to interest John in politics for years, John never really understood his father's fascination with it.

Until now.

# 46

Have you had any further contact with John Luther?" asked Clark, as Rivera worked on attaching a wired microphone to Ryan Morris's chest.

Morris almost laughed at the very notion. "Not a peep."

Rivera was unimpressed by his ego. "You sure about that?"

Morris smiled that smarmy grin of his. "Hey, I'm on your side."

"The only way to be protected is to be completely honest," Rivera said, watching him. She glanced at Clark, who was studying him as well. His expression was blank, but Rivera noticed his jaw was clenched.

He didn't trust Ryan Morris. Rivera was glad.

It was awfully late for a clandestine meeting between John Luther and his wife, but Morris swore it was the time Luther had requested that he bring Monica to the Hotel Blue. There'd been no sign of the preacher yet.

"Hey, if he said he'll show, he'll show," said Morris, defensive. "What more do you want?"

Agent Clark kept his gaze leveled on Morris. "What I want,"

he said, "is for you to give us more information about the activities of Senator Harrison."

There it was at last. The proverbial elephant in the room. After their interview of Shanice Evans, it was Clark who'd posited that Ryan Morris owed his sudden promotion to the maneuvering of Senator Donald Harrison. And based on Morris's reaction to Clark's gambit just now, it looked like he was spot-on.

For the first time since they'd met him, Morris was taken aback and not quick to answer. "I . . . I can't speak to that," he said. "I don't really know him. Look, you've read John's file. He had it in him to do this."

*Everyone does,* Rivera thought. And it didn't escape her attention that Morris had just tried very hard to change the subject. "We're well aware of his history, thank you," she said with a sour note. She finished up with the wire and walked away. Rivera was worried that if she spent any more time in close quarters with this man, she might slug him.

And she was fairly certain that he'd flirted with her at least twice while she was applying the microphone.

Morris pulled his shirt down and stood. "Listen," he said, stepping closer to Clark and taking on a conspiratorial tone, "I don't mean to be disrespectful, but what do they pay you guys for?" He laughed and propped an arm on Agent Clark.

That was it. Now Rivera was certain she would have punched that stupid smile off his face if she were still standing close to him. For his part, Clark looked down at Morris's arm with a threatening gaze.

Morris removed his arm but kept his mouth running. "I mean, prostitution, addiction, gambling . . . it's written all over him. We thought he changed. And we're all about forgiveness and grace. But I gotta tell you . . . this has caused me to doubt my faith a little bit."

While he spoke, Morris opened the room's tiny fridge. Was

he seriously looking for a drink? As if they would let him consume alcohol while he was supposed to be roping Luther in for them! Disappointed to find the refrigerator empty, he turned to the floor-to-ceiling mirror affixed to the wall next to it and examined his appearance.

"But that's the lesson," he concluded.

Rivera watched Clark work. As always, she was impressed with his ability to get people to spill their guts. He switched gears.

"It must be really hard for you to have to take on all that responsibility," said Clark, "especially with no advance notice."

Ryan nodded enthusiastically, as if excited to extol his own virtues. "See, people forget this about Truth Ministries—the size of the thing. It has the same nuts and bolts as a Fortune 500 company. And I'm running it! This ain't no sleigh ride, trust me."

"Oh, I can imagine," said Clark, patronizing him.

Morris seemed to be oblivious. He strode to the hotel room's window and looked out, obviously hoping to spot John Luther approaching. He whirled back around to face the detectives. "All right," he said. "Let's do this."

Rivera glanced at Clark, and for just a second she was sure she saw him roll his eyes.

# 47

Monica.

John's father was dead, murdered as an obvious message, and now all John could think about was Monica. Was she next on the list? Would Donald go that far?

It was the thought that stopped the tears, at least for the moment. His eyes became laser beams, focused on a single target—Donald Harrison. Had Donald really done all this because of his precious bill? Had he murdered two innocent people to get the Faith and Fairness Act passed?

John prayed it wasn't so, but couldn't conjure any hope on the matter. Not anymore.

After driving back into the city, he went straight to the Hotel Blue, intending to rendezvous with Monica. She would be there. She had to be. How would she react when he told her his father had been killed?

The hotel was ahead on the left, and true to his word, Ryan had brought Monica. John knew because Ryan's Corvette was there in the parking lot. It was parked in a handicap space, but whatever. That was just Ryan being Ryan. At least he'd come.

John was about to turn into the hotel's driveway when he spotted an unmarked black SUV parked just outside the hotel, in front of a dumpster. Odd place to park. John lowered his window to get a better look. The white license plate on the back of the vehicle was government-issued.

*Ryan . . .* John grimaced as he pushed down on the gas pedal, speeding past the hotel.

Either Ryan had called the Feds or they had approached him. John hoped against hope it was the latter, because the former would mean that his most trusted lieutenant had betrayed him.

And that he could not fathom.

Mr. Gray had studied countless fighting techniques and styles, trained meticulously with firearms and weapons, and had been a voracious student in the lessons of pain to be able to become the kind of professional he was today. He'd never had the opportunity, though, to watch himself at work until this very night.

The USB drive's surprising footage had at first angered him. The world today with its ubiquitous cameras and constant unblinking eyes. He'd scouted that location days in advance and chosen it in particular for how deserted it often appeared. And still, there'd been someone watching. Filming.

Yet the anger he felt turned to fascination as the video played out. He watched himself move through the steps he'd coordinated in his head. Each and every movement planned and executed with precision. He hadn't lost a step in that respect.

On the screen he sent the girl reeling with a short blow to the head and then followed it up with the syringe. She never felt a thing. Behind her, he could see the passenger side door open and John Luther stumble to freedom, just as planned. After another minute or two of filming, the man emerged huffing and disoriented up the hill, the camera's lens watching him the entire way. Whoever shot the footage stayed silent. Then the man disappeared into the woods once more, and the camera rustled a bit before switching off.

But not until it had moved a few unsteady steps toward a worn-down trailer promising tattoos. Mr. Gray reversed the footage, then paused it when the building came up again. He stared at the screen, nodding slowly. His loose end had a home.

Pulling out both his phone and his Glock, Mr. Gray placed a single phone call. When it was answered, he said, "We have a complication, sir, but fixable."

The voice on the line replied simply, "Then fix it."

Mr. Gray clicked off, slipped on his suit coat, and hurried out to his sedan. He looked at the dashboard clock as he entered and made some mental calculations. Thirty-three minutes to drive there. Fifteen to do the job. Ten to clean the place. Thirty-three minutes back. Should everything fall into place, he'd be back by midnight at the latest. He gunned the engine and was on his way.

It turned out he'd been wrong about the timing. It took him thirty-one minutes to arrive. The stoplights had been in his favor.

Parking once more at the bottom of the hill, Mr. Gray pulled the gun from its holster, just in case of the unexpected, and took the same ragged path up that John Luther had the other night. Above him, the moon glowed silver, the only thing that had gone wrong so far. It would've helped to have had some cloud cover should someone happen to be watching again. These days, someone always seemed to be watching.

This time, though, no one was. He reached the American Woman tattoo parlor in silence, his approach muffled by the music rumbling from inside. Three rusted cars waited outside, a good sign that his target might be inside. The music rattled the frail bones of the building, and a few people let out shouts of excitement. A party. Mr. Gray had one guess what had funded the celebration.

He tucked his gun back in the holster and, making a last-minute correction in his plans, knocked on the door.

Nothing.

He knocked again, louder. This time someone inside turned down the music. Muffled questions were exchanged. He knocked one last time.

Finally the door squeaked open, and a red-eyed shirtless man looked out, an annoyed expression on his face. "Help you, man?"

"Sir, I'm with the task force searching for John Luther, the fugitive who disappeared around here a few nights ago. We're canvassing the area, talking to everyone we can."

"Sure, yeah. Umm . . ." Apparently lying didn't come easily when a person was stoned. "I don't think I saw any . . . uh, fugitives."

Mr. Gray motioned to the party still going on in the back of the building. "How about your friends there? Did any of them happen to see anything suspicious?"

"Kinda late, man," he whined, but when Mr. Gray didn't budge from where he stood at the door, he sighed and called, "Nolan!"

Soon a thin black guy slipped out from behind a curtain and approached warily.

Once Mr. Gray had finished asking the same few questions, the black guy replied, "Man, lots of strange white guys showing up here lately."

Mr. Gray smiled. "So you *have* seen John Luther—the preacher on TV."

"Yeah, we seen him. Was here yesterday. This soiree is in honor of him, in fact."

From the depths of the trailer, two new faces emerged, both of them women. One was blond and looked frail. The other had dark-rimmed eyes and a unicorn shirt on. Mr. Gray looked at both, and when the unicorn girl met his eyes, he saw her recognition. She'd had the camera. The one who'd done such a good job filming him.

"Did you tell anyone else?" he called to her.

"What?" Nolan said.

"Did. You. Tell. Anyone. Else," Mr. Gray repeated. This time the girl shook her head. He believed her.

"That's too bad," he said. In a flash, the Glock was out, and both men went down before they could even cry out. The girls took a minute longer, but the music was loud enough that he didn't worry if their cries had been heard. Just another wild party.

Mr. Gray looked at his watch. Fifteen minutes exactly.

It took ten minutes more, and American Woman burned as bright as the evening's moon.

On a phone call during the thirty-three minute drive home, Mr. Gray made assurances that all complications had been fixed. He made it back before midnight, just as planned.

The only task left for the evening was to destroy the flash drive. But maybe not right away. Maybe he would watch the video one more time.

# 48

Not knowing where else to go, John drove to St. Peter's, entering again through the secret sewer entrance he'd escaped from just a few nights ago. Though it felt to him more like *weeks* ago.

Had he been in a better frame of mind, it would have bothered him terribly that he was filthy and haggard, disheveled strands of hair hanging from his forehead. But this was a night like no other.

A young priest John didn't recognize was in the sanctuary, holding a small midnight mass. A line of about a dozen parishioners was lined up in the center aisle, with the priest standing at the altar and handing out the sacraments for Holy Communion.

John stepped forward and joined the line. He was the last one, and while the priest clearly didn't know him, he didn't deny him the bread and wine. John took them gratefully, ingested them, and then closed his eyes in an impassioned, sorrowful prayer. He knew for some it probably wouldn't be considered appropriate for him to partake in Communion, but he desperately needed a connection to his dad, and this place was all that was left of him.

Would God hear his prayers this night? Would he honor them?

Would he answer?

☖

After the service ended, John remained in his seat. Once all the other parishioners had left, he made his way to the priest's office. His father's office, though he knew this younger priest would be using it tonight.

John opened the door without knocking and stepped inside. The priest stood in the far corner, hanging up his vestments in an armoire. He didn't turn as John entered, so he must not have heard him.

John was so distraught, and his standing in this room only made things worse. Dark, with little more than candlelight to provide illumination, it was like a funeral home late at night. Serene, but eerie and vacant.

"It feels cold in here without him," John said. Had he said it to the priest or to himself, he wasn't sure.

The priest turned with a look of surprise. "Sorry?" he said. As he got a better look at John, he grew visibly concerned. "Sir, are you all right? You don't look well."

John didn't *feel* well. He was pale and nauseous, cold sweat droplets covering his skin. He stepped farther into the room and took a seat in a violet wingback chair.

"He's dead," John said, sickened as the words touched his tongue. "He was executed."

The priest took a tentative step toward him. "Who?"

"Your priest," John said. He looked the young man in the eye. "My father."

The man's countenance changed dramatically. He seemed to have trouble digesting what John was saying. He knelt in front of John and placed a hand on his shoulder. Compassion poured from his features, accompanied by deep concern. Did he think John was a crazed homeless person or something?

"What do you mean?" asked the young priest gently.

John reached into his jacket pocket. "Exactly what I said," he replied. He produced his father's rosary, stained with his blood.

The priest's eyes grew bigger as they fell on the beads. He pulled back his hand from John's shoulder, and John saw the truth swallow him. He looked so grieved, John's heart was pierced all over again. Charles may have been John's biological father, but he was also this young man's spiritual father.

The priest blinked, his eyes filling with tears. "My name is William." He swallowed hard.

*William.* John remembered the name. "The last time I was here, my father spoke very highly of you."

William said nothing but held eye contact with John. He looked to be in shock, struggling to make sense of things, feeling the first onset of grief and disbelief.

"Can you help me, William?"

## 49

Sleep was always impossible to come by in jail. He'd tried the first few times he'd been arrested to at least get some shut-eye, but after the third time, John had given up on that hope. First, they never shut off all the lights. Second, there was the noise—the talking and cursing, the snoring, people going to the bathroom just a few feet away from him. Third was the terrible smell that seeped into his nose and mouth.

So here he was, wide awake after midnight, when a guard came to the cell door and shouted his name.

John was told someone had posted bail. The officer quickly led him out of the lockup area to the check-in desk, where his personal items were returned to him.

Who bailed him out? He looked around the waiting area, but there were no familiar faces. Had Jackie decided to forgive him? Again? No, she'd made her feelings very clear.

John exited the building and found it colder outside than he'd remembered. But then he remembered very little about when he'd been brought in several hours ago.

Parked right in front of the police department's front door was a familiar station wagon, its engine running and spewing visible exhaust out the back. And at the wheel sat Charles Luther, his dad. John tried to remember the last time he'd seen the old man. It had to have been more than a year ago. He certainly hadn't told his dad he was back in the area.

"Thanks," he said with sincerity as he got in the car. "How'd you know I was in there?"

"You're welcome," said Charles. He put the car in gear and pulled into traffic. "Alonso Marquez was on the desk when you were booked. He's part of my congregation and knew I would want to hear that my son was back in town."

John watched the dashboard clock tick by for six minutes while neither of them said another word. Finally he couldn't take it anymore.

"If you want to fuss at me or list all the ways I'm a disappointment, please have at it," said John. "I've got it coming."

"It's tempting," said Charles, a smile playing at the corners of his mouth, "but I'll pass. You're thirty-one years old, John. You're way beyond my disciplinary jurisdiction."

John looked down at his shoes and chuckled. Good ol' Dad. He hadn't changed. In some ways, John hoped he never would. Despite the lectures in the past, John couldn't deny that Charles had always been there when John needed him. Always. John's demeanor turned dark as he pondered that.

"Why do you still help me, Dad?" he asked. "We both know I don't deserve it. I've spit in your face a hundred times. I wouldn't blame you if you turned your back and never wanted to see me again."

"Well, maybe I know something you don't."

Charles turned and looked at him. "What?"

"I know what it means to be a father," he said, his eyes never leaving the road.

John wished he could be more like his old man. Mountains of patience, limitless grace, and never once, despite all John had done, had Charles hurled guilt in his direction.

"Since I paid for your freedom," said Charles without a hint of condemnation or even sarcasm, "would you mind telling me what I spent my money on?"

John's insides withered, and he was certain he'd just shrunk to about two feet tall. He tried hard to blink back the tears, but failed.

"Jackie called the cops," John said, his voice thick and heavy. "I hit her, Dad."

Charles absorbed this in silence as John wept softly.

"Has it happened before?" asked the old man.

John bit his lip and nodded.

"Are you always drunk when it happens?" asked Charles. Even though he was careful to keep the judgment out of his voice, John could still detect the disappointment his dad was unable to mask completely.

John knew his father could smell the alcohol on his breath right now. He nodded again.

"Why? Why did you do it, John? What happened tonight?"

John let out a long sigh. "We were arguing. About money."

Charles nodded. "Gambling again?"

"Yeah," said John. "Jackie kicked me out tonight. She said . . . She wants a divorce, Dad." He began to sob again, his eyes squeezed shut and his shoulders shaking.

After a few minutes, John collected himself and sat in silence again. If it was possible to feel worse about himself than he did at this moment, he couldn't imagine it. And to confess it all to the best man he knew, the priest who was his father . . .

He was drowning in shame.

Charles pulled the car over and stopped in a parallel parking spot.

"John," he said, turning his whole body toward the passenger seat, "I know you think you're the worst of sinners. But you're no worse than me. Or anyone else."

John looked at him but couldn't hold the old man's gaze. He stared forward and shook his head.

"You've been searching for something your whole life, son. And we both know it's not your mother."

No. It really wasn't. John couldn't explain what it was exactly. But it wasn't her. He'd given up trying to find her ages ago.

"If you want my opinion," said the old man, "that thing you've been looking for has been right in front of your nose the whole time."

John looked up as his dad pointed at something beyond the windshield. John leaned forward and peered through the glass. A block ahead and across the street was the silhouette of a small church. Backlit by streetlights, the black outline of a cross stood tall against the night sky.

John sighed. "Dad, you know how I feel about that stuff."

"I know," said Charles. "But just think about it, John. Please. For me."

John had no desire to give any thought at all to religion. He'd been bombarded by that sort of thing during his entire childhood and never wanted to think about it again.

But he couldn't say no to his dad. Not tonight.

"Okay," he promised. "I will."

Charles patted him on the leg. Turning back to the wheel, he asked, "So where can I take you?"

Only one answer came to mind. Before tonight, he would have been humiliated to admit it or say it out loud. But just now, he didn't care.

"Home?" he said. He was dead tired, his last resource of energy tapped out. He sniffed and wiped his eyes. "Can I just go home for a little while, Dad?"

The old man smiled.

# 50

Monica couldn't help wondering why she was bothering to drop Jodi off at school each morning. As if everything were perfectly normal, as if her whole world weren't slipping from her a little more every minute John was away.

Yet life had to go on, and she had a responsibility to keep Jodi away from all this. It was what John would want, and what Monica wanted as well. Jodi was far too young to deal with the madness that was her parents' lives at the moment. As far as the girl knew, her dad was working away from home—called away on a trip somewhere. Jodi hadn't asked how long he'd be gone, and Monica hadn't offered an answer.

As she drove into the school parking lot, she wondered what kind of commentary it was on John's passion for Truth Ministries that his daughter found it perfectly normal not to see him for days and days. Monica turned off the ignition and sighed, thinking about where John could be right now. An ache filled her heart when she realized, for the hundredth time, that she had no idea where he was.

She took Jodi by the hand and walked with her through the steel double doors at the private school, where Jodi was in first grade. Jodi tugged at her hand when Monica led her past her classroom door.

"Sorry, sweetie," said Monica. She hadn't even noticed the classroom.

Was she even really here, in this building? Was any of this really happening? How could it be? Every teacher or parent that she passed in the hall gaped at her, though some of them had the good grace to look away and try to act like nothing was wrong. She hoped Jodi wouldn't notice the strange looks being sent their way.

Why was John staying so far away from her? Didn't he realize they were in this together, and that she could help him?

No. Monica was being too emotional. She told herself to think rationally, and she would know that John was keeping away from them in order to protect them. Plus, she was still under police surveillance twenty-four hours a day. If he came near, he would be caught.

She just felt so helpless, wanting to help him but not being able to—or allowed to. Even though she knew it was unreasonable, even though she was ashamed to admit it, in her weakest moments the worst thoughts and doubts still crept in. When she woke in the middle of the night, and the darkness pressed in on her, she couldn't help but worry that everything they were saying about John was true. He *had* done terrible things in his past. In the years they'd been married, they both knew several men in the ministry who'd fallen—who'd cheated on wives or taxes, who'd become overwhelmed by gambling or alcohol. One pastor they knew from Tacoma had even been arrested for domestic abuse. Good men fell all the time.

No, that wasn't fair. Monica knew her husband, and he was not a man who would murder. Even years ago, at his lowest of lows, when he was drugged out of his mind and drunk all the time, he would never have taken someone's life.

Monica looked around and found herself outside the school's front door. How had she gotten here? Did Jodi make it to her classroom? Had Mrs. Goodwin smiled and spoken to her as she always did when she dropped Jodi off in the morning?

She couldn't remember.

She sighed and walked to the car. On the driver's seat was a piece of paper she didn't recognize. It had probably fallen out of Jodi's backpack or something.

Monica grabbed the paper and slowly sat in the seat. She unfolded the paper and gasped when she recognized the hand-writing—it was John's sloppy, oversized scribbling.

He was here! She glanced at the note and confirmed it. At the bottom of the page were written the words *Love, John.*

Monica spun in her seat, surveying the parking lot and the entire surrounding area. John had left the note in the car for her to find while she was inside with Jodi, so he had to be close by!

She looked and looked, praying for something, even just a glimpse of him. But wherever he was hiding, he was doing it well. She reminded herself that it wasn't like this the first time he'd gone off the grid. He spent so many years running from his father, from God, even from himself. He knew how to be invisible.

She gave up her searching and sank back into the seat to read his letter.

*Monica,*

*I love you so, so much. I hope you still believe in me. I want to see you and Jodi, but I can't—they're watching you.*

*They shot Dad. He's dead, ~~and I don't know if I can keep~~ but I have to keep going.*

*I can't believe he's gone. (Don't tell Jodi yet.)*

*Please pray for me. I miss you both so much. But I have to finish this. One way or another, this will be over soon.*

*Love,*
*John*

Monica's hand was over her mouth. She felt light-headed.

Charles . . . He was dead? But how? Why would anyone kill a priest? It made no sense.

And John . . . He would be devastated—no, *destroyed*—by losing his father. This couldn't be happening, it just couldn't.

How would she break it to Jodi? More and more over the years, Charles had become a part of their lives, and Jodi—who knew nothing of the hurts of the past—simply went nuts with joy over her granddad. But no, John said not to tell her yet. Good, that was good.

No, that was dumb. *Nothing* was good about any of this. Not one thing. Where was God now, when her family needed him more than ever?

She didn't care about the danger anymore. Why wouldn't John let her in?

John made it around to the rear of the school, where the playground was, just as Jodi's class came out to play. They always had a few minutes of playtime first thing in the morning, and there she was.

Monica would be reading his note right about now. He wished he could see her when she found it, hug her after she read it, cry with her when she found out about his dad. At least he could see Jodi for a few minutes, even if it was from a distance.

A locked iron gate stood between John and his little girl, but he could see her plainly. She was skipping through the playground, laughing and playing with the other kids. She was wearing that cute little pink dress, and Monica had braided her hair in pigtails.

John closed his eyes, trying to sear this image of Jodi into his mind. If this was the last time he would ever see his daughter, he wanted it to be this picture of her that he remembered. This one, perfect moment. She was free from the sorrows and dangers he now had to confront, and he was so grateful for that. Her innocence was intact.

He put a hand on the iron bars and leaned in. How he wished he could hold Jodi, feel her little arms squeeze him around the neck, receive her sweet kisses on that one spot she always gravitated to on his cheek. A single tear leaked out as he watched her play.

"Father, please protect my wife and child," he said under his breath.

With a deep breath, John stood up straight and put his sunglasses back on. His father was dead. For better or worse, John was the man he was today because of that man, and John would never see him again in this life. Then there was the evidence that could have exonerated him. It was perfect, iron-clad. He had to assume that Donald had destroyed it by now. Plus, his most loyal colleague, his most passionate supporter, may have betrayed him.

How could he have any chance of winning? Of *surviving* this madness? He still had something to live for. To *fight* for. Two somethings.

And they were enough.

# 51

It wasn't like Agent Carter to disappear, particularly so close to lunch. When he was in the office, Carter's lunchtime was one of the long-standing traditions the man had, and Rivera was worried that she hadn't seen her partner for over half an hour. She'd jumped up to grab a quick mug of coffee, and when she returned, his desk chair was empty and nobody had even seen him leave.

She sat down at her desk and pulled out her file notes. Despite every best intention, this case was getting under her skin. More than that, Washington, D.C. was getting under her skin. And she couldn't say she hadn't been warned.

Rivera had started her career as a local police officer in a small Wisconsin town just west of Madison. She graduated from the University of Wisconsin with dual honors degrees in criminal justice and psychology, and had the bureau on the top of her wish list. But then the hiring freezes came, and she knew her chances of being selected while completely green were almost nil. So she took the closest job she could find, crashed with her parents when off duty, and spent most of her hours chasing down drunk Sconnie high schoolers fishtailing from one side of town to the other. The local sheriff, Beth Gibson, had been perhaps the second best mentor she'd ever had—next to Clark. She'd been the one to warn Rivera that the grass she dreamed of might be greener, but that luxury came at a cost.

"Even in Madison," Gibson had said, "anywhere there's a building with a dome in this country, there's somebody who'll pull strings to get away with murder. Or if not murder, then something that'll seem just as bad. And the movies you see about honest cops who don't play along? They won't kill you—that's all fiction. No. If you don't dance for them, they'll bury you so deep in the organization, you barely have the authority to shut your own office door, let alone stand for what's right." The woman nodded. "Don't know what it is about domed buildings."

Rivera couldn't see the U.S. Capitol building from her desk, but somehow she felt its long shadow stretching ever closer. And then the shadow was there, black and solid and imposing. She looked up.

"Lunch," Clark said, motioning with a thumb.

"Where—?" she started to ask, but he held up a hand to silence her, and she knew better than to ask. Every desk had a set of ears behind it. While she trusted most of them, she knew some of that trust was misplaced. Clark trusted no one. It felt cynical, but it was probably safer in the long run.

They took the stairs rather than the elevator. Rivera guessed that was mostly so he could let off some steam.

"Not doing the usual?" she asked, chasing after him.

This was what worried her most at the moment. Agent Preston Clark, when at his desk during lunch at Quantico, never failed to follow the same routine. He would check his fantasy sports team online, eat a grilled-pork sandwich delivered from the Vietnamese restaurant down the street, and then he'd pull up every crime and automobile database to which he had access and spend the next twenty minutes looking for anything that'd help him hunt down the man who'd killed his wife. Every day he could, he made this search. It was his penance.

"We're going out for lunch" was his only reply.

They hit the ground floor, headed straight for the parking garage, and were soon driving out of headquarters. Rivera would let him explain when he was ready. For now, he kept silent. The drive only lasted four minutes before they pulled into a different Vietnamese restaurant, one Clark usually refused to eat at.

"We're not here under duress," he assured her. He looked around at the place and sighed. "Although I'd feel better about eating here if we were."

But to her, the restaurant looked like nearly every Asian joint she'd ever visited. In the back corner, she saw the reason for their visit. "Director Graves," she said.

"We are not here under duress," Clark whispered again, and this time she caught his tone. Graves wasn't here to pull strings. There was something else going on.

"Agent Rivera," he said, standing, "so glad you could join us. I know your partner here loves Vietnamese food, and I thought it'd be a good opportunity to break bread together. Or break *banh mi*," he laughed, then pointed to the omnipresent sandwich that could be found from here to Hanoi.

Rivera ordered a vermicelli salad with grilled shrimp and watched as her partner sighed his way through the menu, nearly in distress. He finally settled on a simple order of spring rolls and an iced coffee.

"Watching your figure, Clark?" Graves laughed at his own joke and then let his humor fade into an uncomfortable silence. He looked at Clark, who shrugged.

"Agent Rivera, your partner has just been in a meeting to which you were not invited. He was sworn *not* to mention anything said at that meeting, even to you. That order came from

Assistant Director Wesley Walters, and is one I insisted Agent Clark here not dismiss. But . . . since Assistant Director Wesley Walters reports to me—as much as I know he hates it—he's not in a position to give such an order. And I happen to know what was said in that meeting."

The shadow had reached them for real this time.

"Your names are known," Graves began. "And for lowly agents, no offense, that's not a good thing. That means someone is watching you. That means someone is talking about you."

"Do you know where the pressure is coming from?" Rivera asked. She felt her blood rising. Clark sat calmly, and she could almost have punched him for it. Puppets, strings . . . she hated being yanked around by others.

"We do not, specifically. My protégé, Assistant Director Wesley Walters, has a certain talent for hearing things and knowing everyone. You may hear bitterness in my voice as I say it, but I must also give credit where credit is due. That skill is not one that can be learned. He's a natural, and I'm sure, when he's cashed in all his favors, he'll find a way to pay me back for whatever wrongs he thinks I'm paying him. I have no doubt that within a year he'll be my superior. In the meantime, he has control of the information, and we can only make suppositions."

The server arrived with their food, and for a few moments they all fell into silence as they ate. Clark looked miserable. Rivera thought her salad tasted fine. Fish sauce, noodles, shrimp, cilantro, bean sprouts. It wasn't rocket science.

"And so you want us to . . . ?" she finally encouraged. She wasn't sure yet why Director Graves had called them there, except maybe to be a monkey wrench in his subordinate's plans. And that felt just as manipulative.

"My preference in most of these situations is to let God sort out the guilty by who's left standing at the end. So often the sides that tangle against each other in this town are equally culpable, equally dangerous. Occasionally, though, something from the outside gets trapped in their way. And they've forgotten how to play against anything but their enemies."

He was being cryptic, but Rivera could read between the lines. She'd been feeling more and more like John Luther might have been set up. Clark would never let her make such a leap without solid evidence, yet just by agreeing to this meeting she knew he'd been having a similar hunch.

"So, we press on?" she asked. She still wasn't sure what was said in the meeting, but she could sure guess. Assistant Director Walters had likely asked, in a tone that was really a demand, that Clark focus his investigation more fully on Luther as their prime suspect. Anything else that came their way was to be ignored.

"Press on. Absolutely." Graves smiled, and having made himself clear, he pulled the morning's *Post* from his briefcase. Straining to read upside down, Rivera could see the front page article touted the upcoming vote on the Faith and Fairness Act. Senator Donald Harrison was getting himself a *lot* of press over it.

"Changing subjects, sir," she said. "What do you think of this bill that's up for consideration?"

"Faith and Fairness?" Graves said, glancing down at the article. "I would think *everyone* should be for fairness, don't you agree?"

Rivera stopped chewing. Something in the way he'd asked the question gave her pause.

"Fairness is a noble aim," she said, "although it seems like a strange demand to make of things that are often diametrically opposed. Forcing them to coexist, doesn't that render them meaningless? It's like saying 'I want to go up' and being forced to say 'I want to go down' at the same time. You get nowhere."

Graves squinted. "Nowhere indeed."

Clark, who'd mostly just been staring at his sad lunch, took one last small bite, chewed, then swallowed. "Sorry, but our time is up, Director. We should get back before anyone starts worrying about us."

Graves waved them off and settled back to his meal.

Rivera followed Clark across the restaurant on their way to the door. In her mind, she kept hearing the words of Sheriff Gibson, *"Domed buildings. What is it about those domed buildings."*

When they reached the door, Graves's voice stopped them before they could make their exit. "Truth wins, Agent Rivera," the man said. "Maybe not right away. But I pursued this career with that hope. Truth, someday, will win."

Stepping out into the growing shadows of the afternoon, Rivera wished she could believe him.

# 52

17 YEARS AGO

More than anything, John wanted a beer. In all his wanderings these last years, he wasn't sure he'd ever been quite so hot as now, working on this road crew, fixing sections of blacktop that had buckled under the merciless Georgia sun. To his left, a sun-dappled stream snaked its way alongside the road, glinting in the light. A beer and his feet in the water, that was what John Luther wanted more than anything.

"Luther!" the foreman shouted. John startled. He'd been staring off rather than working his pickaxe. He raised a hand to the man in apology but didn't lift his eyes. Eye contact just meant an opportunity for the man to lay into him again.

"Don't make Big Tony angry," said Miles Washington, a short man with the blackest skin John had ever seen. "His wife forgot to pack him coffee this morning, so he'll be worse than usual all day." In the weeks since John had secured this job, Miles was the only other worker to show up consistently and the only other person interested in sharing more than two words with him. What they'd learned over the last days was that they had a whole lot in common—including stints in prison, preachers for fathers, and everyday battles with some kind of addiction. For Miles it was gambling—dice, horses, college basketball, anything. John was just past one year without a drink or a pill. Anything. But the sun today might just be the ruin of him.

"Do you think, Miles," he said, "when you're a millionaire, you'd rather have a house in the mountains or a place on the ocean?" It was a game they'd invented a week ago to distract themselves and to pass the time. Each of them asking outlandish questions of what they'd do when their luck finally turned around.

"Mountains," Miles answered. "But next to a great big lake full of trout and perch for dinner. You?"

John nodded. "My father has a place in the mountains. He says he hears God there in a way he can't anywhere else." In years past, that kind of memory would just have made John bitter, but ever since his father had bailed him out a year ago, something had thawed between them. John still felt restless, still ended up leaving his dad's house after a while. But he sent postcards every few weeks now and even called the old man up last week just to talk. "But me, I'd buy a place in the south of Spain. Learn the flamenco and find myself a señorita."

"South of Spain?" Miles laughed. "What do you know about the south of Spain?"

John laughed along with him and then realized, just for those brief moments, he'd forgotten about his thirst for beer. The rest of the day went on like that. Hours spent dodging his craving, minutes spent enjoying the company of this man he called a friend.

When they finally packed it in, Miles approached John with a look of embarrassment on his face.

"What's the matter?" John asked.

Miles took a deep breath and kicked at the road. "I meant to mention it earlier, but . . . well, it's just strange." John waited, and the man finally continued, "It's my father, the bishop. Turns out he's in town."

John nodded.

"He got in contact with me. Told me he was setting his tent up for a few nights. There's a farmer who's letting him use his sweet-potato field, south of here down on Jackson. And tonight's the last night."

Miles still wouldn't make eye contact with John, who then realized this wasn't just information—it was an invitation. "Are you asking me to come with you?"

Miles shrugged. "I told the bishop . . . my father, that I'd try to swing by. And I *know* you ain't got nothing more important going on."

John couldn't argue that, and he surprised Miles by saying, "Okay, I'll go."

"You will?"

Any other night he probably would have made up some excuse, but the sun still looked like it was directly overhead, and John knew what would happen if he faced the heat alone tonight. It'd been a year and he didn't want to screw up. "A tent sounds cooler than that flophouse where I'm staying. Let's go."

Stopping only briefly to rinse off and change into something fresher, the two were soon headed out of town to the meeting. Down every street a handful of people made their way until there was a stream of folks chatting and laughing and kicking up dust. Half a mile from the tent, three enterprising young men had set up a spit and had barbecue roasting. Nearby a young woman was selling lemonade. Miles and John couldn't pass it up; they ate their dinner while walking the rest of the way to the tent.

Full and exhausted from the day, John took a seat near the back of the tent. Miles disappeared, apparently to go find his father and say hello. Just as he'd hoped, the tent's shadow cut the heat by at least fifteen degrees, and the lightest of breezes even managed to make its way to John's sweaty brow. This, he guessed, would be one of the greatest naps he would ever take in his life.

Only it didn't go that way.

Miles reappeared just as John was about to drift off, all nervous and chattering. Seeing his father had put him on edge the same way seeing Charles always got John's nerves to jangling.

"Said my sister might get engaged. And our old mutt lost an ear to a bobcat, of all things." Miles continued to natter on about places John had never been, people John didn't know, and family history to which John was not privy. John was just about to tell him to knock it off when a gospel choir burst into song from behind them and the show started.

And it was a show.

First the music. Then the testimonies. Then more music. Stories of changed lives. Healed joints. Twenty minutes of quiet prayer, where John *did* doze for a while, only to be woken by even more music—including a woman soloing on "I'll Fly Away," who may have been the best singer John had ever heard in his life. This wasn't a bad way to spend a night, after all. And it was for free. John thought he might have to give Miles some guff for not inviting him to the previous two nights.

Then everything whirled to a halt, and a man who looked a lot like Miles, only with less hair and more gut, sauntered up to the podium.

John waited, expectant. He'd seen revival preachers before, their energy and almost manic shouting about God. He'd enjoyed the show so far and wouldn't mind a bit more before calling it a night.

But Bishop Washington didn't shout or dance or anything like that. The man's voice was deep and low, so quiet when he first started that John actually had to lean forward to hear him.

244

He couldn't exactly say when in the next ninety minutes he began to cry, but at some point he became aware that tears were pouring down his face. At one point, Miles gave him a strange look and then passed over a wadded-up napkin left over from dinner. John didn't bother with the napkin. Instead he just kept listening.

How was it he'd never heard this before today? He knew his own father said these words most every week, yet he never really *heard* them. They just sounded like Charles.

Tonight, in Bishop Washington's hushed voice, they came in a whisper that sounded like the very thing he'd been trying to hear all his life.

"You've been looking," the bishop said. "Looking hard, looking everywhere. Searching for anything that'll last more than a few seconds, more than a few minutes, more than a night. And you might have found somebody, but I will tell you, even they will only last you for their life. But there *is* something, and when you find it, it'll never leave."

On and on the bishop preached. Simple and true. Jesus. And when the call finally came, when the invitation was made, John was the first to reach the stage.

"God has big things planned for you, friend," the bishop said, then nodded in blessing. Afterward, John was given a robe, dunked, prayed over, and sent back into the world with a Bible in his hand and a strange smile on his face, which he couldn't seem to stop.

Miles met him near the back of the tent, gnawing on a wing of barbecued chicken and sucking on a lemonade. "That," he said, "was not why I asked you here tonight." He shook his head and offered the drink. "You thirsty?"

"No," John said, still smiling dumbly. "No, I'm not thirsty at all."

# 53

The giant blue banner with the words *THE SUMAC ALLI-ANCE* glowed brightly, thanks to the spotlight pointed at it. Below the Sumac logo, in smaller letters, it read, *State & Church Unite for Community*. It was the perfect symbol, a summation of Donald Harrison's life's work, and he loved it.

This luncheon marked the culmination of years of hard labor, of pressing on in spite of the seemingly endless obstacles. Congress would pass the Faith and Fairness Act before the week was out. This was more than a banquet for Donald's supporters. This was nothing less than a celebration of Donald's vision and victory.

Pride swelled within him as he took the podium. It was centered on a long table at the far end of the room, right in front of that bold Sumac banner. Positioned emblematically at the table, on either side of the podium, were six of the most respected religious leaders in America. Representatives of every major faith, who had thrown their support behind the Faith and

Fairness Act. Among them, on Donald's far left, was perhaps his greatest victory: Truth Ministries' representative—and newly minted CEO—Ryan Morris.

Donald smoothed out his favorite necktie, a blue checkerboard pattern that always made him feel confident and powerful. "We never thought we'd see this day, did we?" he began. He bore a giddy smile as broad as the table flanking him and probably looked a little silly, but he didn't care. This was it. This moment. This was what his sacrifice and perseverance had been all about.

"But miracles can happen when we as a people unite with one voice!" he continued. "Our opponents boldly stated that we could never have Christians and Jews and Muslims standing together in solidarity. But they were wrong, weren't they? Dead wrong! This is the future of our evolution in this nation, ladies and gentlemen. This is no longer a 'Christian nation.' In fact, it never has been. The question now becomes: How can a government survive and prosper without the steadfast unity of its own diverse religious community?

"It can't," he concluded. "It simply can't."

John's heart and mind were on fire, flames fanned by utter disgust. The sheer gall of this man he'd once called a friend. It was unconscionable. Donald was actually *rejoicing* over his so-called hard work on this precious legislation of his. John wondered how many members of Congress Donald had pressured or bullied or blackmailed in order to get the bill passed.

William had turned out to be a godsend. In less than twelve hours, he'd already helped John in a number of ways. As part of the alliance, St. Peter's had received an invitation to today's event, and William was happy to let John fill the vacancy. The young priest had loaned John his black floor-length cassock and white collar, and he'd been able to enter the Washington,

D.C. Grand Hyatt, find the luncheon, and seat himself at the back of the room, out of the line of sight of anyone at the big table up front, where Donald was giving his speech. Sometimes hiding in plain sight was the last place people would think to look for you.

"Just as Martin Luther King Jr. faced violent opposition when he first birthed his dream of uniting people of all colors," Donald went on, "I have a dream too. A dream of a tradition of faith as diverse as our skins, walking hand in hand toward the light!"

Donald ended his speech with his arms lifted high. John had to admit, it was a strong performance. And full of conviction. Everyone in the room was in awe of the senator, leaping to their feet to give him thunderous applause.

And there was Ryan Morris. He was standing shoulder to shoulder with men and women of authority from various religions, with a broad smile on his face. Ryan was Judas—Judas at the Last Supper, kissing John on the cheek while stabbing him in the back. All while gleefully drinking Senator Donald Harrison's polluted Kool-Aid.

Unable to endure another minute in this room, John stood along with the cheering throng and used the commotion to bolt out of the hotel ballroom door. So many people, all tempted by the same message of equality and freedom. Yet as he descended in the elevator, John could think only of the death and ruin Donald Harrison had dealt in order to bring about his Faith and Fairness Act. With Ryan Morris a naïve but eager accessory to Donald's ambition.

John felt his face harden with outrage. He almost didn't notice the Secret Service agent standing guard at the front door, who spoke something into the radio hidden in his shirt sleeve as John passed by. Something about the man seemed familiar, and as John chanced a glimpse back, the man's flattened profile—as if he'd broken his nose far too often—snapped a memory into place. He'd seen the man on the video the night he'd been abducted. It was the same squash-faced man who'd carried Aaliyah Evans's body into John's vehicle after his escape. The same man who'd been patrolling John's neighborhood, posing as a police officer.

His pulse racing, John picked up his pace, almost running for the parking garage across the street. He skipped the elevator, instead ascending the stairs two steps at a time until finally bursting onto the top deck.

John's fist was clenched tight around his father's rosary beads as he jogged to the car, where William was at the wheel, waiting with the engine running. William pounded the gas pedal before John's door was even shut. They squealed their way out of the parking garage and into D.C. traffic, where William began taking side streets to lose any tails that might be following them.

John took deep breaths, trying to calm himself, but his anger at Donald could not be contained. To be betrayed by someone he once trusted, someone he thought he knew so well . . .

John nodded to himself. He *did* know Donald well. And maybe it was time to put some of that knowledge to work.

# 54

Two hours later, a smiling Donald Harrison treated himself to a well-deserved massage at his favorite Chinese day spa. "My one indulgence," he'd said through the years whenever he'd talk about the place. It always made him happy, and even now, wearing a spotless white terry-cloth bathrobe, he couldn't wipe the grin off his face as he glided into the private massage room.

So John decided he would have to do it for him.

Losing the gray sedan William had spotted after the Sumac luncheon hadn't been easy. They'd circled and weaved through the city streets for nearly twenty minutes before the car slipped too far behind and got trapped at a red light. Even then, John wasn't totally sure the tail was gone. He assumed it was the squash-faced man and the gray-suited man from the video. The two men could've been tracking them some other way, for all they knew. But they had to take the chance. John had this last move on the chessboard, and he had to take it now.

Donald's massages had been a bit of an inside joke between them when they were younger. Every big win or any hard political loss meant at least an hour of getting his muscles kneaded at this quiet little massage parlor. John had no doubt the man would show up here sometime shortly after his speech, and with some help from William in distracting the masseuse, John was able to slip into Donald's reserved room and wait.

The senator was still grinning when he shut the massage room door and turned around to greet his masseuse. He froze when instead he found John sitting in a chair near the door, mostly obscured by shadows. But John knew Donald could see enough of him to know who was sitting there.

He was quick to mask his initial shock, replacing it with the kind of expression reserved for being surprised by a visit from an old friend. "What are you doing here, John?" he said, smiling again.

John wanted to say so many things. He wanted to spit on this despicable man. Instead he just sat there, silent, looking at Donald with his most pointed glare.

He was pleased to see that Donald was visibly rattled. Immediately the man began backpedaling. "I'll make some calls. I'll . . . I'll see what I can do for you, John."

Slowly and deliberately, John shook his head. "No more lies," he said, leaning forward in his seat so that Donald could fully see him—as well as the pistol and rosary beads he held in his right hand.

"Why did you do this to me?" John asked. He was somehow feeling both angry and sorrowful at the same time.

Donald played innocent, trying to keep things friendly. "I don't know what you're talking about."

"I said *no more lies*," said John. "You knew that bill would never stand without my support."

Donald laughed, yet there was a note of bitterness to it. "John, you always had the moves, but you could never hear the music. This is the most crucial piece of legislation since the Bill of Rights! This is heaven on earth for somebody like you. Imagine it, would you? With the flick of a switch you could be preaching to every synagogue and temple and mosque known to man. No more terrorists, no more secrets, because we hold all the keys! Every faith on bended knee before the throne."

"Whose throne?" asked John.

"I'm not your enemy, John. The real enemy is some guy with a nuclear weapon in a suitcase, hiding in a mosque or a temple somewhere. And I can't get to him because I don't have the oversight."

John's ears burned red. Donald had to be kidding. *That* was what this was all about? Terrorism? Was he serious?

John stood and faced Donald, gesturing with the gun. His voice was so thick with emotion when he spoke that he barely got the words out. "You're telling me you killed an innocent girl, you *murdered my father*, and you destroyed my life . . . to protect the nation from *terrorism?*"

Donald regarded him as a slow child, struggling to understand a simple concept. "Sometimes in war there's collateral damage. It's for the greater good."

John's blood boiled over. Remarkably, in this moment of rage, God brought a line of Scripture to his mind. It flowed from his lips like rainwater. "'You, like a tree that bears no fruit, shall be swiftly cut down.'"

Donald frowned, and he shouted in a sudden outburst, "Stop with the Christian platitudes!"

John felt an odd calm settle over him. It had to be God, comforting him, giving him inner peace. But he also knew in an instant how this was going to end. "You called yourself a Christian at one time," he said.

"I warned you," replied Donald, "if you put your personal history out on the street, it would come back to bite you in—"

"Donald," John broke in, speaking slow and methodic, "I want to ask you a question."

But Donald was still having a different conversation. He was shouting again. "You thought you were bigger than the system, but you're not! You thought you could wash yourself in the blood of Jesus and your sins would be removed, but they weren't. You know, John . . . the public doesn't take kindly to a sexual predator on the loose."

John kept going as if Donald had said nothing. "Do you remember what the Lord said to David when Saul was delivered into his hands?"

Donald was irate. "Oh, *stop* with 'the Lord'!"

"The Lord said to David . . ." John turned and pointed with his eyes at an object sitting on a ledge just above the room's door.

Donald followed his gaze to see a digital camera. A camera that had recorded his every word. His eyes grew wide with horror just as John reared back and struck him on the head with the pistol.

"'Deal with him as you wish,'" John whispered as Donald fell to the floor.

John let out a breath and stood to his full height. For a long moment he stared down at Donald, who lay there unmoving on the bamboo floor.

He reached up for the camera, staring into it with righteous vindication. If America wanted a guilty party to blame two deaths on, John had one for them right here.

Live and on camera.

## 55

They didn't have long before the senator would come to and the man's true power would be revealed. How quickly could he and his men find John? He couldn't risk waiting around; he still had one more message to deliver. With William at the wheel, John pointed them southward, out of the city. He was headed home. What used to be home.

Hood up to obscure his features, John was a rolling storm as he burst through the front door of Truth Ministries' headquarters. What had they built here? For years, John assumed he was building the ministry on a foundation of solid rock, as a place devoted to God. But now those who were a part of it had been so quick to turn on him, to seize power and run with it. They'd twisted this beautiful, God-serving entity into a selfish, money-grabbing abomination.

How dare they?

This place was never about man's power. It was about the power of God changing people's lives! It wasn't a cult of personality around John. It was a group of men and women joined together in common purpose—sharing the Gospel with a world that needed it more than ever.

John stepped into the elevator, thinking how this place looked no different from any other time, and yet he saw it with new eyes now. It was different. *He* was different.

He steeled himself as the elevator silently rose.

On the top floor he exited and walked past a ponytailed janitor he couldn't remember, who was removing giant-sized framed photos of John from the walls lining the central hallway. One by one he took the photos down. John wondered what they were planning to replace them with. Photos of Ryan?

As he approached the double doors of the boardroom, he could hear someone's voice speaking authoritatively from inside. It was Ryan. He was praying.

"We are so thankful for your financial blessings, for your abundance of grace, for your showers of mercy, Lord—"

Repulsed, John charged through the doors. The lights were dimmer than usual. The board members were viewing computerized slides on a large white screen.

The room fell silent as he entered, and Ryan halted his praying.

John slammed the door behind him and pushed back his hood, revealing to them his weary but furious face.

"John!" cried Ryan.

With unnerving calm, John gave him a piercing look. "Take a seat, Ryan."

Although Ryan was clearly thrown by the interruption, he tried hard to hold on to control of the room. "John, I don't know what to say. We hate seeing you like this, me especially, but you can't just—"

John produced the gun from his jacket pocket and held it up in the air.

Ryan gaped when John pointed the gun at him.

"I'm only going to ask you one more time, Ryan," said John. "Sit. Now."

Ryan raised his hands and scurried to his seat. "Hey, it's your show."

John joined Ryan at the head of the table, where he looked down at the younger man's open laptop. On the display was the same collection of pie charts being projected up onto the big white screen at the far end of the table. John glanced up at the bigger screen and marveled at the slide labeled *Ministry Donations*, which had been broken down by demographic.

"Your portfolios must have skyrocketed," he remarked to everyone in the boardroom. "Anybody want to see the next slide?"

John scanned the members, who looked to be in shock. Ryan was glaring at him now.

"Hit the button," John said to Ryan.

No one in the room moved, including Ryan, who had control over the slides. The place was deathly silent.

John slammed his empty hand down on the table. It banged so loud that several of his former underlings jumped in their seats. "All right, I'll help!" he shouted.

"John, *stop*," said Ryan, and John heard anger rising in his protégé's voice.

John was about to strike the table again when Ryan finally pressed the button, advancing the slide. Now the big screen showed a bar graph with a snaking line pointing diagonally upward. John couldn't believe it. He knew he probably looked crazed to the board members, but he had no interest in their perceptions of him anymore.

"Now we're talking," he said. "Look at this! Look at those numbers. Not bad for *blood money*. Tell me, was it worth it?" He nodded at Ryan at the head of the table. "Again."

"John . . ."

"Hit the button!" John roared.

Shaking his head, Ryan complied.

John circled the table, working his way back to the projection screen. "Stop. There it is," he said, pointing to a graph on the screen with his pistol. "That's like, what . . . ?" He turned to Dave Wilson, who sat closest to the screen. "Help me out here, Dave—you're the numbers guy. That's like a two hundred percent increase in salary, isn't it?"

Arthur Lewis, another senior pastor on the board, spoke up. "John, please, be reasonable—"

John spun on him. "Reasonable? Is that how you got to where you're sitting today, by being reasonable?"

"John." Dave looked up at John over his glasses with hardened eyes. "Your uncompromising perspective is admirable. You know I've always admired it. But your approach is not always a practical one."

John stared Dave down, sadness rushing through him. Slowly, intentionally, he looked each board member in the eye, one at a time.

"With God's help I built this place," he said. "With my bare hands. Now you're all in bed with the government. You're taking their tax dollars, but do you seriously think they can't silence you anytime they want?!"

# 56

This was getting serious.

Rivera believed that John Luther was innocent, and she could tell that Clark did too, though he hadn't said it aloud. Their current working theory was that Luther had been set up by Senator Harrison, but they had no hard evidence to back it up. Clark was getting pressure from his deputy director for reports, Rivera knew that. And she knew Clark was stalling from giving anything up. She also knew that the deputy director himself was getting pressure. But from who? How far up the bureau's food chain did this go? Without knowing who had the most vested in the case, she and Clark had little recourse on moving forward. Certainly they couldn't request to place the senator under surveillance based purely on one of Clark's hunches.

First they had a bigger problem.

*He's here.*

Clark had received the text only minutes ago from Ryan Morris. Then came the apparently surreptitious phone call that allowed them to listen in on everything.

John Luther was up in Truth's boardroom this very minute,

agitated and dressing down his former lieutenants. Rivera figured those guys probably had it coming. When emotions ran this high, however, the situation was apt to become unstable, and fast. What if the events of the last week had pushed Luther over the edge? They couldn't take that chance.

While Clark drove, Rivera took the passenger's seat, clicked the phone to speaker, and listened to the situation unfold.

Before long they were parked in a secluded corner of the parking structure adjacent to Truth's headquarters. A tactical backup team had been alerted and was only three minutes out. Clark had shut off the van and sat listening in with Rivera. This might be the break they needed, if someone confessed. They needed to assess what was happening, yet Luther was still fuming at the Truth Ministries' board of directors.

"They've got a hook in your back!" said John Luther.

Another voice spoke up. "John, it wasn't always this way."

Rivera glanced at her partner. He mouthed *Wilson* at her. The current speaker was Dave Wilson, Truth's chief financial officer. She remembered reading in Luther's file that he'd met Wilson decades ago, and they'd been friends longer than anyone else on his staff.

"Obviously," Wilson continued, "what happened to you is unthinkable. But as far as this organization is concerned, we're here just picking up the pieces. We were asked to come here for damage control—"

"No! You're being manipulated. Just another pawn! And you don't even realize it because you're too blinded by ambition and greed."

Clark glanced over at Rivera. "He's losing it." He still seemed reticent. "We can't wait any longer," he said.

Rivera didn't want to agree, but she knew that she had to. The man was unstable, and they'd get nothing helpful from him today. She nodded.

Pulling a radio from the clip on her belt, she alerted the team. "This is Agent Rivera. Agent Clark is ordering an immediate breach. Remember, do *not* open fire unless you are fired upon."

John couldn't believe it. Even Dave had turned on him. He'd known that Ryan was a lost cause after seeing him at the Sumac luncheon. But Dave? Dave had believed in him from the very beginning—long before John believed in himself. John had been trying to convince himself that even if everyone else at the ministry had written him off, Dave would still be there fighting for him.

"What good can it possibly do," said Dave, "if we blow our entire credibility on one piece of legislation? The world wouldn't listen to us any longer. We were losing viewers. We'd be spending the rest of our lives wandering in the wilderness, shouting louder and louder. How many people can we reach that way?"

John was out of breath. Sadness fell on him like a waterfall. He appreciated that at least Dave had thought this through and wasn't just blindly following Ryan. But the conclusion he'd arrived at was so far off.

"Have all of you completely forgotten?" he said, quiet and disheartened. He looked around the room at these men and women who used to be his closest friends and confidants. He smiled at them. "There once was a Man who wandered in the wilderness. And he reached more people than you're *ever* going to reach now."

John glimpsed the slide on the screen again. *Money.* That was really what it all came down to.

If money was all they were after, then they could have it. John reached into a jacket pocket and took out the last of his father's cash. There was easily two or three thousand dollars left, and he held up the bills for everyone to see. Then he tossed the entire wad high into the air. He heard a couple of gasps as those in the room froze, watching the bills flutter gently down on them.

John turned to Ryan.

His own personal Judas. Sitting there, looking up at John with fear in his eyes. John felt a momentary surge of power seeing Ryan this way. Justice was so close; he had the gun after all. Yet he couldn't even bring himself to point it at the man.

Jesus forgave Judas.

John shuddered, all his anger suddenly spent.

He tossed the gun onto the boardroom table. It thumped against the table and spun to a stop right in front of Ryan.

John turned and, as he left the room without another word, he heard Ryan's voice behind him.

"That is the destiny of an intolerant man."

# 57

Damage control. It was usually Donald Harrison's second-best mode. He was best at being the proud champion, rousing people with his excitement and his words like he'd done this morning. But so much of politics was damage control, and he'd gotten excellent at it through the years too.

If only the bruise and knot on his forehead would let him focus. He was sure he had a concussion, but he hadn't even taken a moment to get himself checked out. That would come later. What needed to be handled first was the video. The video John Luther had filmed of him confessing to ordering the deaths of that whore girl and also John's father.

Somehow it hadn't made it on the news yet, yet he knew it would happen anytime now. Unless his associates could locate John and get that video out of his hands first. Damage control.

Massaging once more the throbbing bruise, Donald tried to think through all the eventualities. For a second he wondered if it had been a mistake to call the president so soon after his coming to at the massage parlor. Except he knew this was nothing he could hide. One way or another, someone in power would find out about the video. They always did. Demonstrating his loyalty to the president by keeping him in the loop was the smarter move.

Predictably the president was highly displeased. After dressing Donald down a bit, he directed him to "take care of the situation." Which Donald was already hard at work doing. His man had been alerted and knew what to do. Donald had no doubt he'd get a phone call soon, telling him the job was done and that Luther was no longer a problem.

But the phone call still hadn't come, and Donald decided not to take any chances. Someone in his position didn't take such chances during damage-control execution.

As soon as the media got wind of the situation, the press would descend on his home en masse. He had no intention of being here when that happened.

His master bedroom stood littered with clothes thrown everywhere, some in a pair of open suitcases, the rest draped across every available piece of furniture. Donald's wife was flitting about, sorting through armfuls of clothes. Across the room, their television was tuned to cable news, and Donald feared their going to "breaking news" any minute now. Once more his phone rang and once more Mr. Gray was calling to say they hadn't yet located Luther.

"Well then, where is he?!" Donald shouted into the phone. The man wasn't a ghost, after all.

As Mr. Gray replied, the doorbell rang downstairs. Donald gave a quick look outside, fearing a streetful of news vans. But there was nothing, other than a single jogger running alongside a golden retriever. With a sigh he went to answer the door.

"He can't be *that* hard to find!" Donald said, restating what he'd been shouting at Mr. Gray since he'd first called ninety minutes ago. Donald descended the winding, open staircase that led to the ground floor. "Listen to me. Clean this up. Whatever it takes. Are we clear?"

He reached the entrance and swung open the door. In the doorway stood Mr. Gray, holding his own phone to his ear.

"We're clear," said Mr. Gray.

Donald's breath caught in his throat, and he tried to slam the door shut, but Mr. Gray was too fast, positioning himself over the threshold. Donald was shoved back onto the floor as Mr. Gray flung the door open wide and stepped inside. Donald looked up to see Mr. Gray pulling out his Glock 22 and taking aim.

From above, Donald heard a scream. His wife stood at the top of the stairs.

Mr. Gray swiveled his gun upward and shot twice.

The screaming stopped.

Donald had no time to look up or even think of her, because in a flash Mr. Gray had the gun trained on him again. He opened his mouth to say something, anything, to beg for his life or offer Mr. Gray money, but he never got the chance.

The last thing that went through his mind before the gun fired was the single phrase *All for nothing.*

# 58

John saw the FBI men entering the stairwell from two flights above. He still couldn't allow them to catch him. He couldn't trust them. Senator Harrison's influence certainly reached down into the bureau, and he couldn't trust that they'd ever allow him to release the video. No, this needed to get to the media, and now.

He diverted quickly to the third floor, weaving through a roomful of cubicles. Several employees stood as he ran by, shocked and scared. He had no time to slow down. Using an external fire escape at the rear of the building, he was soon on the ground, dashing toward the car, where William waited with the engine running.

As they speeded down the road, his mind was racing along with the car. He'd put off this decision long enough. It was now time to decide where to go next. Should they take their chances and take the video to the police, or should they head straight for a TV news station?

John glanced at William. He was so grateful to the young priest for his assistance. No one could ever replace his father, but William had been there for him in his darkest hour. And it wasn't like the priest was obligated to help him. He was risking his life for John, and he barely knew him.

John turned and thanked him, patting William on the arm as the man drove. That was when the unmarked white sedan rammed into John's side of the car at high speed.

The burgundy car spun a full circle, with glass, metal, and rubber flying everywhere. The scents of burning rubber and hot metal filled John's nostrils as he fought to hold on to consciousness. A nasty gash on the side of his head was sending a stream of blood down through his sideburns, cheeks, and neck.

William seemed okay, since John's side had taken the brunt of the impact. Dazed, John looked up. The front right corner of the car was crushed in, but remarkably the engine continued to run. Yet all such concerns were erased when a very familiar man in a gray suit stepped out of the white car that had slammed into them, drew his side arm, and pointed it straight at John—all in one fluid motion.

"William!" John cried.

But there was no time. On the other side of the windshield, the man stood a mere ten feet away from John. There was nowhere to hide, nothing John could do as the gray-suited man pulled the trigger.

John was terrified. This couldn't be how it ended, not like this . . .

Miraculously, after piercing the windshield, the bullet missed its mark. John gasped when instead the bullet ripped through the left edge of his seat, barely an inch or two from hitting him.

William wasted no time but pushed down hard on the gas pedal. The rear tires spun in place for a few seconds, until the car gained traction and peeled away from the gray suit.

John leaned to his right to get a glimpse of the man through the side-view mirror. He'd barely caught sight of him when another bullet struck the car, from behind this time, and traveled through the rear window and into the back of John's seat.

Instantly John was thrown forward against the dashboard.

The car's momentum then yanked him back into his seat again . . . but something wasn't right. A sledgehammer had knocked into him from behind, and now there was a pain in his chest. John felt his upper abdomen and pulled back his hand to find it completely covered in red.

"John!" cried William. "You're bleeding!"

The young priest pushed the car even faster, tearing down the street at a dangerous speed.

"Hold on! The hospital's not far—"

"No!" cried John, wincing through the pain. "I'll be all right."

William looked at him, his eyes wide with panic. "But John—!"

"There's no time," said John, sucking in air. "The church . . . Please, we have to . . . get back to the church."

🏛

Ten agonizing minutes later, William stopped the car at the curb around back from the church. The car had barely come to a halt when John opened his door and staggered around to the other side. William got out as well and put out his hands to steady him.

"We have to get you help!" insisted William. "You're bleeding—"

John shoved the digital camera into William's hands. "I need you to do this."

William hesitated. John could see that he was concerned only with helping John.

"Please," said John, gritting his teeth. "They have to see it. Show them. Show everyone. For me. For my dad."

While the worry never vanished from William's face, finally he agreed and accepted the camera. "What about you?"

John gave him a weak smile. "I'm the target."

William understood. While he handled the video, John would make sure that Donald's minions pursued him instead of the priest. William placed a hand on John's shoulder, then ran into the church with the camera.

John slid into the driver's seat, trying to ignore the excruciating sensations all over his body. He pulled away from the curb and drove off.

These guys wanted him dead? Fine. John knew how to run. He'd done it for thirty-some years of his life. He'd run from his dad, from God, even from himself. He could run for years, if he had to.

If they wanted him, he was going to make them work for it.

# 59

Any reason to hang up the phone on her mother would have worked for Monica. She was looking around the house, trying to find Jodi, but she'd gone upstairs to do her homework. Monica had had the TV on all day, watching and waiting for any new information about John. At the moment, though, they were just showing a current weather map of the United States, and the weather was the last thing on her mind right now.

Monica had been on edge all day after finding John's note in her car. She looked down at the kitchen counter again where the note lay and read it again. *One way or another, this will be over soon*, it said. How soon? Monica had pondered that question all day.

She wanted so badly to call the police and report that Charles had been murdered, so they could try to catch the killer. But she didn't know how or where he'd been killed, and anything she reported now would probably get blamed on John. Monica couldn't take that chance.

The nagging doubts had lingered, despite her fervent efforts to keep them at bay. She believed John's letter. She believed he was innocent. But still . . . there was no evidence to prove it. Not yet anyway.

To her knowledge, he'd never lied to her. But there was a first time for everything. What if . . . ?

She shook her head, shooing the thought away.

Ten minutes ago, her mother had called for the sixth time today. Her mom was confused so easily nowadays, and she was still trying to get her head around the charges that had been filed against John. She'd always loved John like her own son—she even insisted on supporting John's ministry out of her retirement fund, despite their continual protests—but now that he was a fugitive, she was more baffled than ever.

"I can't understand why they don't just get that man on the television to find out who really killed that girl," she said into Monica's ear.

Monica sighed, cradling the phone in the crook of her neck. She knew that the "man on the television" her mom was referring to was in fact the main character from the TV show *Monk*.

"Mom, that—"

Monica's eyes connected with the TV in the living room, where Diana Lucas had just appeared with a huge *Breaking News* graphic underneath.

"Mom, I need to go. I'll call you back soon," she said, then hung up the phone. She rushed into the living room and turned up the volume.

". . . stress that the raw, unedited footage you're about to see has not been verified as evidence in the charges against John Luther," said Diana Lucas. "But our public submissions department has concluded that this video is authentic. Take a look."

Diana was replaced by a view from above of what looked like a massage table. A man in a bathrobe was standing near the bottom of the screen, close to the camera, while John faced him from a chair to his right.

Monica's heart ached at the sight of her husband, so gaunt, so hurt, so despondent. She prayed Jodi wouldn't come downstairs just now, to see her father like this.

"*Why* did you do this to me?" asked John, his voice so full of pain that Monica's eyes promptly filled with tears.

Those final tiny doubts that had plagued her vaporized the instant she heard those words escape his mouth. She didn't have to hear anything more.

She knew.

She also knew she might never see her husband alive again.

# 60

Luther was long gone. He'd escaped them again.

Rivera was almost glad. She trusted the other agents on her team, but tensions were running so high around this case, with so much pressure on everyone from the top down thanks to Capitol Hill, that itchy trigger fingers were inevitable.

She stepped out of the van as Clark approached. He'd just been up to Ryan Morris's office, debriefing various members of the Truth Ministries' board of directors who'd been present when John Luther interrupted their meeting.

Clark shook his head. "Nothing useful. Most of them were cagey. They're still in shock. Morris kept pushing Luther's 'instability,' but his stock with the others seems to be plummeting."

Rivera raised an eyebrow. "Shocking."

Clark held out a nickel-plated pistol. "Luther tossed it to Morris before he left."

Behind Clark, the six-member team of agents they'd sent into the building returned in a pair of black SUVs. One of them reported that the building was, as suspected, clear. There was no sign of Luther.

"So what's he thinking?" she mused. "Where does he go next? Home finally?"

Clark shook his head. "More likely he's gone to see the good senator."

Rivera's phone rang. She excused herself and stepped away.

A few minutes later, she returned to Agent Clark, who crossed his arms as he listened. "That was a friend at the local PD. Said he just heard a report that there was a two-car collision a mile west of here about twenty minutes ago. A witness claimed that a white sedan with tinted windows intentionally smashed into a burgundy car with two men inside—one of whom matched the description of John Luther."

"Could the other one be his father?" asked Clark.

"No," said Rivera. "Luther's driver was described as a *young* white male."

Clark nodded. "So . . . the preacher's found himself a friend."

Rivera sent him a meaningful look. "There's more."

Clark waited, listening. Three other members of the ground team wandered over to hear.

"My friend just got a second report from a local badge, who saw a damaged burgundy car turning onto Route 16, heading up Kings Mountain. Said there was a bullet hole in the windshield, and the driver was bleeding from the head."

"He's being chased, and he's unarmed now," Clark said, his voice tense. He paused, looked into the distance. "Kings Mountain . . . where did I just see that name?"

Rivera thought for a moment, then snapped her fingers. "Doesn't Luther's father have a cabin up there?"

She locked eyes with Agent Clark.

Clark whirled on the six other agents and gestured toward the SUVs. "We're rolling! Everybody load up right now!"

# 61

John had so little time left. He could feel his life draining away with the blood leaking from his body.

If he could just make it to the cabin, he might be able to prolong this enough to . . . to what? What was he hoping for here? That he might be able to hide long enough for someone to come to his rescue? He had *minutes* left, not hours. That he might evade his pursuer and get the drop on him? John had left his only weapon back in the boardroom.

If William had come through and sent the video to the media, then it was safe for him to go home, to the authorities, or to the hospital. But he had no way of knowing if that was done yet. Perhaps they'd sent someone after the man. So John had no choice but to run. His only other option was to lie down and die or let the man in the gray suit catch up with him and finish the job.

The pain had become so fierce, it would be awfully easy for him to give up the fight, to stop his running and let things play out however they would. But he couldn't do that so long as there was even the tiniest of chances that he might survive this ordeal and so be with Monica and Jodi again.

He forced himself to keep driving. Both hands on the wheel, one of them still clutching his father's rosary, and fighting the increasing pain all the way up Kings Mountain. He pushed the car as fast as it would go. In the distance, on the road behind him, John caught sight of a white car. But then the road curved, and the car vanished before he could get a good look.

Was it *him*? Probably.

"Come on, come on!" he muttered to the car, willing it to go faster.

William would come through. He had to.

The job was almost done; it would be over within the hour.

Mr. Gray had the preacher in his sights. Less than half a mile separated them on the rural road leading up to Kings Mountain. Mr. Broad was on his way, heading toward Luther from the opposite direction. The plan was to box him in, and then finish this thing once and for all.

Obviously the fool was headed for his father's cabin. He must've thought that his being there would give him some kind of advantage. Or maybe he just wanted to be in familiar surroundings when he died.

How bad was the wound he'd given Luther? It was impossible to tell until he got a closer look. But he was certain that his last bullet had made contact. Instincts built on more than two decades of service to his country told him that when the hollow-point bullet left his Glock, it hit Luther in the chest. And it was very likely a mortal wound.

Mr. Gray considered shooting out the tires of Luther's car, but decided against it. Truth be told, he was enjoying the pursuit. His job was usually so clinical, so surgical in its speed and precision. It was nice to leave standard procedure behind.

And he respected the man's fight. The senator had made a

mistake in underestimating Luther—a mistake Mr. Gray never made. Prey was prey until it was dead, and the senator paid the price for forgetting that lesson. Worse, his memory and legacy were going to be tarnished because the public would soon be learning about his role in the recent deaths.

Still, the man in the Oval Office wanted John Luther dead. It was probably a personal grudge at this point, but that information was well above Mr. Gray's pay grade. No matter, for it had no bearing on how he did his job.

The job was all that mattered. He'd taken care of the girl, the priest, and the senator. Only the preacher remained.

Soon that loose end would be neatly tied up too.

# 62

One look at the gas gauge told the tragic tale: John would never reach the cabin. Already the Volvo was starting to sputter, and in just a minute or two it would go no farther.

Thinking fast, John stopped the car on the side of the road and got out, stumbling into the cover of the woods. He pressed one hand to his chest, trying to stop or at least slow the bleeding—even though he'd already lost so much blood that it might not matter anymore.

The bullet had gone straight through him, since he was bleeding immediately from the front after being struck in the back. He didn't want to think about how much he was bleeding back there too, or about what the bullet might have damaged on its trip through his body. The pain was too intense to tell. It couldn't have been his heart—he would have died almost instantly. But there were other vital organs in the vicinity—lungs, liver, stomach—and wounds to any of those could certainly be fatal for him.

John's heart thumped harder when he heard the echo of a car door slamming not far behind him. As best he could, he broke into a run. In truth it was more of a sped-up hobble than a run.

He came across a dirt path, and something deep in his memory stirred. It was almost as if he'd been here before.

He stopped and spun in place. He'd heard a branch or a twig snap. Were those footsteps?

Taking a gamble, John turned onto the dirt path and pushed himself to run a little faster. Around a bend in the path he reached a clearing where the skeleton of an abandoned greenhouse stood atop a raised, round wood platform. The dome-shaped structure was empty, the glass panels gone. Only the geometric frame remained, outlining the structure that once stood there.

John jogged around the dome, not quite believing his eyes. He *had* seen this strange structure once before, years ago, the first time he'd run away from his father. And now he'd stumbled across it again. Only this time he wasn't sure he would escape.

He had to stop when a sharp pain deep beneath the bullet wound stole his breath away. He doubled over, using the raised wood platform for support. It was a relief not to have to hold up his own weight for a moment.

The moment ended when a gunshot rang out, and a piece of wood splintered just a few feet away from his head.

He looked up. At the far end of the clearing stood the gray suit, his gun raised. And the man wasn't alone—his police-car-driving accomplice was right there with him.

John breathed a quick prayer and took off running.

# 63

Agent Rivera loved driving. She'd proven to be quite adept at it too, even in highly charged situations. So good that Agent Clark let her take the wheel anytime they were in the field.

Through her dark sunglasses, Rivera spotted the three cars on the side of the road just ahead and slammed on her brakes. Almost as one, she, Clark, and the other six agents poured forth from their vehicles. She circled the car to join her partner while checking the ammunition on her side arm. The other agents did the same.

It was during their ten-minute drive there that the call had come in. CNW had broken the news that Senator Donald Harrison had framed John Luther for the murder of Aaliyah Evans. All to push a pet bill of his through Congress. Reportedly there was a video of Harrison confessing, which had been arranged by Luther so as to exonerate himself. That had taken some serious guts on the preacher's part, to confront the man who'd taken everything away from him and basically trick him into admitting what he'd done—on camera. It was smart, impressive, and the sort of tactic her partner would have employed in a similar situation.

In that moment, she and Clark knew their target was no longer John Luther. He was now free from blame. Their target was the muscle who'd been working for Harrison. His henchmen, be they hired thugs or government agents. It didn't matter. They'd betrayed their country as much as Harrison had, and they'd already proven themselves as extremely dangerous.

Orders had come in straight from the highest office at the Hoover Building. These men trying to kill John Luther had to be stopped, and at any cost.

On Clark's orders, the unit deployed some of its heaviest weaponry, including standard rifles, shotguns, and one sniper rifle. The agents under their command donned the black protective gear they reserved for the most dangerous of situations. A few of them even wore balaclava masks.

Rivera followed Agent Clark's lead, sticking to her navy-blue FBI track jacket, although this time they both wore ballistic vests underneath.

With speed and silence, the team entered the woods.

Another hundred yards along the dirt path, John came upon another clearing. There was a small storage shed full of debris and rusty steel barrels that looked as though it hadn't been seen by human eyes in quite a while. The camp had obviously been abandoned years ago. The path continued beyond the shack, and John kept moving.

The woods closed in around the path, and soon there were overlapping branches sticking out in John's way. He was forced to slow down, duck, and weave his way through the undergrowth.

Slowing down killed his momentum and forced his adrenaline to subside. The pain hit him again full force, and random moments from the last week flashed through his mind. Was this his proverbial "life flashing before his eyes" moment? Or were his emotional defenses simply being stripped away, allowing thoughts and feelings to surface after days of suppression?

He remembered shaking hands with Donald Harrison in his dressing room and embracing him in a friendly hug. This memory was then replaced with a mental image of Donald standing at the Sumac podium, smiling with his arms held aloft in victory before a standing ovation.

He thought of Ryan's pep talk the night of his last televised sermon. How ironic that Ryan had advised him to "forget the politics," when Ryan had been unable to focus on anything else when he took over the ministry.

And that night, the fateful moment after his sermon when he was approached by Aaliyah Evans and the man trying to kill him now, who posed as her father and asked him to have their photo taken with him. That strand of recollection led inevitably to mental flashes of Aaliyah with her hands all over him, taking pictures shortly before she was killed.

His most painful memory was seeing his father's dead hand— the hand which still held his rosary beads—with the old man's blood pooling on the hardwood floor below him.

That memory and the pain he'd endured lately were too much for John, and he stumbled on a low-hanging branch. He hit the ground hard, and his first attempt to stand back up failed as soon as it began with him right back down, flat on his stomach.

*"People are looking for a symbol,"* his father had told him the last time they spoke together, in the park. *"Someone who'll get back up when he's knocked down."*

Squeezing his father's beads and drawing strength from his words, John pushed against the ground until finally he was back on two feet. The woods spun around him, but he shook away the sensation and pressed on.

Ahead he found the end of the dirt path and felt another sudden sense of *déjà vu*. He remembered this path and knew where it would lead. Soon enough he found a small, weather-beaten shack and a platform he knew led to the swimming pool. Only it no longer glistened like an oasis. It lay empty, cracked and vacant. This camp that had once been his salvation now looked like a graveyard. His graveyard.

John staggered onto the wood deck and began limping across it. He was thinking the empty pool might make a good hiding place, with its being partially belowground, when he reached the end of the deck and came face-to-face with the gray-suited man.

# 64

A split second after looking into the cold eyes of the man who'd been hunting him for almost a week, John was lifted into the air and thrown to the ground. He landed on his back, his head making a cracking sound against the old wood of the deck. The blue sky above and the surrounding trees swirled in and out of focus, darkness creeping into the edges of his vision like the tentacles of an octopus that was swallowing him whole.

The next thing he knew, the gray suit was yanking him up by his jacket collar until he was on his knees.

John closed his eyes and silently prayed, *If this is the end, my spirit's ready to enter the gates of heaven. But if it be your will, let me live to hold my precious ones again.*

When he opened his eyes again, he was staring into the black barrel of a revolver. Holding it was the second man, the gray suit's comrade, and John saw murder in his eyes.

This was it.

Agent Rivera caught up to her partner just as John Luther was tossed on the ground like a plaything. Luther was bleeding from the abdomen, had a sizable gash on his head, and was very likely delirious from the loss of blood. Did he even know what was happening to him?

Two men were there with Luther—the one attacking him, and a second man who stood behind Luther, holding a revolver. So this was them. The men working for Harrison. They didn't look like mercenaries or professional hit men. They looked like Secret Service.

Which meant that Senator Harrison had tasked his own personal Secret Service detail with eliminating the girl and framing John Luther.

Unless . . .

Unless their orders came from higher up.

That was a sobering thought, and not something for pondering right now. Rivera filed it away for another time.

Agent Clark took point, silently working his way forward, using the trees for cover to get as close to the tiny cabin as possible. Rivera followed his steps precisely, readying herself to back him up when he made his move.

The two men had Luther on his knees, execution style.

It was time.

Agent Clark moved out into the open, his weapon drawn, and stepped forward onto a twig. He'd done it on purpose, and it made a loud *snap*.

The two assailants turned in his direction. Luther lazily did the same. He was pale and barely conscious now.

"Put the gun down!" ordered Clark.

The men looked at each other with surprise, then scanned their surroundings. They were taking in the situation tactically, just as Rivera would have done. There were eight agents all together, moving in to surround the cabin. She doubted the two men could see their sniper, who'd taken up position a little farther away.

"On the ground! Now!" barked her partner.

The one holding Luther up produced a badge clipped to his belt.

"We're United States Secret Service," said the other one.

That was irrelevant as far as Rivera was concerned.

Clark too. "I said *put the gun down*!" he yelled.

The one who'd spoken put a hand in his pocket. "I'm just reaching for my ID," he said. "I'm putting my weapon down."

The other one let go of Luther and bent over to drop his gun on the ground.

"On the ground!" Clark repeated.

Rivera didn't like this. Something felt wrong about it. . . . Clark had to be feeling it too.

"We're all on the same team, pal," shouted the first man, the one wearing a gray suit.

As his friend bent over to drop his gun, Rivera saw the first man give him a hand signal.

She opened her mouth to warn Clark, but the second man was too fast. He had his revolver up and fired a perfect marksman's shot into Agent Clark's forehead.

*No!*

Rivera ran to her partner, found him crumpled on the ground. He was dead from the instant the bullet struck.

She glanced up to see the second man taking aim again with his revolver, but he had no chance of getting off a second shot. The sniper hit him three times, center mass. The bullets shredded through his chest, and he collapsed. Rage surged through Rivera as he landed on the ground with a hard thump.

When she looked up again, the first man was gripping a backup gun, pointed at her.

He fired.

# 65

John watched in horror as an FBI agent was shot and killed. His second attacker fell to the ground behind him. Then the gray-suited man was shooting again, and John heard a scream. He followed the sound to a female FBI agent, who was doubled over, lying on the ground and cradling her leg.

But she didn't stay down. With a cry of fury she propelled herself up to a sitting position, raised her gun, and shot back.

The sight gave John a fresh rush of adrenaline. As the gray suit made a run for it, John crawled on all fours to the end of the deck and launched himself over the edge, sliding down the sloped wall into the empty pool.

When he recovered from the hard landing, he propped himself up against the side of the pool. He heard several hurried footsteps not far away, in a rush to chase down their target.

Still holding his chest with one hand, John looked down at his wound. His shirt and pants were soaked through with blood. It hurt to breathe, and his breaths were coming too fast. He tried to slow them but couldn't. Lying next to him, also smeared with blood, was the cell phone his father had left him. It must have slipped out of his jacket pocket when he slid down into the pool. John picked it up, his fingers trembling.

It was over. He was dead already. He merely had to wait for death to finish its work.

But maybe he had just enough time left . . .

His limbs so heavy they were hard to move, he lifted the phone and hit speed dial. The number he'd programmed and had wanted to call a thousand times. The line was ringing as he placed the phone to his ear.

There was a click, followed by a small, beautiful voice. "Hello?"

"Sweetie," he whispered.

"Daddy!"

It was Jodi. As far as she was concerned, it was a normal day and her daddy was calling home just to talk.

"Hi," said John, anguished but smiling.

*Thank you, Father, for letting me hear my little girl's voice one more time.*

"I drew a picture at Sunday school," she told him excitedly. "Do you want to know what I drew for you?"

John was so overcome he could barely choke the words out. "Of course I do."

"Who is it?" said a voice in the background.

Monica!

"I'm talking to Daddy" was Jodi's casual reply.

John heard shuffling sounds, and then Monica grabbed the phone. "John!" She was already crying.

"Hey, beautiful," he said, still smiling.

"John, they're dropping the charges! It's all over the news!"

John's chest deflated in measureless relief. He closed his eyes. "You saw it . . . Good."

She knew. Monica was still talking, saying something about the president getting involved in absolving him, but all that mattered was that she knew he didn't do it. Now and forever, she knew he was innocent.

"Monica," he said, straining to speak, "I want to apologize for shutting you out. You are the love of my life, and you deserve so much better."

Tears spilled out on both ends of the phone line, Monica's coming with the short, gasping breaths that happened when she tried to stifle her crying.

"Listen," John said. "If I don't make it out of this, I want you to be free."

"No," she replied adamantly, though her voice was quivering. "You're coming home, John. It's over and it's time for you to come home to us."

John couldn't hold it in anymore. He was done. He had nothing left to do, no time left to live. He didn't know how to tell her that he was dying, that they would never see each other again in this life, that he wouldn't be there to watch Jodi grow, guide her into adulthood, walk her down the aisle at her wedding, station himself in the waiting room while she gave birth to their grandchildren.

He put down the phone and let the tears rain.

It was done. He was ready to let it all go. . . .

Until he heard footsteps shuffling across the deck planking above.

# 66

Agent Rivera was on her feet, pushing through the pain. There was only one thing she knew for certain, just one thought cycling through her mind over and over again.

The Secret Service man was going down, and she would be the one to take him out.

She was hobbling across the deck, scanning the area with her gun drawn, when a man's thick, muscular arm seized her in a choke hold from behind. The gun fell from her hands.

Rivera struggled violently against his iron grip and belted out a wrathful growl. But it was no use. The man was too strong.

A dozen feet away, the remaining members of her team scrambled into position, weapons raised at the Secret Service agent. But he wheeled her around to block their shots while aiming his own gun at her head.

"Stand down!" he ordered the FBI team. "I'll kill her!"

Rivera was livid. She bared her teeth, fighting this loathsome member of humanity and wishing she could end his life with nothing but her own hate.

With all his remaining strength, John used his final moments to climb up the edge of the pool, his hands and arms so shaky he could barely hold on.

In the late afternoon sun, something shiny caught his eye on an outcropping about a mile up the mountain. He squinted and tried to focus. It was a window in the side of a building. A log cabin. A familiar log cabin.

His father's home away from home.

Lying there on the deck right in front of him was the revolver that had been pointed at his head just minutes ago. Still holding the rosary beads, he picked up the gun with the same hand and aimed it.

The gray-suited man stood not far away with his back to John. It was the perfect opportunity to end this. And that man was threatening to kill the FBI woman.

He hated himself for thinking it, for needing to do it, for having his finger on the trigger. All of this had begun because everyone believed he was a killer. He'd sacrificed everything—even his own life—to prove that he wasn't. And now he had to be a killer in order to save a life. If these were the choices people had to face in this world, maybe it was best that he leave it.

His face twisted in anguish, John pulled the trigger with his last ounce of strength.

When the shot rang out, the Secret Service man let go of Rivera and fell. She knew right away that he was dead, without even checking his pulse, and a surge of satisfaction flowed through her. Along with tremendous relief that she'd survived.

Still . . . Clark was dead, her partner and mentor. She couldn't compute that fact. Not yet. That would take some time.

She glanced out at her FBI team, wondering which of them had circled around and taken out her captor from behind. Thankfully she counted six. They were all there, looking back at her, nodding. She let out a sigh.

Rivera turned then and saw John Luther. He was peeking over the edge of the empty pool with a revolver in his hand. His eyes were rolling back into his head, and his grip on the edge was slipping.

She rushed over and reached for him, but she was too late. He fell and collapsed at the bottom of the pool. And there was a long red trail of blood tracing from the spot where he'd clung to the pool's edge all the way down the wall to a puddle of blood beneath his broken body.

# 67

A full moon shone down on the emergency room parking lot as Monica haphazardly steered the family car into the lot and screeched to a halt.

Her mind raced, fearing the worst and knowing it had to be bad since he'd been rushed here. She sprinted from the car to the glass double doors, which opened far too slowly, and then up to the check-in desk.

Incredibly, no one was behind the desk. Then, on the other side of the room, she saw a familiar face. The woman was sitting in a wheelchair with her leg propped up.

"Um, it's Agent . . . Rivera, isn't it?" she asked.

Rivera looked terrible. Her hair was a tangled, matted mess, she looked impossibly tired, and she was grimacing in pain. But her expression softened when she locked eyes with Monica.

"Mrs. Luther," she said. "It's okay. He's alive."

Monica felt weakened by the news. "He is? Are you sure?"

Rivera nodded. "The doctors said that if it had been even ten minutes more . . . He should be out of surgery by now if you want to see him. I can get you into his recovery room."

Monica ran the backs of her hands across her eyes, wiping away tears. "Thank you. Thank you so much. For everything." Monica looked about. "I should thank your partner too. Where . . . ?"

Rivera looked down, and immediately Monica knew why.

"Oh," she said, struggling for words. "Oh no. I'm so sorry . . ."

Now it was Rivera's turn to wipe away tears. She nodded in gratitude for Monica's sympathy but said nothing.

Monica placed a hand on her shoulder and prayed aloud for her, right then and there.

Afterward, Rivera took her hand and gave it a gentle squeeze. "Come on," she said. "It's this way."

She led Monica in her wheelchair through a set of locked double doors—which she got opened by showing her FBI badge to a staff member—and into a large round area with twenty or so patient rooms fanning out from it.

"He's in 109, over there," said Rivera, pointing. "When he wakes up, tell him I said thank you."

Monica looked at her. "What for?"

Rivera's eyes met hers. "I went into those woods today to save his life. He saved mine instead."

With that, she spun in her chair and rolled away. Monica watched her go, amazed at her words.

Quickly she found the room, and a nurse led her inside. Monica's hands flew up to cover her mouth when she saw John. He was sleeping in a hospital gown, lying on his back, with a respirator and other equipment she didn't recognize hooked up to him.

A young man sat in a chair beside the bed. His head was bowed as if in prayer, but he looked up when Monica entered. He jumped to his feet and offered her the chair.

"It's an honor to meet you, Mrs. Luther," he said, offering to shake her hand. "Your husband's a remarkable man."

Monica reciprocated his handshake, trying to figure out if she'd met him before. He didn't look familiar at all.

"My name is William," he said. "I work—I *worked*—with John's father. At St. Peter's."

"It's nice to meet you, William," said Monica, putting the pieces together as she took a seat in the chair. "You . . . you helped him?" she asked, looking at John.

"Yes," said William. "After Father Charles . . . well, I've already made sure the authorities know about him. They've taken the body from the cabin."

*Charles . . .*

Monica teared up again. Without really thinking about it, she was on her feet again and throwing her arms around William's neck.

"Thank you," she said, sobbing against his shoulder. "Thank you for helping my husband."

# 68

TWO WEEKS LATER

The Truth Ministries' headquarters building loomed large in John's window as the car came to a stop near the front entrance.

Monica put the car in park and turned to her husband. "You sure you don't want me to come with you?"

John glanced at her, almost amused at the thought. "You'd have to smile and hug and pretend like you're not holding a grudge against these people."

Which she was. John was in the process of letting go of the hurt and betrayal he'd suffered from these men and women, but Monica hadn't progressed quite that far yet. She was still furious at the lot of them.

"I assure you," she said with a sly grin, "I wouldn't have to do *any* of those things."

John chuckled and opened his door. "In that case, you're definitely staying in the car. I won't be long."

On the top floor, John emerged from the elevator, cane in hand, to find the same ponytailed janitor he'd seen the last time he was here. Only this time he was hanging the framed posters of John back up on the walls.

He knew he looked better than when he'd been here two weeks ago. Monica had helped him to get into his favorite navy-blue business suit, a crisp white shirt, and a red silk necktie. She told him he looked "terribly handsome," yet he saw new wrinkles on his face alongside the healed-over scars.

John walked slowly down the hall, leaning on his cane, and his heart sank when he saw what was waiting for him. Outside his office was a gathering of a couple dozen staff members, all of them applauding his return. There were a few wrapped gifts and even a cake.

What was this? They were throwing him a party? They were acting like he was a cancer survivor or something.

Ryan wasn't among them. His contract had been terminated by the board the day after John was cleared of all charges. John had heard a rumor earlier in the week that Ryan had already started a new ministry of his own, somewhere in the South.

"We thought you were dead," said Arthur Lewis, who'd been named interim chairman of the board.

There were so many bright smiles, but John couldn't bring himself to conjure one. It felt beyond strange being back here. "So did I," he replied.

Walter Bailey, another board member, spoke up. "We're being flooded with donations!" he said. "It could be our best quarter ever!"

John had no reply to that. He couldn't shake the odd sensation he'd felt upon entering the building.

"It's so good to see you, John," said Walter. "You look great."

"No. I don't," John countered.

They were posturing for him, and he was already tired of it.

Walter seemed to notice his discomfort. "We prayed for you constantly," he offered. "We prayed over what to do."

Then John's oldest friend in the world, Dave Wilson, stepped forward from the crowd, smiling like everyone else. "Now that you've been cleared of the charges, we'll reconvene as soon as possible and get you reinstated."

Although John saw their mouths moving, all he could hear was their support of Ryan and the Faith and Fairness Act, their condemnation of him and their lust for government earmarks. Clearly the whole letting-go thing was still a work in progress.

Walter was talking again, and John had already missed some of what he'd said.

". . . normal, it'll be like nothing ever happened!" he said, beaming. "And we've got some ideas for the next quarter that we think you're going to be extremely excited about. Some incredible outreach opportunities!"

A part of John wanted to join in with their enthusiasm. But he just couldn't. Not even a little.

"We've gotten cards and letters from all over the globe, like never before," said Dave. "This level of support is unprecedented! The whole world is standing behind you, John. I firmly believe that God is going to take what happened to you and use it as a testimony to reach millions more for him."

A chorus of amens echoed across the gathering.

Everyone was watching him, waiting for him to say something, every eye expecting him to share in this joyous occasion. But John simply wasn't interested.

"Excuse me," he said as he weaved and pushed his way through the crowd. "Excuse me. Excuse me . . ."

He hobbled to his office, entering it for the first time in weeks. He glanced around the room. Where was it? He'd come for just one thing, and he was sure he'd left it in this room.

There it was, on his desk.

An old, tattered Bible. His father had given it to him years ago. Holding it gave him strength, determination, purpose. And, he realized, a strong sense of what would come next.

A moment from his interview with CNW just days ago flashed to mind. Diana just couldn't seem to believe that he was willing to take a stand.

"So if it comes to that, are you telling me you would be willing to fall on your own sword? For this?" she'd asked, incredulous. Sometimes people worked so hard to make a thing complicated, when really some things were actually very simple.

"Diana," he'd said, barely holding back a smile, "if you take away a man's right to speak his mind in a country founded on that very principle, you don't really have a country, now, do you? So there's really no sword left to fall on, is there?"

She hadn't had a follow-up question to that.

Simple, though, didn't mean easy. Nothing would be easy— the past days had shown him that much. A storm was coming, and it was simple to say one should stand firm in the face of its wrath. But when that wind began to howl . . . it would be far from easy to do so.

With one last look around his office, he carried the Bible back out into the hall. Walking faster than before, he brushed past the partygoers and didn't look back.

They were all sycophants, swaying to whichever way the wind blew. Would he ever be able to trust them again? Could they ever regain his respect?

Today that was inconceivable to him. But, he told himself, didn't everyone deserve a second chance?

After all, few men understood God's amazing grace and forgiveness better than John Luther.

The next day dawned, and John found himself staring into Monica's wide, alert eyes. He didn't want to guess at how long she'd been up. It was to be his first full day back to work and he could only guess at the whirlwind of thoughts racing through her mind. She said nothing, but instead just smiled at him and slipped from bed to begin their day. Coffee first. A shower. The ritual would begin once more.

John heaved himself up to a sitting position—it took so much effort to do such a small, simple thing—and let the joy wash all over him again. The last time he'd been in this position, he'd been leaning against the edge of a drained pool, watching the life flow from him, heartbeat by heartbeat. He didn't expect to see this room again. He didn't deserve to see this room again.

But if his life had taught him anything, it was that *deserve* had nothing to do with it. "If we all got what we deserve," his father would say on occasion, "there'd be no one left alive to complain about not getting what they want." At the time, he thought the old man was just ragging on him—and part of him was—but it was also at the heart of his world view. A world infused with grace, where only God's goodness meant anything. A sharp pang made him wince, but John realized it wasn't his wound that ached. It was his soul. He hadn't yet had the chance to even begin mourning the loss of his father and everything his death had cost them both. It would come in its own time—the pain and then the healing.

John had his eyes closed, thinking about his dad, when he heard giggling coming from his bedroom door, followed by the padding of footsteps.

*Jodi . . .*

One of her favorite games was to try to sneak into her parents' bed without waking them. She got the biggest kick out of them waking up and their delight at finding her there in bed with them. Only she rarely could stifle her giggles, and for a girl with small feet she often made a surprising amount of noise.

John played along, even giving a fake snore. A minute later when she climbed in next to him, her frigid feet grazed his legs, and he startled for real.

"Surprise, Daddy!" she shouted, then stuck out a tiny fist. John offered his fist too, and they bumped them together. It had been their solution when the doctor warned that hugging, even though meant with love, could aggravate his wound. For now, fist bumps would have to do.

Monica returned from the kitchen with two mugs of steaming coffee. "Two more minutes, sweetie, and then Daddy's got to get ready for work."

Jodi nodded and held out her first again.

He couldn't do it. Not so soon. Not when this was all he'd stayed alive for. He couldn't just jump back into the routine.

"Change of plans," he said and then asked for the phone.

Half an hour later, despite the worry expressed by the few people he'd talked with at Truth Ministries, he was out the door with his family. Monica wore a slightly dazed expression while Jodi gripped her daddy's hand as if she'd never let go.

He'd return to the ministry. Someday. And probably soon. But today he was with his family. Today he *was* living. Tomorrow the world could find him again.

"Where to?" Jodi asked, looking up at him.

"I think . . ." John said. "I think this is your day to drive."

And so she did. First was a stop downtown to pick up donuts for breakfast, then a visit to the zoo, where they all had to choose their favorite animal. Jodi had selected a lumbering black bear because she said it walked a little like Granddad. John and Monica shared a look. They'd told Jodi her grandfather had died—not mentioning how—but the news hadn't seemed to quite connect.

"It's okay," she said when they asked her how she was doing a few days later. "I'll see him in heaven."

Her granddad still found his way into her thoughts, and John wondered when the little girl would finally realize he was gone. Maybe at his funeral. Or maybe she already had. Maybe heaven was the right answer, after all.

The zoo was followed by a picnic, which was followed by a matinee of a movie Jodi had been "dying to see." Already his little girl was sounding like someone so much older. They ate popcorn and stayed all the way through the credits, not wanting to miss anything the filmmakers might be trying to hide from them.

Jodi yawned, and John could see their perfect day was reaching an end. He switched his cell phone back on, which he'd turned off when they'd left the house, to check the time and found himself staring at an unthinkable hundred-plus emails and seven voice mails. He thought the world would find him tomorrow, but it had managed to sneak in a grasp at him today.

"At least listen to the voice mails," Monica said, who'd been watching him. "You never know."

Three were from media outlets wanting to follow up on his story. Those he could pass on to the ministry's publicist to tackle. The fourth was from a literary agent telling him how he *must* get his story out there. That got deleted immediately. The fifth surprised him, a short message from Miles Washington, a voice he hadn't heard in years. The man had seen the stories, seen what had happened, and was just glad John was all right. And that if he wanted to call back, Miles might not get the call because he was staying at a cabin in the Tennessee Smoky Mountains, doing some fishing.

Monica asked him why he was smiling, and he waved her off as the sixth voice mail began. This one he also recognized, the Southern drawl like honey in a warm sun.

"Mr. Luther, this is the president, and I have a matter of some importance I'd like to discuss with you. . . ." The message went on, requesting that John get back to him as soon as he could. John felt his whole body tense and could feel his wound once more. This, more than anything, had brought him fully back to reality.

But it was the last message—a short follow-up from one of the president's staff who was calling to arrange a time to meet—that chilled John for another reason. "We're really hoping you get this scheduled shortly, Mr. Luther," the voice said. "So, please, call us at your earliest convenience. And we do hope you enjoyed the movie with that lovely wife and daughter of yours."

John looked around, eyes wild, though he knew there was nothing to see. They were all alone in the theater at this point. The credits had ended, and the two most important people in his life were staring at him with concerned expressions.

And John knew. It wasn't over yet. It might never be over.

# Epilogue

Near the back of the White House press room, John leaned on his cane for support with one hand and held tight to Monica's hand with the other. The president was at the podium, under the bright lights, extolling the virtues of John Luther and Truth Ministries and decrying the deplorable actions of the late Senator Donald Harrison.

All told, seven people had lost their lives to Harrison's madness. A teenage girl. A priest. The senator himself, along with his wife. A highly respected FBI agent. And two officers of the Secret Service.

John was grateful not to be the eighth. And yet . . .

Something was still nagging him about the whole thing. A thought that had occurred to him while he lay in his hospital bed for days on end.

What if Donald hadn't been the true architect of all this?

Words from his father still rang in his ears: *"Aside from the president, I don't know of many people who are better equipped to withstand a bullet like this."*

John couldn't shake the feeling that that was exactly what

was happening. Even here, now, at this press conference the president had personally asked him to attend. It just felt like . . .

Damage control.

Watching the president speak now, with his good-old-Southern-boy charm and homespun smile, John was more sure of it than ever. Everything about the man felt counterfeit.

Then again he *was* a politician. And it was the business of politicians to manufacture personas that matched what the public wanted in their leaders. Maybe John was just being paranoid. But he didn't think so. Every ounce of his soul told him the president was guilty of murder.

"Decide what you're going to say yet?" whispered Monica.

John sighed, shook his head.

It had been a topic of great discussion at the Luther house over the last few days. Would John stand up in front of the world and do the song-and-dance routine that the president expected of him? Or would he go up on that stage and blow the whistle on the man who'd been at the heart of this entire sordid affair?

"Well, I do," said Monica, eying him with confidence. "I know exactly what you're going to say."

He looked at her. "Oh? What then?"

"I can't be the one to tell you," she said. "You have to figure it out for yourself. And you will. When you step up to that podium, you'll know exactly what to say."

Was she serious? Monica was enjoying herself. That much was certain. Or she could have been teasing him about his indecisiveness . . .

"What makes you so sure you know what I'm going to do before I do it?" he asked.

She leaned in. "Let's just say that in all the years I've known you, you've never once disappointed me."

He smiled at her. He'd spent every waking moment of the last two weeks with Monica, and he still couldn't get enough of her. What was he thinking, all those years that he'd excluded her from the ministry, from everything that was happening in his life?

Still holding her hand, he gazed into her eyes. "Thanks for coming with me."

Monica gave his hand a squeeze and looked back into his eyes. "Thanks for asking me to."

It was time. John gave Monica a peck on the lips and then pulled away to the spot just to the side of the stage, where he'd been instructed to stand.

"Ladies and gentlemen," said the president, "it is with great pleasure that I introduce a longtime friend of mine: Pastor John Luther."

Polite applause came from the reporters and journalists filling the room. But John's eyes were locked on the president, who with a wide smile walked across the stage and gave John a hug.

It was for the benefit of the cameras. Most of what this man did was.

John was taken off guard when the president leaned in close and whispered in his ear, still grinning, "Very few men defy their own government and survive. But you did, John. And now everybody in the world wants to hear what you have to say. So let's play nice, shall we? *Real* nice."

John felt shell-shocked as the president stepped aside, clearing the path for him to walk to the podium. Dozens of cameras flashed as he stepped forward and gripped both sides of the podium. He was a preacher preparing to deliver a sermon again. The only question was which sermon would it be?

Any lingering doubts he had about the president's culpability had just been erased. But outing the leader of the free world on national television could put him—and his family—right back in the crosshairs of the nation's powerful elite.

Did he dare go off script?

John Luther glanced at the president one last time before

letting out a slow, steadying breath. With grim determination he stared out at the press corps.

The cameras flashed once more in unison, and then the room turned deathly silent. Nearly all were leaning forward as they anticipated his address.

John Luther peered into the blinding spotlight until everything had dissolved into a greater light and he heard the whisper he'd hoped would come. He heard the whisper, and his heartbeat quickened.

He heard the whisper and he knew: *I will not be silent.*

# Questions for Conversation

1. Do you feel your rights as a believer have been limited? Has this changed over the years? What do you think the future of religious freedom is in America?

2. Compare America's religious freedoms with what you know of other countries' values. In what ways do we stand tall for freedom, and in what ways do we fall short?

3. The Bill of Rights explicitly protects religious freedoms while also providing for a separation of church and state. Do you feel religion should be more represented in government? Where is the balance between being a nation under God and not forcing your faith on nonbelievers?

4. Romans 13:1–2 says, "Let everyone be subject to the governing authorities, for there is no authority except that which God has established. The authorities that exist have been established by God. Consequently, whoever rebels against the authority is rebelling against what God has instituted, and those who do so will bring judgment on themselves." How do you apply this verse when government stands in opposition to your faith?

5. What areas of American life today are particularly vulnerable to limitations of religious expression? How is faith

being challenged in the areas of same-sex marriage, workplace regulations, and public schools?

6. Have you ever been wrongfully accused of something? What emotions did you feel? How did you get through that situation?

7. How did John Luther's past help him in the novel? How did it hurt him? Are you more cautious when you know someone has a complicated and dark background?

8. What do you think Senator Harrison's true motives were? Are there some causes more important than an individual person's life?

9. What do you think it is that John Luther says in his address at the end of the novel?

Interested in Gathering More Information
on Protecting Your Religious Freedoms?
Check Out These Resources.

**Alliance Defending Freedom:** A unique legal ministry that has brought together thousands of Christian attorneys and like-minded organizations who work tirelessly to advocate for the right of people to freely live out their faith in America and around the world. http://www.alliancedefendingfreedom.org

**American Center for Law and Justice:** Focusing on U.S. constitutional law, European Union law, and human rights law, the ACLJ and its affiliated organizations are dedicated to the concept that freedom and liberty are universal, God-given and inalienable rights that must be protected. www.aclj.org

**American Conservative Union:** An umbrella organization harnessing the collective strength of conservative organizations fighting for Americans who are concerned with liberty, personal responsibility, traditional values, and strong national defense. www.conservative.org

*If we ever forget that we're one nation under God,
then we will be a nation gone under.*

President Ronald Reagan

**Robin Parrish** has written for over a decade as a journalist on the cutting edge of Christian culture, from books and music to film. He is the author of the DOMINION TRILOGY and suspense novels *Offworld*, *Nightmare*, and *Vigilante*. Robin and his family live in North Carolina.

**Daniel Lusko** attended film school at the New York Film Academy and directed the multiple hit documentaries *Inside the Revolution* and *Epicenter*, based on Joel Rosenberg's *New York Times* bestsellers. Over the past two years, Daniel has directed his first action/adventure feature film *500 MPH Storm*, as well as the gritty crime drama *11 Seconds*. He is also writer and director of the thriller *Persecuted*, produced in collaboration with Gray Frederickson (*The Godfather*, *Apocalypse Now*). Daniel and his family live in New Mexico.